THE TRAUMA CHILD

A thriller

C.G. TWILES

HURACÁN
PUBLISHING

Chapter One

The killer would pass by without notice.

I'd had a glass of wine at dinner, and because I drank so seldomly, it had given me a quick buzz that hadn't yet worn off, dulling my usual state of hyperawareness.

Not to mention we were with Kevin. He was only a few inches taller than I was, but he worked out frequently, so his shoulders were bulky, his biceps well-developed. And he was a man.

His presence quelled my sense of being constantly on high alert, something I'd had since I'd moved to the city—or perhaps since long before that, perhaps since when I was a young teenager and noticed that strange men were focused on me with intense, violating eyes.

This feeling was heightened when Arial was with me, because she was always my first priority. Back when she'd been in a stroller, I'd felt impaired and vulnerable. Even now, I couldn't flee, couldn't fight back if my child was with me. Because everything would go into protecting her.

But Kevin was with us. I could relax.

We'd just sat on a bench. It was dark but not late. It was cold but not too cold. There weren't many people in the park. But still… it was a city park. Always people somewhere. It wasn't risky at all, sitting on a park bench at seven p.m. Though, within minutes, I'd realize the bulb in the cast-iron Victorian-style streetlamp was out.

Kevin reached into his backpack and slipped out a flat package wrapped with silvery-blue paper. I don't know why he hadn't given it to her in the restaurant. I guess he'd forgotten.

Arial delicately unwrapped the paper, careful to preserve its corners. I knew she'd want to reuse it later for an art project. Inside was the next installment in one of her favorite book series, Benny and Belinda. The siblings were former stray cats who'd been saved by a family and were living the good indoor life.

This one was called *Benny and Belinda Go to Paris*. I'd never been to Paris (or even outside the country) but somehow two stray cats managed it. Arial had been asking for the book for weeks, but I knew Kevin had bought it, so I'd been putting her off.

"Thank you, Kevin!" she said, squeezing the book to her chest as if it were a fluffy, stuffed toy.

"Happy birthday, munch," he said, using his nickname for her, short for munchkin. "Welcome to the last year of your first decade."

She leaned sideways, hugging his arm. It was something I'd seen her start to do with him, beginning maybe a month ago. I wasn't quite sure how I felt about it yet.

Kevin and I had been dating for six months. I was still trying to adjust to having a man in my life. A man who wasn't Jed. A man who was actually here. A man who called when he said he would, didn't cancel visits at the last minute. A man who was interested in Arial, her activities, her crafts, her school day.

A man who bought *Benny and Belinda Go to Paris* not because I'd asked him to (I hadn't) but because he knew she liked the series. Because he asked her questions about herself and then listened to the answers.

"Can we read it tonight, Mom?" she asked exuberantly as I slid the book into my mini backpack, trying not to bend it.

"Of course. Let's get going so we can get in bed and read it."

The man must have passed by us as we'd sat. I'd lived in the city for almost a decade, so I was pretty attuned to the vibrations of strangers. You can tell a lot simply by the way a person walks. There's a casual, relaxed walk. There's a tense, wiry walk. And there's a full-on angry walk. One that veers, lunges, and jerks spasmodically. Those are the walks you stay away from.

I didn't notice that type of body language on the man. I didn't notice him at all until he suddenly careened off the pathway and attacked the lone metal garbage can, sending bottles and plastic bags scattering everywhere. A small but loud act of violence.

Kevin put his arm out to protect me and Arial, who was in the middle of us. Then the man, from about fifty feet away, turned and shouted something incoherent in our direction.

My heart began to thud, the fibers of my body electrifying with adrenaline, with the fight or flight reflex. I normally carry pepper spray, but because I'd brought the mini backpack and not my usual tote bag, I didn't have it with me.

"It's cool, man," Kevin said, his arm still straight out, trying to shield me and Arial.

We'd blundered straight into confrontation. Normally, if I see a person acting erratically—something not unfamiliar in the city—I quickly move away. Cross the street. Switch train cars. Or just walk in the other direction. But this time it was as if the man was a wave, and we were standing on the shore, and he crashed over us without warning.

My concern was Arial. I put my body in front of hers, as I saw Kevin had put his in front of mine. Despite my every molecule screaming that we were in trouble, that we would not get out of this unscathed, there was a large portion of me that expected the stranger to continue on his way. This is what the mentally disturbed normally do—they bluster, then leave. But not this time, not this time.

"Calm down, buddy," Kevin said, his other arm raised at the man placatingly.

But the man was lunging towards us. I thought he hit Kevin. Punched him. Or pushed him. Because Kevin pitched backward, and he was on the ground.

Chapter Two

"*M*om!" Arial screamed.

I'd never heard her scream like that, never heard that level of shrill hysteria in her tone. I felt torn in two. I needed to grab Arial and get her away from this danger. But Kevin was on the ground, something bad had happened to him, and I needed to help him, too.

I tried to do both things at once. I pushed Arial behind me with both hands, then cried, "Kevin!" But it came out a hoarse whisper. My throat muscles had spasmed with fear.

The man was standing over Kevin, his fists clenched, as if waiting for Kevin to get back up so they could continue fighting. I realized I should try to memorize what the man looked like. Memorize his face so I could describe him to the police.

But it was so dark, so dark. The antique streetlamp on this stretch of pathway was out. And he was wearing all-black clothing, the top of his hoodie squeezed around his face. My eyesight had deteriorated and I'd kept putting off getting glasses because of the cost.

The man could be anyone.

My phone was in my knapsack, which was strapped to my back. There was no possible way I'd get the phone out of the zippered compartment before the man would get to me. For I knew I was his next target.

"What the fuck you staring at?" the man shouted at me.

"Please!" I said, holding up my shaking hands. All I wanted was to protect Arial. That's it. I'd have to deal with Kevin later.

"I'm the devil!" the man yelled.

Then he suddenly sprinted down the path, into a dark stone tunnel. As fast as he'd approached, that's how fast he disappeared. I sank to my knees and pressed my trembling hands on Kevin's light jacket. My palms slid into wetness.

Kevin had been stabbed.

Chapter Three

"*What* do you think? This is where I used to sleep, you know."

"It's cute."

She didn't look too impressed. I considered giving her the larger room—my grandparents' old bedroom. But no. She was the child. I was the adult. I had to keep reminding myself of that because right now I didn't feel like one.

Running back to my home town. And taking it a step further—running back to my childhood house, as if I was trying to burrow back into a time when I was the one being taken care of.

I still didn't know how Beckett had managed it, but I intended to ask him when Arial wasn't around. Either he or Jed had pulled some strings. I was accustomed to them pulling strings and relied on it more than I wanted to, because I had nothing else to rely on.

The house had gone out of the family after Grandma's death. It had been remortgaged and the bank had simply taken it. I was eighteen, Arial was one, and we'd moved to the city. Jed had put us up in a small one-bedroom in an (as they say) "up and coming" neighborhood. I went to CUNY, studying business.

I'd chosen business because it was nice and vague and had an easy-ish schedule. Not like chemistry or computer science. I don't know how single mothers can major in chemistry or computer science. There were nights I was up until the wee hours as Arial cried with an ear infection, stomach ailment, or some other malady. I couldn't then have the brain power for anything complex. I barely had the brain power for business.

Within months of the move, Jed and I were done romantically. I was fine with that, it had been my call, after all, but I needed his financial support. And I kept hoping he'd tell his wife everything so he could help raise Arial, be a real parent to her. *Help me.* Be the one to stay up all night with her as she sobbed. Couldn't *I* be the one to get eight hours' worth of sleep occasionally? I'd settle for six.

At some point, I gave up on that, too.

A few months before Kevin's death, I'd been laid off from the home organizing company that barely paid enough to buy groceries. A recession had hit and people wanted to cling to their possessions not rid themselves of them.

Jed had been picking up many of the bills, which Arial and I were entitled to, but I still hated it. I'd been determined to switch gears, stand on my own, get into something better-paying, like public relations. Or to get my real estate license. I'd looked into becoming an electrician but electricians went to school longer than doctors.

Then everything came to a screaming, ghastly halt when we walked through the park on Arial's tenth birthday.

"We can paint it," I said to her about the room. "Any color you want."

"Purple?" she suggested, mischievously.

"I don't think so. Let's keep things light and cheery, okay? Purple will make the room seem smaller. And if you ever want a different color, that will be almost impossible to paint over."

"Yellow!"

"Yeah, that's sounds good. Yellow like the sun. When the sun comes out, it gets warmer. Flowers and plants grow. It's like a new start, boo. Exactly why we moved."

My most regular nickname for her had been "munchkin," which Kevin had adopted, shortening it to "munch." Now I didn't want to call her that, concerned it would continually remind her of Kevin.

So, I called her an assortment of other pet names— "boo" being the most common one, short for boo-boo. She'd once said "boo-boo" about a hundred times in a row when she'd scraped her knee and I'd called the resulting cut her "boo-boo." She liked the word. If she noticed I'd stopped calling her munchkin, she didn't say.

There was a lot we didn't talk about. I still wasn't sure what was the most appropriate way to usher her through something so horrendous, so unsuitable to be thrust on a child. Talk about it? Or do what I preferred to do, which was fold into myself, curl into an emotional fetal position, as if I'd been stabbed, too?

There's a primal instinct to shut down after a trauma —to go deep inside and try to heal, as you would staunch a wound to keep it from bleeding out. But that isn't what society wants you to do these days. It wants you to stand on a stage, lift your anguish high for all to see and give their opinions on.

And so, everyone kept telling me to bring my daughter to a therapist. And bring myself to a therapist. Therapist, therapist, therapist. That was the solution for everything.

But I wasn't ready. I couldn't stand the idea of being further poked and prodded about all the details of that night. Especially as I'd had to recount them over and over and over for police and the district attorney. They'd asked me the same questions so many times that I felt they were trying to trip me up, trying to catch me in some sort of lie.

I no longer wanted to hear one word about that night.

The movers had set up our spare furnishings: Arial's twin bed, my double bed, the ratty couch, an old flat-screen TV, an old DVD player, a small desk in the spare room. And my favorite, though impractical, possession: an antique, hand-painted, globe lamp I'd inherited from my grandparents. For years, I'd kept it safely tucked away at a friend's place, worried Arial might knock into it while executing one of her spontaneous pirouettes.

But I'd have to buy more furniture, including a kitchen table. We'd come from a 600-square-foot one-bedroom apartment with two closets into a 1,500-square-foot ranch house with three bedrooms, albeit small ones, a closet in every room, a windowed porch, and a finished basement.

Not to mention a half-acre of property and a small tool shed that currently contained no tools. I'd have to acquire a lawn mower, a rake, a shovel. Things you didn't need when you lived in a city apartment. And things I didn't have the money for.

Arial's boxes with her clothes, posters, artwork, paints and drawing materials, books, dolls, toys, and games were stacked in the corners of her room.

"I'm worried about Daddy," she said. "Isn't he going to miss us?"

"Not at all," I said, throat tightening. "He would completely understand why we had to leave. As soon as we can, we'll go visit him."

She looked unconvinced.

"Why don't you find some things to unpack, boo?" I asked.

After helping her open the box with her art materials, I went back outside to find Beckett. He'd driven us to Orchard, Connecticut, a four-hour ride from the city, in his SUV.

I figured he'd want to turn straight around and head back, to try to beat rush hour traffic, though I didn't think he would.

He was wandering through the front yard, examining the lush lawn with its smatterings of large lilac, azalea, and hydrangea bushes. The same bushes that had been here when I was a kid. It was a glorious time for the yard, redolent with crops of lily-of-the-valley, and wild roses and orchids.

I was thankful the family who'd lived here hadn't ripped everything out. For some reason, people now wanted a smooth lawn with no plants, no vegetation, no character. The family had also kept the original interior touches of the house intact. I knew I'd like them.

"Thanks for driving," I said to Beckett. "Now that she's out of earshot, I meant to ask how you managed to get the house."

Beckett was a distinguished-looking man, in his forties, with heavy, wiry eyebrows, and dark-brown hair graying along the temples. He was always tan, presumably from a tanning bed, and well dressed, even now when he wasn't working. He never, ever spoke about any kind of personal life. I'd come to believe he simply didn't have one.

He was Jed's right-hand man, his chief general counsel, and knew more about Jed than Jed knew about himself, probably. But Jed wasn't very self-reflective.

"The family had a little girl who was undergoing cancer treatment," he said.

My eyes went wide and I covered my mouth. "Oh no."

"I have a contact at the Mayo Clinic. I asked the family if they had any desire to go there, and they did. Then I offered twenty percent over what the house was worth. Which, to be honest, was still less than a studio in Brooklyn."

"Then you should have offered them thirty."

He guffawed as if that was funny, even though I

wasn't joking. I felt as if we'd pushed a little girl with cancer out of her own home.

"I hope that's what they really wanted, Becks."

"Oh, it was. No worries." This was his *everything's fine* voice, which he used frequently. He wouldn't have the job he had otherwise. He needed to remain calm while the world burned. And, in his line of work, it burned all the time. "They really did want to go," he insisted. "They've got the best pediatric cancer specialist in the country. The money didn't hurt. They weren't going to get that offer anywhere else. It's a buyers' market these days."

He started to meander back to his vehicle and I followed.

"How's Arial doing?" he asked.

"She's okay. It's a lot for her to take in. She has friends she'll miss. But I couldn't go back in that park, I just couldn't."

"Understandable."

"Her class is always in the park. All the classes are. How am I supposed to live in Brooklyn and not go near the park?"

I supposed many people lived in Brooklyn and didn't go near the park. Like Beckett, who claimed he was allergic to trees. Who's allergic to trees? He seemed fine right now, with trees everywhere.

But I couldn't live in a city and not have a parcel of nature to escape to. And Arial would need to be in the park for classes, for recreation, for events. I'd need to pick her up and drop her off. No, I couldn't do it.

I turned to glance at the house, again grateful that

the family who'd bought it at auction from the bank had renovated it without destroying it. I'd been so pleased to see that while they'd painted the living room dark gray—a trendy color but one that wouldn't have been my personal choice—they otherwise hadn't changed much.

The wide to-the-ceiling kitchen cabinets were now green and not white but were still the originals. The smaller glass-and-wood cabinets lining the ceiling in the living room, hand-built by my grandfather, hadn't been ripped out.

Even the long counter that separated the kitchen and living areas was still there, though the family had mercifully torn out the crumbling laminate top and replaced it with butcher block. For the most part, they had improved the little ranch house without stripping it of character.

It was the only place I wanted to be. The only place I felt safe.

The man who'd killed Kevin was sitting in jail, awaiting a trial. But because there were no cameras inside of the park, and my description of him was so unhelpful, it had taken weeks for cops to identify him and locate him.

In fact, the only reason they eventually did find him was thanks to Arial. She'd remembered the man's dark hoodie had the words **BOSS MAN** scrawled on the chest.

I'd been so busy staring at his face in a futile attempt to memorize his features that I hadn't noticed the very thing that would lead to his arrest. But Arial had. And, unlike me, she'd also been able to pick him out of the lineup.

Those weeks the killer had been missing were hellish. I could scarcely bring myself to go outside, worried I'd run into him. And that, while I wouldn't recognize him, he'd recognize me and finish me off.

Nor did I want Arial outside for the same reason, so she'd been pulled from school. We'd holed up in the apartment, using delivery for food and necessities. It was no way to live, even with friends coming over, even with Jed (Mommy's "friend") making appearances.

There had been times in the past when I'd learned that, for one reason or another, he'd been nearby our apartment and hadn't even stopped over to see Arial. But following the murder, he'd come by spontaneously once a week or so—a big effort for a man who generally made no effort.

He always sneaked through a narrow, garbage-can-laden side alley, then took the service elevator to the apartment he rented for us in a four-story brownstone. It was a building with no surveillance cameras, something getting increasingly difficult to find. He promised to do what he could to pressure the police to keep up the hunt for the killer, but both of us knew he couldn't appear to have an unwarranted special interest in either me or my daughter.

Judging by his ashen face and nervous demeanor, he was on edge that the glare of media attention would somehow shift to him. Luckily for him, the media was uncharacteristically gentle with both Arial and me. *Unprovoked attack* was the term it kept using for Kevin's murder. *Unprovoked*. As if there was any provocation that could have justified what happened?

While the large daily tabloids printed my name in connection with the case, they all respected Arial's status as minor, and did not print hers. Nor did they scrounge around for pictures of us to blast all over the place.

I think Jed was irrationally worried that if thousands of people saw Arial's face, at least one of them would conclude the child in the park had a resemblance to City Councilman Jed Thompkins.

Married City Councilman Jed Thompkins.

Not only did I want to return to my hometown to bathe in my nostalgic childhood memories, I also wanted to reconnect with my roots. My grandparents were gone but there were people in town who'd known them. I wanted to be around those people.

The city had always felt rather soulless to me, but now it felt downright evil. An unfair assessment, perhaps. Millions of people lived in the city their entire lives without anyone they loved being murdered in front of them.

Besides, anything could happen anywhere, right? Hadn't my parents been hit by a drunk driver in rural Vermont, of all places?

Still, it didn't matter. The city had lost all charm for me. I could no longer be there without reliving that night in the park, endlessly replaying it, continually analyzing what I could have done differently that would have saved Kevin.

Could I have acted insane? Insane enough to scare off

an insane killer? Why hadn't I put my pepper spray in my pocket before we left the apartment? Why had we walked through the interior of the park when we could have as easily walked the perimeter, with all its lights and cars?

And, most of all, when we saw the man violently attack a garbage can, why hadn't I grabbed Arial's hand and insisted we all run, run, run?

Over and over again, I'd see the man as his arm jutted up and down with the stabbing motion I mistook for a punch, and then I'd see the man as he lunged towards me and shouted, "I'm the devil!"

I'm the devil.

In that moment, I'd assumed I was dead. That this was the way it would end for me, in the park I'd walked through hundreds of times without incident, life taken by a knife-wielding stranger. All that went through my mind was Arial, Arial, Arial. Who would take care of Arial?

"I can't be there," I said, swallowing down tears. "It's sad to hate a place you used to love, but that's the way it is."

Beckett put a hand on my shoulder. He wasn't a touchy-feely guy, so the gesture was unexpected but welcome. "You don't have to convince me, Neely. This is why I did what I could to get your house back."

I stared off at the ranch's white vinyl siding and dark blue window shutters, wanting to make sure Arial was still inside.

"Jed must be happy winning the primary," I said, lowly, not wanting my words to travel over to the house and through the windows, even though they were closed. "Now he's a shoo-in for mayor."

"No such thing as a shoo-in," Beckett demurred. "Can't be complacent. Soon as he gets back, it'll be go-go-go until November 7."

"Gets back?"

Beckett's expression fell. He looked uncomfortable. But I was used to that look on him. He was stuck in the middle between Jed and me—never knowing how much he should say, how much he should reveal, and what he might say or reveal that, in his mind, was perfectly harmless but that would set me off.

"They're in Rome," he said, avoiding eye contact by pretending to inspect broken pavement on the small turnaround driveway. For whatever reason, the family who'd lived here hadn't repaired it. Perhaps they'd been planning to when they learned news of their little girl's cancer. "A trip for Gia's birthday," Beckett went on, clearing his throat. "But after that, it will be wall-to-wall campaigning."

"How nice. Know what Arial did on her birthday? Watched a man get murdered."

"Neely…" he murmured, apologetically, then couldn't seem to decide what to say after that, so he drifted into silence. Finally, he stammered, "I—I thought he got her a bike."

That was code for *I know he got her a bike because I'm the one who picked it out.*

"Becks, imagine there's a mansion where a family lives. They keep a dog in the barn. They never let the dog in the house—not through rain or snow. Every once in a while, the man of the house comes out, stands on the porch, and tosses the dog a bone. Maybe it's a nice, juicy bone. Maybe it's better than nothing. But the dog is still in the barn and it's still a bone."

He was staring at me with a pained and slightly mystified expression.

"She gets a bike; the other kids get Rome," I said. "My child is not a dog!"

My voice burned with recrimination, as it usually did when I talked about Jed. It was especially galling because I knew that Jed's mother's side was from Italy, so the country was a special place for him. A special place he experienced with his wife and two other children, not with Arial.

That's really what got me. Not that they were in a beautiful city halfway across the world, but that they were all there *together*. Arial deserved that, too.

My daughter—*our* daughter—shouldn't be a dirty secret, hidden from the world. She was such a great kid. She was gentle, empathetic. She loved animals and would get so excited when we'd see dogs in the park that we'd stand for an hour watching them romp in the dog run.

She had a sublimely sharp memory. If I forgot where anything was, I only needed to ask her. She was thoughtful. If a friend got sick, she'd want to make a get-well card, with colored-paper cutouts, glitter, and paint. She'd spend hours on a card, just wanting someone to feel better.

She loved to read and draw, devoured science and stories about volcanoes and icebergs and asteroids, and even liked math, something she must have gotten from Jed. These days, I could barely count my own fingers.

She didn't deserve to be treated like a second-class child. Sometimes, when I looked at her and she didn't see me watching, when she was intently playing with her dolls or sleeping, she'd appear so angelic, so perfect, that I'd rage that any man would help make this precious creature, then sweep her to the farthest borders of his life, as if she were a dust bunny. Or—as I'd already taken pains to explain to Beckett—a relegated-to-the-barn dog.

"But we got you the house, right?" he asked. I could tell he was hoping reminding me of this would get me off the Arial-is-a-neglected dog analogy.

"She doesn't need a house, Becks. *I* needed the house. What *she* needs is a father. You realize if that maniac had gotten me too, she'd have no one?"

"Look. Things will be different after the election. I know he'd like to do more for her."

"Oh, please," I scoffed. "It will be even worse after the election."

I sensed Beckett didn't completely sympathize with the situation. I sensed that, deep down, he was thinking *What did you expect, getting involved with a married man?*

I hadn't told him the full truth, the whole sordid story. Just how young I'd been when Jed and I had gotten involved. That I'd been so young, I didn't even know what was happening until it had happened. Jed was smart enough to wait until I was the age of consent, but we'd met before that—when I was fifteen. He'd gotten his hooks into my mind long before he got them into my body.

I glanced over my shoulder, wanting to make sure Arial hadn't slipped outside. But mostly, I wanted to draw comfort from my childhood home.

Just looking at it brought my grandparents into my minds' eye. Simple but long Sunday dinners. Iced tea on the porch in summer, listening to the loud buzz of cicadas. Winters by the glowing, crackling fireplace. Running out of my room on Christmas morning, down the long hallway, and seeing the tree lit up and the many gifts my grandparents would spend much of the night wrapping for me. They didn't have a lot of money but would buy small gifts on sale throughout the year.

The house was the one—the *only*—place I'd ever felt truly loved.

"Becks," I said, in almost a whisper. "Once she began asking where her father was… and asking so insistently… I didn't know what to do…"

He crossed his unruly brows. I tightened my arms around my abdomen, which was churning with the realization that I was about to tell him something awful. It was also colder here than in the city. I'd have to buy Arial and myself warmer jackets for winter. Yet another thing I'd have to ask Beckett for, like I was a child asking for my allowance.

"Well…" I said, chewing my lip, fumbling over these shameful words. "I brought her to a grave inside Greenwood. I'd seen it once before… a young guy who died in the towers. He has a memorial bench there by the lake. It's just beautiful."

The apartment Jed had rented for us was a five-minute walk to Greenwood Cemetery, one of the most famous cemeteries in the world. It was a rolling country-side of old and new graves and giant mausoleums, almost 500 acres, with everyone from Stephen Whitney to Jean-Michel Basquiat permanently resting there.

Arial and I loved to roam its green, hilly landscape, seeking out interesting and significant graves. The young stockbroker who'd died in the World Trade Center was one I'd stumbled across.

"I told her he was her father," I finished.

Beckett looked bewildered, as if he didn't under-stand what I'd said. Maybe he wasn't going to respond, and we could forget it. Or perhaps what I'd told my daughter hadn't been such a big deal. Maybe he'd shrug in that *shit happens* way of his and say, "Well, of course you did."

"What?" he said, a quiet intensity building in his tone. He shot a side glance at the house—no doubt also wanting to make certain Arial wasn't approaching. "You *what?*" This time louder and sharper.

"I didn't know what to do. He won't acknowledge her and she kept asking about—"

"Neely, I told you, after the election—"

"Oh, bullshit. First it was state assembly. Then city council. Now mayor. Next it will be president. When exactly will be a good time to tell the public he has a secret daughter? He'll have to resign if he tells after the election."

"Maybe. But then the Public Advocate will take over. If he tells now, that Nazi will win."

By "that Nazi" he meant the other party's candidate. If it was anything I'd learned by being on the periphery of politics, it was that everyone thought they were the good guys and that everyone else were the bad guys, and there was no in between. In politics, there wasn't room for gray areas, for nuance. Nuance did not win elections. Neither did trying to see things from the other point of view. Demonizing, catastrophizing, pointing fingers, and name calling is what won elections.

Beckett squinted at me disbelievingly and dipped his voice again. "She thinks her father died on 9/11?"

The way he said it, as if he could scarcely believe I'd do something so morbid, made me feel like the worst mother in the world.

Yet it was mostly Jed's fault. Yes, I'd had an affair with a married man. But I'd been a goddamn child. My brain had been so nebulous, so mushy, I didn't know that a man would lie about his marital status. I didn't know that when you found out about his marital status, he'd lie about something else—like that his wife was sick and wouldn't be around much longer. Nor did I have any idea that a man like this could seem perfectly nice, charming, and moral, and yet be rotten to the core.

"What do you want me to *say*?" I asked, annoyed with how whiny my voice sounded. "I had to tell her something. She kept asking. He was no help coming up with what to tell her. Do you think a little girl doesn't want to know who her father is? So, I picked a guy who kind of looks like Jed. They have his picture on the memorial bench. I came out with it one day and then couldn't take it back."

Beckett kept shaking his head disapprovingly, staring off towards a hill that sloped down to a watering hole where I'd spent most of my summers. Where I used to meet up with Jed in his silver Mercedes.

I'd been so thrilled that a handsome, erudite, older man who owned a shiny Mercedes was interested in me. I hadn't paid attention to how he insisted that I not tell my friends or family about him. I hadn't paid attention to how if he took me somewhere, it was always somewhere dark, like the movies or the back of a dim restaurant. But mostly, we'd stay inside his expensive car, parked down at the pond, at the very end of the road that led into it.

Nor had I paid attention to how he always had to be home fairly early, because I had to be home fairly early, too.

I was so young, so naive, so stupid. I didn't have parents who may have warned me of these types of men. I grew up with old folks. World War II generation. They thought people were essentially good and heroic. It never would have occurred to them that a man from a "good family" who had a summer home in the town next door, a man almost forty years old with a wife and two young children, would chase after a high school girl and take her virginity.

When it became obvious that I was pregnant, I'd told my grandparents the father was a boy from a different town, a boy I did not want to be with or name.

They were disappointed. Very disappointed. But they also made it clear that any child of mine was a child of theirs, and we'd get through this together. In fact, my grandmother, after a suitable period of worry for my future, seemed downright enthusiastic with the idea of having a baby around the house.

They were also too naive to know they should have hired a lawyer and gone after the father for child support. Only, because I refused to identify the father, I hadn't even given them that option.

I'd only realize much too late that the remortgaging of the home they'd lived in for decades, that my grandfather had built with his own hands, had likely been to continue to financially support myself and then the child I was bringing into the world.

They only thought they needed to step up and take care of things, and they did so until I moved out two years later. Officially to attend college in the city, but in my mind, to be with Jed, who would make a family of us.

He never did.

"Is this something you want me to tell him?" Beckett asked. "That she thinks her father is dead?"

I closed my eyes, took a very long, deep breath, then hissed, "I really don't give a shit. And I doubt he does either."

"She'll need to know the truth someday, and then what, Neely?"

"Know the truth about what? That she has a father who doesn't care about her? I'd rather she thinks he died on 9/11."

"Okay," he sighed, rubbing his eyes. They were turning pink in the corners. Maybe he really was allergic to trees. "I guess you did what you felt you had to do. I'll let you tell him, if you decide to. Because I have no idea how to..."

He trailed off into astonished silence before adding, "Wow, these trees. Did I ever tell you I'm allergic?"

"Anyway," I said, unable to resist a last dig before he disappeared. "I hope Jed is having fun with his—" I hooked my fingers in the air, "*real* family."

Chapter Four

"*C*an Matilda come visit?"

Matilda was Arial's best friend. She didn't make friends easily. It had been a relief when, at the age of eight, she'd met popular extrovert and class queen Matilda, who took a liking to the quieter, more introverted, more artistic Arial.

"Yes, of course," I said. Matilda's mother, Rachel, had ended up being one of my best friends, too. But I knew how tenuous friendships could be, how they were often forged out of convenience.

I liked Rachel well enough, but would she and I have been friends if we didn't have daughters in the same class? Probably not. I had a friend who'd moved to Queens a couple years ago, and I hadn't visited her once, nor had she visited me. And that was only interborough travel.

I doubted any of my friends would be making the four-hour trek to the wilds of Connecticut any time soon, especially as the town wasn't even on the Metro-North railroad.

You had to take an Amtrak train to Hartford, then rent a car and drive another half an hour. But Arial didn't need to know the harsh truth of the importance of convenience to relationships. When school started at the end of summer, she'd make new school pals, then stop asking about her city ones.

"Arial," I said, sitting cross-legged with her on the floor as she plucked dolls out of a moving box, lining them up on the floor for inspection, making certain they'd survived the trip. "You're really going to like it here, I promise. This is Mommy's hometown and I know you don't remember Grandma and Grandpa, but it's theirs, too. There's so much fun stuff to do."

"Like what?" she asked, dubiously, scrunching up her nose. While she highly favored me in the looks department, her nose—a bit wide, freckled, with a bulbous tip—was her father's. Her real father, not the doomed, young stockbroker who died in a terrorist attack.

I was glad she looked far more like me than Jed. Because I didn't know how a strong resemblance between them would go unremarked upon when she got old enough to contemplate the facial features of "Mommy's friend."

"Well, there are orchards all around here." I swept my arm towards the walls of the room. "Grandma and Grandpa would take me blueberry, apple, strawberry, and peach picking. Pretty much any fruit imaginable is grown here. Exactly why the town is named Orchard.

They have a strawberry supper at the church every year. It's kind of famous, people come from all over the state for it. It should be coming up pretty soon."

"Church?" she scrunched up her nose again, fiddling with her yoga Barbie doll with its tie-dye leggings, twisting her into what appeared to be quite painful positions.

"Yeah, church. It's very casual, more like a social club. Hey, I used to have to go to Sunday school. I won't make you do that."

"I'll do it." She shrugged.

"Well, okay, we can talk about that later. This is about making friends, not about religion."

She said nothing, intent on pulling Barbie into a backbend.

"On top of that, summer is almost here, and there's a pond right down the hill. And listen, boo," I said, putting my hand on back-bending Barbie so I could get her attention. "You can ride around on your new bike. All by yourself. Just like I used to do. I don't need to helicopter parent you like I did in the city."

I wasn't sure if she understood "helicopter parenting" but she didn't ask for clarification.

"In fact," I went on, "when I was a kid, Grandma had one rule: be home by dark. We can't go that far with you, not yet. But you'll have a lot more freedom here than you did at home—I mean, in the city. Know what this kind of freedom is called?"

"No."

"Free-range."

"You mean like the eggs?"

"The eggs? Oh, you mean the chickens. Yeah, like the chickens."

"Why is it called that?"

"Because it means you'll have more freedom. I'll be free, too. From having to watch you every second."

Rippling underneath every sentence were the unspoken promises, *It's safe here. No one will hurt you here. No one gets murdered here. We'll be free here. Free from danger.*

"That would be good," Arial said, her little face serious. "I like being free."

I smiled. How could she even know what freedom was? Other than running around the big lawns of Prospect Park when she was with her class—and even that was watched over carefully by her teachers—she'd thus far had a zero free-range childhood.

"Then, when summer's over, you'll go to the same school I did," I continued in my quest to impress the town's many attributes on her. "Did you know in high school, I was a cheerleader?"

"No way, Mom!" Of everything I'd said, that got her attention the most.

"Yep, it's true. You can do that too if you want. Or dance. I'm sure there's art classes. We'll get you into gymnastics. And you can join the theater club. We used to put on plays every summer. Listen, it'll be great, I swear. Heck, look at that yard," I pointed out her west-facing window, the one that overlooked the backyard. The property led down to the dense, pine-filled woods, which thankfully hadn't been torn up for tract housing. On the drive here, I'd noticed that various places in town that were once lush forest were now filled with rows of bland, identical box-houses. "You can go out and play any time. All alone. Can't do that in the city."

The family who'd lived here had put up a jungle gym set. Monkey bars, a slide, one swing, a small fort on top. For their little girl. The one who, tragically, had cancer. But the she was now at the Mayo Clinic. I had the fiercest hope that would make all the difference.

"Look at that jungle gym," I said. "It's all yours."

I was aware of how pushy, how verging-on-desperate I sounded. As if I was trying to convince her of something I myself wasn't convinced of.

I wanted to enjoy one summer before trying to figure out what kind of job I could get here in the country. I needed a job, even if it meant working at a restaurant. Or a pizza joint, like I'd done when I was a teen. I couldn't always be reliant on Jed for money, especially as I knew it was being funneled through some dicey means that could be discovered—and possibly halted—any moment.

The funds appeared in an online account every month, one that was connected to Beckett's—not Jed's —bank. It wasn't enough to make me rich by any means, but it paid the bills, and Arial and I lived frugally. Unlike Jed and his "real family," who traveled the globe, who were photographed out at high-end restaurants, Broadway shows, and galas. One Christmas, a postcard went out to all his constituents—on the front were Jed and his "real family" skiing in the Alps. I also got the postcard. I didn't bother to tell him this was insensitive but I did ask him to take me off his mailing list.

Sometimes I wondered if there was anything illegal

about the money I was getting—if it was diverted from campaign contributions. Other times, Jed was so indifferent that I vaguely posited that Beckett felt sorry for me and was giving me his own money.

"Yeah, but I have no one to play with," Arial said.

"You'll meet kids at church, the pond, school, the playground in the center of town. And my best friend Debbie has a kid. He's younger than you, only six, but I'm sure he'd like to play. His name is Nashua. Isn't that a cool name?"

"It's stupid," she said petulantly.

This was unlike her. She never called anything stupid, and she loved oddball names. Her Brooklyn class was full of hipster monikers: Hopper, Zephyr, Magnus, Zelda. It had taken me forever to memorize them.

She often said she wished she had a more unusual name, that Arial was "kinda boring."

But I figured this uncharacteristic pronouncement meant she was still reeling from the move, and the horrific thing that had spurred it.

"Boo, we don't call people or their names stupid," I gently corrected.

"I thought Matilda's mom was your best friend."

"Debbie is my best *childhood* friend. She lived right down the street until she got married and moved across town. She's excited to meet you."

Arial was still twisting yoga Barbie into splits, refusing to make eye contact. "It's fine," she sighed. "I'll get used to it. Can we get a dog now?"

"Maybe later, boo. Once we get settled."

I didn't want to tell her that dogs cost money and I

didn't feel like I could ask Jed for more right now, not after he'd just bought us a house.

She pouted briefly but then said, "We can really pick blueberries and strawberries?"

"You bet. I'm going to look up all the orchards and all the seasons for all the fruits."

I gave her a quick hug and pressed my lips to the side of her sweet-smelling face. "It's going to be awesome. I promise."

Chapter Five

I awoke when I heard what sounded like a hard thud against the wall. The sound mingled with a sound in my dream—Kevin's head hitting the concrete pathway in the park.

While I don't remember this collision making any discernable noise in real life, in my dreams, it always did. I'd had the same dream almost every night since Kevin died. Watching him crumple to the pavement as I reached out for him, feeling if I could stop his fall, then I could stop everything that was to follow.

The killer was nearby. I sensed him, but didn't see him. I could also sense Arial behind me, and I was terrified to move from the spot, to move closer to Kevin, lest the killer turn his attention to my child.

I opened my eyes and took in the room, relieved to be out of the nightmare, and to be somewhere I felt, in my bones, was safe. My grandparents' old bedroom.

The family that moved in afterward had painted over the walls, but I could still feel my grandparents' presence. I even felt I could smell the tiniest bit of them —a comforting blend of my grandmother's Chanel No. 5 perfume and my grandfather's Old Spice aftershave— but that had to be my imagination. They'd both been gone for seven years now, dying in the same year, as if they couldn't live without each other.

I didn't expect to hear the sound again. It had likely been the reverberations of the sound in my nightmare. Kevin falling, Kevin hitting the pavement. Kevin gasping "Mom," as I held his hand and screamed for help. *Help, help, help.*

Mom. That had been his last word.

When I saw his mother at the funeral, I debated whether to tell her this. I hadn't ever met her before and wasn't sure if it would be too much for her to bear, knowing that she had been the last thing to streak through her son's mind before he died.

But in case this knowledge would give her comfort, I told. I could scarcely get the words out I was crying so hard. She had said nothing, her face etched with unbearable grief, grief so pronounced it made her look slightly inhuman.

Thud.

This time I was up in a flash, casting aside my thin blanket, my only thought for Arial. The sound seemed to be coming from her room, which was right next door. Perhaps she'd fallen off the bed. She'd done that once when she was younger and it had scared the daylights out of me. She was now big enough that something like that shouldn't happen, but she'd been through so much lately.

In fact, a month ago, she'd wet the bed. Jed and Beckett were already in the process of buying my childhood home, so I'd let that incident go, thinking all would be well once we got out of the city.

I cracked open her bedroom door, heart pulsing hard. Her room was dark, so I turned the dimmer light up slowly, wanting to illuminate the room enough to see if she needed help, but not so much as to wake her if she was asleep. The family hadn't changed the dimmer light from the original, and it still made a barely-detectable, high-pitched ring when turned on.

She was in her bed, back turned to me. Her blanket was kicked off and bundled around her feet, and her favorite pink nightgown, with its frilly white collar, was hiked up so I could see her flowered panties and the inches of bare flesh above them.

I stealthily moved closer to the bed. Her knees were bent; she was nearly in a fetal position. I leaned over her —not sure if what I thought I was seeing was what I was actually seeing.

Yes, her thumb was in her mouth. She'd had a very brief period of thumb sucking when she was about one year old, but that was it. I was astonished to see how her thumb rested snugly inside of her lips.

The poor thing. She'd suffered so much lately that she was regressing. First wetting the bed, now this. I needed to find her a counselor. It was time. We were safely out of the city and I could turn my attention to other things besides escape.

I supposed I could use a therapist too, but I loathed the idea of it. I didn't want to talk about that night, to hear myself describing it. Didn't want to continue to root inside my brain, unable to stop the questions. Could I have done something? Why had we walked through the park? Why had we stopped on the bench?

Arial looked so babyish and innocent with her bare, chubby legs hiked up towards her belly and her mouth wrapped around her thumb. Impossible to believe in three short years, she'd be a teen. And in five short years, she'd be the age I was when a middle-aged man began pursuing me for sex.

The same thing wouldn't happen to Arial, that was for sure. I wouldn't let it. I knew all the signs to look for and I'd keep my eyes ferociously peeled for them. If a predator dared to come near my baby, he'd regret it.

I had no idea what the noise had been. My best guess was that Arial had kicked the wall in her sleep. It was odd that this had been loud enough to snap me out of slumber. Her bed was pushed against the opposite wall to the one that split our bedrooms. But there was no other explanation for the sound.

I was now realizing how thin that wall was; perhaps not the ideal partition that should divide a single mother —one who might want to eventually, sometime in the vast future, have sex—from her daughter. But these days, there was certainly no risk of that. I was celibate as a nun and intended to stay that way.

I leaned over farther, making certain that her eyes weren't open. They weren't. I smiled to myself. Nothing to see here.

As I pulled away, Arial turned and latched onto my wrist. It happened so suddenly that it scared the shit out of me and I let out a little gasp-scream. Arial's eyes were wide open, but they appeared unseeing, staring right through me.

"I killed him," she said, her voice strange and foggy. "He deserved to die, the cheating son-of-a-bitch. Are you happy?"

I was in utter shock. I tried to wrest my arm away; she had it clamped so strongly in her small hand that her nails were painfully cutting into my skin.

"Arial!" I rapped out. I wanted to be loud enough to wake her but not so loud that I'd frighten her. "Honey, wake up!"

She let out an odd laugh, unhooked her fingers from my wrist and rolled to the wall, crimping into the fetal position. She closed her eyes and pushed her thumb back into her mouth.

Chapter Six

*T*he next morning, I was exhausted but got up before Arial to make her buttermilk pancakes. She normally woke up about seven a.m. and so did I, but this morning I was up at the crack of dawn because I hadn't really been able to fall back asleep after what had happened.

I'd never heard Arial speak like that and had no idea where she could have learned that kind of language. I'd caught myself saying *shit* in front of her, but that was all. And *cheating* son-of-a-bitch? The second part was bad enough but how did she know about cheating?

I was extremely concerned that this was a side effect of what she'd witnessed. For the first couple weeks after the murder, she'd hardly spoken. I'd been a wreck myself and hadn't been adequate emotional support for her.

The district attorney's office had assigned us a social worker but I'd stopped calling her back because Arial began resisting the appointments. I didn't want to press her. She should only talk about that night if it was something she wanted.

But had that been the wrong decision? By not dragging the terrible thing we'd seen into the daylight and forcing us both to stare at it unmercifully, had it burrowed deeper into her consciousness, where it festered and expanded?

What did she mean, *I killed him*?

I assumed she meant Kevin. On some level, did Arial believe she was responsible for what had happened? Because we'd been out celebrating her birthday? Because we'd sat on the bench so Kevin could give her the gift?

The idea that she might consider herself responsible had never occurred to me, not in a million years. Did I need to come straight out and tell her that nothing was her fault?

The soothing smell of buttermilk pancakes filled the air. Grandma used to make them for me and between inhaling the familiar buttery scent and standing in the same kitchen I'd had so many wonderful dinners in, the peculiar incident from the night before began to seem less dire, the uncharacteristic language something she must have heard in a movie. Or online. I tried to keep track of everything she watched but it was probably impossible.

I glanced at the underside of my wrist, where my daughter had drawn blood with her sharp, little nails. Two Band-Aids covered the tiny but deep gouges. I was glad I'd bought a box of them yesterday, wanting to be prepared in case Arial took a tumble off her jungle gym or bicycle.

"Mom?"

She stood at the end of the counter that separated the kitchen from the living room. Her dark chestnut hair was tangled, her hazel-flecked brown eyes with their enviable fringe of bristly lashes blinking at me. I jumped up from the table and gave her a long hug.

"How did you sleep, boo?"

"Fine."

"I made pancakes. Buttermilk. Like Grandma used to make for me."

"Ohhh. Sounds yummy."

She scooted into the nearest chair and stared at me expectedly. We had a new kitchen table, bought only yesterday at the Goodwill. Cheap, and yet made of durable oak. I'd also picked up a large folding table and wood chairs to eat on the porch when it got warmer, a couple of throw rugs, and some pots and pans.

The Goodwill in town was a goldmine; there were plenty of wealthy people in Orchard who loaded it with upscale second-hand goods. I was already preparing to raid it for Arial's school clothes and supplies. I had no shame about buying her things at a thrift store. Arial had heard my lectures about how second-hand was better for the environment and she was on board with that.

Normally, she got out her own plate and utensils but I'd only unpacked those last night and she probably didn't remember where I'd put everything. Unusual for her. She had a photographic memory for where things were placed in our old apartment, which came in handy because I was the type who could lose whatever was in my hands as I walked from one room to the next.

I retrieved maple syrup from the fridge and set it on the table, then layered two big fluffy pancakes each on two plates. After Beckett had left yesterday, I'd driven twenty minutes into the town center and shopped at Whole Foods. There hadn't been a Whole Foods in town when I'd lived here, but it had opened up sometime in the past few years.

It took Arial no time at all to notice the Band-Aids on the underside of my wrist. "What happened?" she asked, reaching out to gingerly touch them.

"You don't remember?"

"Remember what?"

"You were having a bad dream. I came in and tried to wake you, but you didn't wake up. You kind of grabbed my wrist in the middle of it."

"I *did*? You mean I grabbed you? I *hurt* you?"

"Just a little. From your nails. It's not a big deal, hon. You didn't mean to do it. It was an accident. I only want to make sure you're alright and that if you're having bad dreams, you tell me. You can always come sleep with me if you want."

"Mmm, I don't need that," she said, somewhat distastefully.

"Okay, just checking." I paused and watched her eat. She finished off one pancake and started on the other. I was satisfied to see that her appetite was hearty.

"Arial," I said, forcing myself to confront things in a way I should have done earlier. "If you ever want to talk about Kev, I'm here to listen. I know it's been extremely hard for you. I know how much you liked him and he liked you."

She said nothing but slowed down her eating, staring into her plate. I felt guilty that I'd just stunted her appetite. I should have waited until after breakfast.

"If you don't want to talk, that's fine, too. There are times I don't know if I want to talk about what happened or not. It's all so confusing. Would you be interested in speaking to someone who isn't me?"

"Like who?" she murmured.

"Like a therapist. Similar to the lady we met at the district attorney's office. Sasha. Remember her? But someone here in town."

She pushed a piece of pancake around in a glaze of syrup. "I don't really want to talk to anyone," she said. "Do you?"

"I probably will soon. I've just been trying to get my bearings. To—to kind of right myself. It's—it's been so... so very hard. There's no book that tells you how to deal with this kind of thing. Well, maybe there is, but I haven't read it. But, Arial, listen." The tone of my voice conveyed that I wanted her to look at me, so she turned her eyes up. "You know what happened was nobody's fault, right?" It occurred to me it was the fault of the killer, but I plowed on, "And certainly not *your* fault. You don't think that, do you?"

"No," she said, sounding convincing.

"Good. It was just a terrible, awful thing that happened. A horrible tragedy. I know it made the world feel unsafe." I reached out and squeezed her small, soft hand. "But I absolutely promise you that we're safe here. Nothing, I mean nothing, will hurt us here."

"I know, Mom."

I got up and hugged her, kissing the top of her head. Her hair had that slightly musty odor that meant it was time for a wash.

"I love you very, very much," I said, placing my hands on either side of her face. Besides Jed's nose, she had his brown eyes, not my blue ones, but the goldish flecks around the irises were her own. "I'll always love you. And nothing, I mean nothing, will ever hurt you. I promise that. You can count on that. What you had to see was something no one should see, let alone anyone your age. But you will never see anything like that again. Ever. I swear it. Okay?"

She nodded. "Okay, Mom."

Chapter Seven

The next day, I sat with Debbie on a bench at the playground in Orchard's center. The playground was across from the high school, where Debbie and I had attended all four years, and where we'd been good friends. A lot of my childhood friends had moved out of town but not Debbie.

She had flaming red hair, skin of the palest white, and freckles everywhere. In high school, she'd been involved in a toxic relationship with a football player who constantly cheated on her. I could never understand why she stayed with him, but she did, even as he hurt her over and over. The way I remembered teenage Debbie was that if she wasn't smiling ecstatically, she was crying.

But now there was no trace of that time. My friend appeared confident and contented. She had a successful furniture flipping business. She was married to her college boyfriend, a cardiologist, and only had positive things to say about him.

And she had an adorable six-year-old son, Nashua. He had a shock of fuzzy red hair—clearly inherited from her—squishable chipmunk cheeks, and seemed to be sweet and loving.

I hadn't known how Arial would be with a boy so much younger but to my relief she immediately seemed to like him. Within minutes of arriving, the pair had planted themselves in the playground's large sandbox and had a game going.

There were only a few other children in the playground. If this had been Brooklyn, it would have been teeming with kids, parents, and nannies. But in a place like Orchard, most homes had backyards, so there wasn't any need to travel somewhere to play.

"They're getting along," Debbie said, nodding at the sandbox. They were using shovels to fill the back of a plastic dump-truck with sand. The shovels had already been in the box but Debbie had supplied the dump-truck.

"I know. It's great," I said.

The idea that I could hang out with one of my oldest friends while our children entertained each other was gratifying.

It was a clear, brisk day. Summer was rapidly approaching, but today was firmly clinging to spring. Arial had her pink sweater jacket wide open. I resisted the urge to call over to her to zip it up, not wanting to interrupt whatever friendship was budding between her and Nashua.

"It's awesome to have you back," Debbie said, giving

one of her big, toothy smiles. "Any particular reason you left the city?"

I stalled silently, staring past the sandbox to the cloudless, solid blue sky. Although my name had been in the media, unless you were deliberately searching for me, or a story happened to come up as you were online, you wouldn't have seen anything.

Which I was grateful for. I didn't like the idea of everyone in town knowing what had happened to me. I wasn't even sure how much to tell Debbie. Today was a pleasant day and telling her what had happened was going to put a dark pall over everything. But I didn't want to lie either.

"I had—it was a bad experience. It's—I don't know, I don't want to go into detail. But I really wanted to move back."

"No problem," Debbie chirped. "I didn't mean to pry."

"Who do you still see from school? Give me some gossip."

Debbie went on to tell several stories about mutual high school acquaintances. I'd moved to the city shortly after graduation, several months after September 11, with the acrid odor of burning piles of ash and metal still hanging in the air. I hadn't kept up with the local happenings. But the people she started naming were bringing back memories.

Jake Carter, a popular baseball player both Debbie and I had had crushes on. He'd married another girl from school, but they were divorcing.

Arabella Finesse. One of the prettiest girls in school.

Her wealthy parents had bought her a clothing store in the new shopping mall where she sold her own designs. Fitting, as she'd been voted "Most Fashionable."

Tommy Jacoby. A big drinker who became a bigger drinker after graduating. Debbie said he'd become paralyzed after getting drunk and leaping off a cliff at one of the local watering holes.

After his accident, the town passed an ordinance banning swimming in the area—a disappointment as I'd grown up swimming there and looked forward to introducing it to Arial. I felt terrible for Tommy. I really hadn't known him well. Only remembered his name and his shaggy mane of blond hair.

Arial and Nashua appeared to become bored with the sandbox. They trundled over to us, Arial leading the way. Both had flushed cheeks from the fresh air, the kind of healthy glow that I was glad to see, and that made me feel I'd done the right thing by insisting we exit the city.

"Mom, can Arial sleep ovvverrrrr?" Nashua asked. He was at the age where most utterances sounded like a whine.

Debbie looked surprised. "Sleep over?" She glanced at me. "That's an interesting idea."

"How do you feel, Arial?" I asked hesitantly. She hadn't had any sleepovers since the tragedy, and only a few before that. Her nightmare from the other night was freshly lodged in my brain. I wasn't sure it was a smart idea to have her away from me all night. "Is that something you're interested in?"

"Yeah, Mom, I want to sleep over," she asserted. "I want to see Nashua's trains."

"It's really up to Debbie," I said, still not convinced this was the greatest idea but not wanting to forbid it. Maybe Debbie would do me a favor and put the kibosh on the plan.

"Why not?" Debbie said, enthusiastically. "There's the cot we can put in Nash's room. Do you mind sleeping on a cot, Arial?"

"No, I like it," Arial said, though she'd never slept on a cot before.

THAT NIGHT, Debbie and I sat in her kitchen drinking wine as Arial and Nashua played in the large stepdown playroom. Debbie had certainly made great decisions in her life. Not only marrying her college boyfriend, Jack, the cardiologist, and running a successful business remodeling furniture that she sold out of an antique store, but having this enormous, custom-built home in a luxury subdivision in the hills.

The house was too huge and impersonal for my tastes—I preferred the small ranch my grandfather had built—but in every other way, Debbie had an enviable life.

It had been a long time since I'd had any alcohol—in fact, the last time had been a glass of wine at Arial's birthday dinner. I associated wine with what happened that night and couldn't completely banish the idea that if my senses hadn't been slightly dulled with alcohol, I'd have picked up on the danger faster, and moved us out of harm's way.

Or I nursed the fantasy that, had I been one-hundred percent sober, I could have disarmed the man. Hadn't I taken self-defense classes over the years? But every single thing I'd learned in classes had fled that night—the only thing I'd done was get in front of Arial, then stand in shock, my hands behind my back in an attempt to keep her safe.

There was another reason I didn't drink these days. I suspected if I went down the road of burying my pain in alcohol, I'd continue down that road until I ended up in a ditch. I couldn't do that to my daughter. She only had one parent, and she needed all of that parent.

But when Debbie took a bottle of white wine out of her enormous stainless-steel fridge and poured two glasses without asking if I wanted any, I'd eyed the wine hungrily, experiencing that forgotten tingly anticipation of instant relaxation that alcohol offered. Though, as I had to drive home, I determined to keep myself at one glass.

Before coming over, Arial and I had gone home for several hours. She'd packed an overnight bag and we had an early spaghetti dinner. I was still unsure allowing her to spend the night somewhere else was the right thing to do. I dreaded a middle-of-the-night phone call to come pick her up.

But she kept reassuring me that she wanted a sleep-over. It was surprising since Nashua was so much younger. But he was a chatterbox extrovert, exactly the kind of child Arial was drawn to. And between my hoarding her at the city apartment after the tragedy, and us moving here, she hadn't seen any other children in months.

"Cheers to being home," Debbie said as we clinked glasses. She'd taken us on a tour of the house and then set the kids up in the playroom. We could hear Nashua's elaborate train set whirring on its double loop.

"Cheers to that," I said.

After half a glass of wine, I was already quite buzzed. I couldn't bring myself to tell Debbie about Kevin, because for the first time since that night, I was having a good time and didn't want to ruin it.

But I did do something else. Something I hadn't done with anyone but Beckett. I began to open up about Arial's father. Of course, I didn't tell Debbie his name, but I admitted he was rather high-profile, and much older, and he was the reason I'd moved to the city shortly after graduation.

"I always wondered," she said. "You kind of disappeared after Arial was born. You never wanted to tell me who he was. I'd always thought it was an older guy from around here."

"Close. He—well, he had a summer home here. He's—damn, I might as well tell you." I hopped up and went to the doorway that led to the sitting room. Right beyond that was the playroom. I wanted to make sure Arial wasn't in earshot. Then I returned and drew my stool closer to Debbie. "He's married."

I could tell by Debbie's face that she was surprised but trying to appear non-judgmental.

"I didn't know it when we got involved," I insisted.

"Once I knew, he lied and told me his wife was dying. Ten years later, she's still quite alive."

"Jesus," Debbie breathed, eyes wide.

"I fell out of love with him years ago but rely on him for financial support, especially as I got laid off about six months ago."

"Is he still married?"

"Yep. His wife has no idea. It's a really messed up situation. So, Arial doesn't know who her father is. I mean, she's met him. She thinks he's a friend of mine. But… I should tell you this in case she mentions it to Nash… I told her that her father was a guy who died in the World Trade Center." I shook my head, which was fuzzy with the wine. "It's so bad. But she kept asking and I couldn't tell her the truth."

I couldn't tell what Debbie thought about all this. We had been good friends in school, but hadn't seen each other in almost a decade. Everything coming out of my mouth made me sound like an awful, immoral human being. And it might sound even worse to a woman who'd suffered a lot in high school because her boyfriend was a chronic cheater.

"I want to make a new start here," I said. "I'll tell her the truth soon. It's just so complicated."

"It does sound complicated. The guy thinks his wife will divorce him if he tells her?"

"There's that. But also, he has a job… it's a sensitive one… and this kind of news wouldn't go over well. He'd probably lose that job."

"I don't know much about this topic, but shouldn't he be paying child support?"

"He should. But he's spooked me. If he loses his job, his only income, he won't be paying hardly anything in child support. It's better off this way, kind of under-handed. At least until I can support both of us."

"Is—is he—famous?" she asked, eyes glinting excitedly.

"Um, not really. Maybe a little."

Debbie's look of intrigue deepened. I realized she probably thought he was a movie star.

"It's—he's a politician. In New York."

"Oh, I see," Debbie said, though her tone was a bit flat, bordering on disappointed. Hardly a movie star.

"If this comes out, he's convinced it will destroy his career. The public thinks he's a big family man. The sad part is, he *is* a big family man. Just not with Arial. He comes over occasionally, tries to make small talk with her, gives her a gift, then leaves. He doesn't know anything about her. Doesn't ask about her grades, her likes and dislikes, her friends. Are there worse fathers in the world? Of course. He's not abusive or cruel. But he's *indifferent*. That's its own kind of cruelty."

"Oh, man." Debbie shook her head and sipped her wine. "That's rough."

"I should have had more sense, more brains. I'm not proud of any of this. My only defense is that he got me very young. Very young and naive."

"I get it. But, if you don't mind my saying, Neels," she said, using my nickname from school. "It seems at some point, Arial needs to know the truth, right?"

"Right, right," I agreed, intensely ashamed of every-thing I'd said, even though she didn't sound judgmental.

"But there's another thing. Um." I paused and sniffed at my wine. A small stalling technique. "Something else happened. I can't give her any more shocks to the system right now."

Debbie's wide eyes were plastered to my face, waiting.

"It's so hard to talk about. I'm scared she might come barreling into the room and hear it. I just want her to have fun tonight. She hasn't had fun in so long. I'm grateful she's found a little friend already."

"I understand. No worries," Debbie said, valiantly changing the topic. "Hey, you remember Jordy Collins?"

"Sure. I remember hanging around Jordy's house a lot back in the day. What's she up to?"

"She's living in——"

A piercing wail split the air. Debbie and I simultaneously bolted from our stools and dashed toward the playroom. It sounded as if Nashua had hurt himself. Debbie, who was moving with the adrenaline of a mother who heard her child was in trouble, was ahead of me.

When she hit the playroom, she hurled herself towards Nashua, who was flat on his back on the floor. He kept screaming as if his life was ending. She scooped him up while I looked around for Arial. She sat calmly on the couch, tinkering with a small, red metal train.

"Arial?" I said loudly to be heard over his cries. "What happened?"

She had the oddest look on her face, far away and dreamy, as if she was staring at something I couldn't see. Nashua continued to cry like only a small child can cry.

At that age, it can be difficult to know if a child is truly injured or being more dramatic than warranted. I hoped right now it was the latter.

"What, what, what is it?" Debbie was saying, patting all over his body, checking for injuries.

"She pushed me!" he hollered.

I looked over. Debbie stood with him on her hip. He was pointing at Arial with a chubby finger.

"She pushed me!" he repeated, face scarlet and tear-stained. The floor had carpeting, the first thing I'd noticed when we left them to play, so at least he probably wasn't hurt.

"I'm sure it was an accident," Debbie consoled.

"No!" he cried. "She-she did it on puh-puss!"

"Arial," I said, firmly, trying to bring her out of her trance. "Tell me what happened."

She finally looked at me. "Nothing," she said.

"Nothing?" I snapped, incredulously. "He said you pushed him. Is that true?" I took the little metal train from her hands so she'd pay attention to what I was saying.

"Nope," she said.

"Mommy, Mommy, Mommy," Nashua gasped, then wailed, "She, she, she pushed me off the table." He pointed at the table in front of the couch. It was scattered with Legos, metal trains, and pieces of unidentifiable plastic.

"Why were you on the table?" Debbie asked patiently. "We don't stand on the table."

"She, she, she said she could fly. She, she, she flew

round and round. And she said, get on the table. I'll make you fly. But she pushed me off!"

"Did you do that?" I demanded.

"Nope," she said, still calm. Too calm.

"Arial, please don't lie to me."

"I didn't. I swear it."

"Liar!" he screamed.

"Okay," Debbie said. "You're not hurt, are you?" She was testing all his limbs. "Nothing's broken. You just got scared."

"Mom," Arial said. "I want to go home."

"Yeah, that's probably for the best." Debbie and I exchanged a *so much for the sleepover* look.

She, she, she flew round and round.

I pictured Arial jumping off the table, winging around the room with her arms outstretched. I'd never seen her pretend to fly before but perhaps hanging out with a young boy inspired her to do something more rambunctious. Could this have also spurred her into taking it too far, pushing him off a table? Trying to make him "fly"? She was old enough to know humans flying around a room wasn't a real thing.

I'd never known her to do a bullying thing like shove or hit another child, but something about her eerie calm made me half-wonder if she'd actually done it.

If she *had* done it, perhaps the residue of her trauma had deepened. I'd spent hundreds of hours watching her on playgrounds and never seen her act aggressive with another kid. In fact, on multiple occasions, I'd had to intervene as a rowdier child shoved, pinched, or otherwise mauled her while she stood with a slightly stunned expression, as if she couldn't believe there were children who behaved in such a way.

"I can't imagine her pushing him," I insisted to Debbie even though doubts were pricking me. I knew I sounded like one of those parents who refuses to believe their kid could be anything less than an angel. I'd been in arguments with parents who'd objected to my light scolding of children who bullied Arial, even though they must have witnessed it with their own eyes.

I'd told myself that I would never be one of those parents—if *my* child misbehaved, I'd correct it. I'd refuse to be blind to a child's faults because faults were completely normal. A child needed to be molded and guided, not coddled to the point of corruption.

I suppose this was another consequence of being raised by elderly people. They never had an issue firmly but lovingly disciplining me if I acted unruly. Once, I'd stolen a small toy from a local general store. My grandmother marched me back inside and forced me to present it to the store's owner with a tremulous apology. I'd never stolen again.

And yet… now I found myself in the position of wanting to defend my child despite ample evidence she'd misbehaved. Because I simply could not imagine Arial pushing a small child off a table. But having seen Nashua sprawled on the floor, his face crimson with indignation, it was unlikely he was faking.

"Things happen," Debbie said. She bounced Nashua on her hip, then slung him down to the floor with a look that said he was too heavy to hold for long periods. "I'm sure it was an accident."

Chapter Eight

"Mommy, are you mad at me?"

The roads were pitch-dark and twisty. I'd had a glass of wine so I was being ultra-diligent, driving slowly, hands gripped tightly on the wheel. Nor had I spoken to Arial about the incident since we got in the car. Mostly because I didn't want to be distracted.

"Mommy?" she persisted. "I didn't push him. Honestly, I didn't. I don't remember it."

The high beams picked up a dirt road to the side so I maneuvered into it and shifted into neutral. The car was a rental. I hadn't yet bought one. I didn't have the money to do so. Jed was in Rome with his "real family" and hadn't put enough funds into Beckett's account. So I was paying an exorbitant amount for the rental and piling it onto my already overtaxed credit cards. Another thing for me to be irritated about.

"Arial, first you said you didn't do it, now you're saying you don't *remember* doing it?" I asked.

"That's the same."

Only if you're a politician, I thought. I hope she didn't inherit that trait of Jed's, twisting words to fit his narrative.

"It's not quite the same," I said. "I know you've been through a lot, boo. But Nashua is a little boy. Just a baby. And you're a big girl. So you can't lay hands on him. Do you understand?"

"But I don't remember it. We were sitting on the floor playing with his trains. Then he was on the other side of the room, crying. Like out of nowhere. It was so weird."

"Are you telling me you think he was pretending to be hurt?"

"No. I—I don't know. I just don't remember any of it. I feel like, if I *did* push him, then it wasn't—like it wasn't me who did it."

"It wasn't you?"

"Yeah."

"Honey, you've lost me. Listen, I'm not mad at you but it's wrong to put your hands in a bad way on any other kid. You know that. We've had these talks. You've always been good about it. So, I'm giving you the benefit of the doubt. I know things have been difficult and maybe you're not feeling yourself."

She put her sad pout on, so I placed my hand soothingly on her arm.

"We can't have anything like that again, okay, boo? I'm not saying you did it. But in case you did it, and don't remember, then we've got to lay down the rules

again. Remember that book *Hands Are Not For Hitting?*
They're not for pushing either. *Comprende?*"

"I know, Mom. I know all that."

* * *

AT HOME, I waited until Arial was in bed, then slipped
into a light jacket and walked into the front yard to call
Debbie. I didn't want to make the call inside the house.
It was a small house and Arial could overhear me.

"Is he okay?" I asked when Debbie picked up.

"He's not hurt. Just shook up."

"If she pushed him that's no Arial I've ever seen. I'm
really sorry, Debbie."

"They're kids. Things will happen." She chuckled.
"He keeps saying she knows how to fly."

I moved to a lawn chair I'd set in the middle of the
front yard, anticipating that I'd need to make private
calls. I'd been making private calls with Jed since Arial
was a toddler and had gotten to be an expert at slipping
into secluded areas so she couldn't hear me. The half-
moon was enamel white, with low, flowing clouds undulating past it like a ragged cape.

Debbie was being polite but I could already tell she
had no intention of inviting Arial to sleep over again
any time soon. I couldn't blame her. What I was about
to reveal might excuse my daughter's behavior but it also
could cement the idea that she was defective with
trauma. But I felt Debbie should have an explanation.

"I don't know about flying, but she hasn't been the
same since the incident I mentioned, what happened in

the city. The reason we moved." I took a deep gulp of a breath, stared at the brilliant moon some more, then plunged ahead. "I was dating a guy. For about six months. He was really kind and good, and I liked him a lot, but mostly, I think I kept dating him because he accepted and got along with Arial. She really liked him."

I paused and watched the thin, dark clouds as they streamed faster past the moon.

"I can't even tell you how hard it is to find a guy like that, at least in the city. Most of them want sex on date one. I lived in a one-bedroom with my kid. We had two beds in one room, with a fake wall in between."

"Yikes," Debbie said.

"Finding a man who is okay with taking things incredibly—I mean *incredibly*—slowly in that area... it wasn't easy. I'd have to hire a babysitter and then I'm paying for sex. I'm keeping an eye on the time, you know?"

Debbie laughed even though this was a true statement.

"He was a saint. On her birthday, we brought her out to her favorite Italian restaurant. We walked home through the park. And, um... he was attacked."

"Attacked?"

"Yes, he was, ah..." Hot, prickly tears jabbed behind my eyelids. I swallowed hard, pushing them down inside of me. "Killed. Murdered."

There was a very long silence on the other end of the line. So long that I began to wonder if the call had dropped.

"Neels…" Debbie said faintly. "I'm so sorry. I had no idea."

"She saw it. She was right there."

"Oh my God. That's horrific."

"She—she's had some instances where she's been 'off.' But I never would have allowed her over if I'd thought she would get physical, put her hands on Nash. She says she doesn't remember pushing him. I believe her. But I believe him, too. So, I'm stumped as to what happened."

"Has she seen anyone? A therapist?"

"A few times. We were assigned a social worker by the crime victim's advocate. But I didn't like going outside while the guy hadn't been found. Then they arrested him but, I don't know, I stopped with it. I got preoccupied with moving. That became the thing I thought would solve everything. And honestly, it was so hard to talk about him. It still is. But I've been thinking of starting up again."

"I can recommend someone," Debbie said, her voice soft with empathy. "A woman in town. Jack and I went to her a few years ago when we were having some issues. We even brought Nash to a couple of sessions. She counsels kids, too."

"Great. Can you email me her name?"

"Absolutely." She sighed. "Arial has been through so much. Her father. This."

"I know. I'm terrified that she'll never be the same. She was so happy-go-lucky before all this."

"She's young. The young are resilient. I'm

concerned for you too, Neels. My God. What you've been through. Is there anything I can do?"

I stared up at the moon, with the transparent, ragged clouds flowing faster and faster over it, and listened to the breeze lightly rattling the tree branches all around the property. It sounded as it did when I was a child. I took strength in the sounds, the fresh smell of the lawn, the low-hanging moon. Everything I saw, heard, and inhaled brought me right back to my childhood, when I was safe.

I was safe now. Arial and I were both safe. I had to believe that. I *did* believe it.

"Be a friend, I guess?" I asked her.

"Of course, Neels. Always have been. And the kids can get together again. Of course they can. But we probably need to keep an eye on them next time."

Chapter Nine

I was astonished to see the district attorney standing on my doorstep. District Attorney Andres Acosta. "Call me Andy," he'd told me when he and I first met, the day after Kevin's murder. But I'd never called him Andy. He was too intimidating to be anything other than "Mr. Acosta."

He was a large man in every way—tall, broad-shouldered, hefty around the middle. The kind of man who made me feel it will get done, the killer will get convicted.

His hair was chunky and all gray, and he appeared in his late fifties. He dressed sharply, always in a dark suit with a bright tie. Right now, the tie was light blue. I was not only confused to see him on my doorstep, but surprised that he was all dressed up as if he was standing inside his office.

"Oh, hi," I said, reluctantly opening the screen door. "Did you call me?"

"No, ma'am, I didn't," he said. "Was passing through and thought this should be done in person."

Was passing through the middle of Connecticut? Sounded strange but what did I know about the man's schedule? I was nervous he'd come all this way to give me some execrable news, like that the killer had escaped jail or that his office had decided not to bring charges after all.

I didn't want to speak where Arial could hear us, so I asked him to hold on while I checked that she was in her room thoroughly engaged with an art project involving her little jars of paint and wood tongue-depressor sticks. Then I ushered him out to the front lawn, and walked him down the crumbling pathway to the small turn-around drive. His sleek black town-car was parked there.

"Would you like to sit in the car?" he asked.

"Uh, sure."

The inside of the car was top notch, everything gleaming and modern. District attorneys must make decent money or this was a city car.

"Sorry to spring on you like this," he said. "I wanted to alert you to a couple of updates."

It was terrifically odd he hadn't called me, and instead had driven all this way. This in and of itself made my stomach go queasy. I knew without question he was about to give me some kind of unwelcome news.

"The perp definitely had mental issues," he said. "He had an incident in the park about a week before, where he chased after someone with a bottle."

I nodded slowly. Not a big surprise.

"The victim never reported it and came forward a few days ago. Parks department said there have been other issues with him over the years, knocking over garbage cans, things like that. He sleeps in the tunnel. But he'd never been institutionalized."

I nodded again, fearful about where this was going. There is no way Acosta drove all the way here to tell me the guy had mental problems. That was already clear.

"According to your statement, he said, quote, 'I'm the devil,' correct?"

"Yes, exactly."

"See, what I'm concerned about," he said, tapping a wedding band on his ring finger. "Is that the defense will plead not responsible by reason of mental defect. And, given his history, the plea might work."

My stomach turned. It was as I'd feared. Something was going to stop Kevin from getting justice.

"What does that mean? He'll go free?"

"If the plea is successful, he'd go to a psychiatric facility."

"Would—would that be bad?"

Acosta turned his dark eyes on me. They were eyes that had seen it all. "I don't think he's insane," he said. "Issues, yes. But legally insane to the point where he didn't know right from wrong? Where he didn't know that killing was immoral and against the law? He knew enough to stash the knife inside a hole he'd dug out in the tunnel. He knew enough to wipe down his fingerprints. He knew to stay out of the park for several days afterward and hide out with relatives. He knew what he'd done was wrong, he absolutely knew it."

"So—so then what?"

"If he ends up in a state hospital, they can only hold

him for as long as he's deemed legally not sane. It probably wouldn't be long before he's out. A few years, maybe."

"What?" I gasped.

Staring out the window, I slowly shook my head at the unfairness of the world. How does a man get the life snuffed out of him for no reason and the person who took that life, that beautiful life, won't even be properly punished? In a few years, the killer would be free to roam around and possibly kill again?

"We don't want that," Acosta said. "We're going to fight it with everything we've got. But I wanted to ask you—do you remember anything else he might have said that night?"

"He said, 'What the fuck you staring at?'"

Had Acosta forgotten that part already?

"And he yelled something before he came over to us. I have no idea what he said or whether he was even speaking to us."

"Right. Anything besides that?"

"Mmm… I don't think so, but it was all a blur. All I could think about was protecting my daughter. I was so scared he was going to come for her."

"That's perfectly understandable, Ms. Pfau." He sighed, and turned his head to stare across the street at the ballpark, which had started to get lively with Little League games but was currently empty. He wasn't looking at me as he said, casually, "Mr. Huang was half-Asian, correct?"

"Uh, yes."

He turned towards me. "Did you two discuss that?"

"Discuss?" Confused by the question, I furrowed my brows and couldn't help laughing a little. "Not really. I don't think it came up at all."

"Is there any chance the perp said something about Mr. Huang's ethnicity?"

"About his—about being Asian?"

"Yeah."

"Um. It was really dark. I doubt the man even noticed that."

"But, say, if the perp *did* say something like that… then it's a bias-motivated crime. Additional charges. Much less chance of a successful legal defect defense. If you're coherent enough to be racist, then you're damn well coherent enough to commit murder. It's important that if he said something along those lines that you report it to us."

My mind was whirring, yet sluggish at the same time. It was taking me a while to figure out what was happening. I didn't know if the district attorney was triple-checking that I remembered everything the killer had said… or if Acosta was…

Suggesting I lie?

Now I was the one who couldn't make eye contact. Squeezing my hands in my lap, I stared off down the sidewalk that stretched to the end of the street. A woman with a stroller headed towards us. I just kept staring at her, noting her clothes, her hair, the type of stroller she was pushing.

"I don't, um, I don't know, but, um…" I stammered.

The woman turned at my drive, where the sidewalk ended, and headed back where she came from. Just out for a stroll with her baby. What was her life like? Did she suffer the same kinds of emotional earthquakes I was suffering? She looked so carefree. Why did some people get so much thrown at them and others lived long, healthy, serene, fortunate lives?

"You'd let me know, right?" Acosta said. "I understand if you'd want to leave that part out, not want to bring race into it. But it would be vital information. It could mean the difference between justice and injustice."

"But I already told the police everything I thought he said," I said, practically whispering. "Wouldn't it seem strange if I remembered more?"

"Not at all. Once the shock starts to wear off a little, people often remember other details. More memories come. It's pretty standard."

"Oh."

"Think about it," Acosta pressed. "I know it's hard to go back and relive it. But we don't want this guy on the street any time soon."

"No."

This is why Acosta hadn't called me. This is why we were sitting in his car.

He didn't want any record of this conversation.

Chapter Ten

*T*he psychiatrist's office was on the ground floor of her historic home on Quarry Road, with an eye-popping view of the river. Given how upscale her home and office appeared, I was surprised she took my anemic health insurance, which cost a small fortune but finding doctors who took it was akin to the proverbial needle in a haystack.

If it hadn't been for her accepting my insurance, I may not have even booked with her based solely on her name, Dr. Nora Bertussi. Because Bertussi's Pizzeria is where I'd worked as a waitress on weekends following my junior year. (Years later, I'd realize why the owner paid me in cash—I was too young to be legally working in a restaurant.)

It was also where I'd met Jed.

He'd sit at a corner table by himself and order the sausage and pepper hero with a dark beer, and read what seemed dozens of newspapers and magazines he kept in a briefcase. I'd wait on him, fascinated and impressed by a man who read so much. None of the boys I knew read. They played sports and video games. Increasingly, I had nothing to talk with them about.

But Jed and I could talk… and talk… and eventually we fucked. Why we could talk so much and not discuss birth control was a mystery. I've come to realize even the most intelligent men can be dumb as rocks when it comes to sex.

And, no, he hadn't been wearing a wedding ring.

"Please sit where you feel most comfortable," Nora said. The office was decorated in neutral colors—white walls, white couch, a cushy black club chair, and a black-and-white armchair. There were a few oil paintings with banal and tranquil depictions of nature. The décor scheme seemed chosen to be as innocuous as possible, with absolutely nothing that could trigger an emotionally fragile client, even a loud color.

Nora looked to be in her sixties, with blondish-reddish hair in a fashionably messy bun, and eyeglasses hanging around a glass-beaded strap. I chose the end of the couch to sit on and Nora lowered into the club chair across from me. I noted several fidget devices placed on the glass coffee table. I refrained from picking one up.

We only had forty-five minutes, so I tried to bring her quickly up-to-date on the major events—Kevin's murder, the move to Orchard, Arial's recent behavior, including the dream with her saying *I killed him*, and her squeezing my wrist until she drew blood. Also, the alleged pushing of Nashua off the table.

Nora diligently took notes and appeared the perfect

combination of sympathetic but composed. She'd very likely heard much worse in her time.

"I'm thinking she needs to see a therapist," I said. "Maybe she and I could come here together. I'm not sure how that works."

"With minors, we can have mutual and solo sessions," Nora said. "It's important for the child to be able to have free expression without a parent around, so she's not anticipating what the parent wants to hear and saying what she thinks will please the adult. Other times, it's preferable for the parent to be present, for the child to have that safety and support."

Nora balanced her glasses on her nose as she examined her notes, then took them off, staring at me with kindly and intelligent blue-gray eyes.

"I have no doubt that Arial is suffering major trauma from Kevin's death," she said. "Witnessing something like that is horrendous enough for an adult let alone a child. May I ask, where is her father in this?"

I should admit the entire truth about Jed and how we'd gotten involved when I was still a teenager, but was loathe to do so. And the part about me telling Arial her father had died in the World Trade Center stuck in my throat, refusing to budge out. Both things were so bad that I felt the therapist's attention would immediately divert to me—that I would become the sole cause of Arial's mental health issues.

"He's around but Arial doesn't know him as her father. He stops by occasionally, pretending to be an old friend."

"Oh?"

I sat twisting my hands, feeling a few beads of sweat pop on my brow line. What was the point of coming to a therapist and then lying to her? Or lying by omission?

"See, I got pregnant at sixteen, when I was a senior in high school," I said, eyeing the fidget devices. "I skipped the first grade so I was younger than the average."

The look on her face was impassive, as if this was news she'd entirely expected to hear. I plowed on: "He was much older, married, and an assemblyman in New York. Right up until this day, he hasn't told his wife or the public. Now he's..." I debated revealing his identity but figured the session must be confidential. "Now he's running for mayor. And he'll probably win."

I also weighed telling her that I'd met him at Bertussi's Pizzeria—I'd later learn the place was owned by a distant relative of Nora's whom she hardly knew—but decided this tidbit was irrelevant.

"Arial has no idea that he is her father?" she asked.

"No. Here's the even worse part." I cringed—physically cringed—then admitted to the lie about the young stockbroker who'd died on September 11.

Nora kept taking notes, nodding slightly, completely nonjudgmentally. I wondered what she was really thinking. Could anyone be this unruffled about what she'd just been told? She'd either heard some major crap in her day or she was a master at remaining expressionless.

"Some of this very likely plays into her trauma," she concluded. "In her mind, her father goes to work one day, enters what should have been a humdrum, routine day, and dies horrifically. Then she meets a father figure, and he also dies under extreme and horrific circumstances during what should have been a routine event, walking through the park. More than most people, she'll think that merely going on about life is highly risky."

"Oh, God," I moaned. "You're right. I hadn't even put that together."

Now I truly abhorred myself for telling my child that her father had died in a fiery terrorist attack. What the *hell* had I been thinking? I finally snatched one of the fidget devices and began spinning the outside with my forefinger.

"She's going to have deep abandonment fears," Nora said. "Especially when it comes to male figures."

"I guess I…" My voice lumped in my throat, and I squeezed the fidget device hard to keep from blubbering. "… thought was better she thinks her father died than that she knows the one she *does* have doesn't love her."

The therapist's face remained placid but one foot, encased in what could only be described as "sensible shoes," began bouncing a little. Maybe I'd finally earned her disapproval.

"I'd say that's not true," she said. "Having a relationship with an absent or inadequate parent can be difficult. But relationships like that can be worked on and healed. Can't do that with a deceased parent. Besides, the truth is always best."

"I know. I just don't know if I can handle the millions of questions she'll throw at me. Where is Jed, when is Jed coming over, why is Jed traveling with his other kids and not her, why is Jed spending holidays with his other kids and not with her. All of this will become solely up to me to answer because he won't. And I'll have to do it over and over."

The thought of having to answer all these uncomfortable questions made acid fizz in my stomach. Speaking them aloud, I realized that *this* was the real reason I'd said her father was dead. For my own convenience.

"It's unfortunate that these are things you'll have to talk through with her," said Nora. "But I still think it's best that she knows the truth."

"Right but… then there's the chance she tells it all to a friend or two. And those friends tell their parents. The next thing you know, everyone knows. I'm relying on him financially. Wouldn't it be worse if I tell her the truth but then ask her to keep it a secret?"

"Perhaps right now isn't the most advantageous time," Nora said, fingering her beaded glasses strap. "But I don't know when *would* be. Eventually, she'll find out, and it will be a lot more hurtful if she finds out years from now. When I counsel children who've been through traumatic events with parents, it's not so much the difficulties the children find hardest to heal from, but the deceptions. Children need to know, above all, that they can trust their parents. Since you're essentially Arial's only parent, that means trusting *you*. You've let this untruth go on for a long time. I strongly encourage you to take some time and sit with how to gently and lovingly usher Arial into the truth."

Nora was a nice woman but the tap-dancing around what she was trying to say irked me. I wanted to snap *Just say 'stop lying to your daughter!'*

But I was hardly one to demand forthright language from anyone.

The session was over before I knew it. As Nora guided me to the door, she said, "I have a little homework for you."

I grimaced. I'd loved school but despised homework. Seeing the look on my face, she smiled. "It's good homework, I promise. I'd like you to take a little time for yourself."

"Myself?" It was like I'd never heard the word before.

"Yes, you know how on an airplane they always tell a parent to put the oxygen mask on first in case of emergency, *then* help the child afterward?"

I didn't want to admit I'd never been on a plane so I just nodded.

"It's important that you take care of yourself. Important not only for you but for Arial. Here's the homework: do something for yourself. Go to a spa. Join a book club. Get your nails done. Whatever it is. But it has to be something that's only for you."

Do something just for *me*? Who was supposed to take care of my child while I was me-timing around town? I almost sarcastically suggested I drop Arial off here while I did this but worried that Nora might actually agree.

As she opened the office door, I dazedly concurred with the homework assignment but, in reality, I had no idea how to do it.

Chapter Eleven

*B*y the time I finished with the psychiatrist, went grocery and pharmacy shopping, and returned home, it was nearing eight p.m. and already mostly dark.

Weighed down with bags of food and hygiene products, I was a little uneasy as I headed up the cracked pathway to the house. The living room light was on but couldn't see anything else through the one large window that took up most of the living room wall facing the street.

"Helllooo," I called as I entered.

Amara, Arial's babysitter, stood up from the couch, where she was sitting with a reading tablet. She'd come recommended by Debbie and attended the local high school.

She was sixteen and very pretty, with black corkscrew curls piled atop her head, giving her at least six inches on an already tall figure. I imagined, based on nothing but her striking looks, that she must be popular at school.

"Hi," she said, smiling.

"Everything go alright?" I asked, a touch of nerves attacking my voice, making it sound girlish. It was the first time I'd left Arial with a babysitter since the murder.

Amara tucked her reading tablet under her arm and glanced toward the hallway. "Sure. We read for a while, then had hot chocolate. She painted most of the evening. About half an hour ago, she said she wanted to be left alone so she could make you a surprise."

"Oh?"

"She didn't want me to see it. Should I have stayed with her?"

Amara looked at me beseechingly. The poor girl must be wondering why I appeared concerned. It was normally perfectly acceptable to leave a ten-year-old in her own bedroom in her own house. Amara had no idea that Arial was suffering any kind of trauma and had had a couple of small behavioral episodes. Nor had I instructed Amara to keep her eye on my daughter every second of the babysitting job.

"Of course not, no worries," I said, placing the grocery bags on the table. "She had dinner?"

"Yes, at six, like you said. Mac-n-cheese, broccoli, and yogurt. I did the dishes."

Amara came over and indicated some dishes on the wooden drying rack. This girl was a find. No wonder Debbie liked her.

"She ate well. She's a great kid."

Relief surged through me that all had gone smoothly. "Fabulous. You ate, too?"

"Oh, I'll grab something on the way home." She put her tablet inside of a tote bag she retrieved from the couch and took down a cardigan from the standing coat rack.

"Well, thank you so much, Amara," I said, digging in my bag for money. I handed her four twenties. Perhaps I should go into babysitting for some extra cash myself. I'd hoped babysitters would be cheaper in the country but no such luck. "Hopefully we'll see you again."

I turned on the outside light and watched Amara head up the pathway to the little car she'd parked in the drive. Then I decided to see what Arial was up to before putting away the groceries and making something to eat.

ARIAL WAS SITTING on the floor, with her small jars of acrylic paints, her palette, and brushes spread out on her drop cloth. Instantly, my eyes were drawn to the wall behind her. On the white paint, in lurid red block letters, were the words DIE YOU SLUT.

I gasped and clapped my hand over my mouth, eyes wide at the graffiti. "What the——" was all I could get out of my mouth.

"Mommy!" Arial screeched in her usual *I'm glad you're back* greeting. She held up a green cardboard sheet with a glittery design on it that I couldn't decipher. Not when I was still standing in astounded horror at what I was seeing on the wall. "I'm making a book!" she cried. "It's for you!"

"What the——" I wanted so badly to let rip a *fuck*. It took massive willpower not to have the word bullet out of my shocked mouth. "What is on the *wall*, Arial? What *is* this?"

She looked bewildered for a few moments before following the direction of my pointed finger. Then she turned back to me, a vacant look on her face.

I walked into the room, right up to the wall, and stared at the words as if still half-expecting them to morph into something else, into something cutesy and child-appropriate. I was accustomed to Arial's handwriting and this looked like hers.

"Why did you do this?" I demanded.

"I didn't do that."

"Arial," I snapped. "I'm *sick* of this! And where are you learning this language?"

"I'm not."

I drew one finger over the D in the word DIE. The paint was dry so she must have written this a while ago. She'd deliberately sent Amara out of the room so she could deface the wall.

"I seriously can't *believe* this," I said. "This is *not* acceptable."

"Mom, I didn't do it."

"You're the only one in the room!" I stalked over to her paints, and looked down. One of the brushes lying on the drop cloth still had red paint clumped on the bristles. I pointed at that too. "That looks like the culprit!"

Arial sat with her little shoulders glumly slumped.

"Are you telling me this wasn't you?" I demanded again.

"It wasn't," she said quietly, lower lip pushed out in a pout.

"Then who was it?"

When she didn't answer, I stomped out of the room, determined to calm down before I did something I couldn't take back. I'd never hit Arial before. Not ever. But I had the urge to spank her on the butt. Just one quick not-too-hard crack. But I didn't believe in corporeal punishment. I did not think laying hands on a child who couldn't fight back was remotely fair. But, by God, I was tempted.

She's traumatized, she's traumatized…

I kept repeating this to myself as I hunched over the bathroom sink, staring at my pale, distressed face in the mirror. Then I returned and stood in the doorway of Arial's room. She was obliviously back to painting.

"Arial." My voice was clipped but I managed to hold my white-hot anger in check. "You're going to put those paints away, clean up, and I'm taking them from you. You have lost your painting privileges."

"Whyyyy?" she whined.

"Put those paints away. *Now!*" This time I used my *don't you even think of messing with me* tone, reserved for the most serious of infractions.

And I'd never seen an infraction this serious from her.

Chapter Twelve

"Thanks for coming over," I said, opening the door.

A rather handsome man, about my age, stood on the small steps. He looked vaguely familiar. I'd called Deluxe Painters in the morning and spoken to a man whose name I didn't ask. He said he'd come over soon to see what I needed done and give me an estimate.

Last night, I'd spent about an hour trying to scrub the offending words off the wall with no luck. Neither soap nor detergent nor fingernail polish remover put a dent in the blaring red paint.

The whole wall would need to be painted over. Because the wall was an off-white, with the barest undercoat of beige, I'd have to match that exact color, something I had no idea how to do. If I couldn't match it, the entire room would need to be repainted. Though I'd promised Arial that she could select the color for her room, I no longer felt she had that privilege. Not after what she'd done.

The painter stood in my living room, his head of dark shorn hair almost scraping the swirly popcorn ceiling. If he did a good job in Arial's room, perhaps I'd hire him to get rid of that, too. The popcorn ceiling brought back a lot of nostalgia but not enough to make me like it.

"Do I—do we—?" I said, wagging my fingers at him. "You look familiar."

"Don't recognize me, huh?"

He smiled. He had a great smile, enviably white but natural-looking at the same time. Probably the best smile I'd ever seen on someone who wasn't on a movie screen.

"Sorry, no."

"Salem Collins. Jordy's little brother."

"Oh my God! Salem!"

Now I remembered Jordy's younger brother. Always skulking around Jordy's house, popping his head around corners at inopportune times, spying on whatever mischief his sister and I were getting up to. Whether we were making prank calls, whispering about making out with crushes, or sneaking beers out of her father's garage fridge, Salem always seemed to be lurking nearby, trying to catch us in the act. He never tattled that I was aware of so maybe he only wanted to be part of things. Now I felt a little guilty that I hadn't been nicer to him.

I certainly didn't recall him being so good-looking but most boys aren't at the age I remembered him— twelve or thirteen. I only recalled his name because it was an unusual one. Jordy would shout at him, "Get out of here, Salem, you witch!"

At the time, I hadn't put it together that she was referring to Salem, Massachusetts, site of the infamous burning of doomed women accused of being witches. I wondered what made his parents decide on that for a name.

"You look so different," I said, taking in his tall build, the jeans torn at the knees, the snug white t-shirt showing off a gym-toned body, and the dark blue hoodie with white paint streaks on the sleeves.

He made circles with his fingers around his eyes. "Used to have glasses."

"Oh, right!"

"You look the same."

The way he said it, it sounded like a compliment.

Now I was reluctant to show him the writing on the wall. It would have been embarrassing enough to show to a stranger—and I planned to blame it on the family who'd moved away—but to show it to someone I sort of knew?

"Come, ah, see the room," I stammered.

As we passed the kitchen, I shot a glance out of the window above the sink. It had a clear view of the back-yard and Arial on the playset's swing. Although I'd spent hundreds, maybe thousands of hours playing in the backyard as a kid with zero oversight, times were differ-ent. I hadn't yet become accustomed to allowing my kid a free-range lifestyle. I'd been peeking out of the window every fifteen minutes or so, making certain she was still there.

"This was here when we got here," I said, laughing uncomfortably, indicating the message on the wall. "Maybe someone broke in and did it. I tried to scrub it off but couldn't manage it."

His eyes were taking in the room, noting all the girly paraphernalia, swiftly putting it together that a child lived in the room. A child who must be aware of having DIE YOU SLUT on her wall. Once again, I felt like worst mother of the year. The decade.

"She insisted on this room since it overlooks the woods," I said, stridently. Then I shrugged. "She's heard worse on TV."

Salem sidled over to the wall, digging at the paint with a finger. "Once paint dries, it's like glue. I could try some turpentine."

"Well, I've been wanting to paint over everything anyway. There are some stains along the ceiling."

I drew his attention to some mysterious charcoal-colored smudges. The family who'd lived here probably used this room as an office and someone smoked.

Salem peered at the writing again. I inwardly cringed each time he focused on it.

"I'd have to use a heavy-duty stain blocker, primer, then emulsion paint," he said. "Or you could go darker."

"I'd really prefer to keep it light. Sunny. I want a cheery mood in here." I laughed, indicating the writing. "This is not cheery."

He turned and laughed with me. "Nope. Definitely not cheery."

* * *

"IT WAS NICE SEEING YOU AGAIN," I said, watching Salem climb into his pickup. As he did so, I couldn't stop myself from stealing a glimpse at his backside. It was suitably gawk-worthy.

"Tell Jordy I said hi." My voice was overeager and slightly breathless. "I'd been meaning to get in touch since I moved back but I got distracted."

I crossed my arms, rocking on my feet, and tried to sound as casual as possible. "Maybe the three of us could meet up for a drink sometime."

In the forefront of my mind was Nora's "homework assignment"—her directive that I do something for myself. Drinks out with Jordy and her (let's face it, quite hot) little brother should be enough. I couldn't believe how much he'd changed, and for the better. I'd hardly noticed him when he was a kid other than to absorb that he was nosy and nerdy.

He closed the door of his truck and stared down at me. "She's not in town anymore. Married a Canadian and moved to Nova Scotia."

Now I remembered that Debbie had been about to tell me some news about Jordy right before Nashua's cries had shattered the air. It must have been about Jordy's move.

"I didn't know. That sounds like an interesting place to live."

"She seems to like it." He grinned. "I'm booked up this week but got some time next for the room. What works for you?"

"That works." I laughed too airily. Since he'd side-stepped the question of meeting up for drinks, I guessed he wasn't interested. Which was fine. Too soon for me, anyway. I'd find time to read a book that wasn't written for a ten-year-old and make that my homework. "Open schedule right now," I said.

"I'll bring over some swatches and get started on the blocker."

"I, uh, forgot to ask your estimate?"

"Let's see…" He drummed the side of the vehicle with his long, slim fingers. "For you?" He grinned down again. "Since you're a friend of Jordy and all, I'll give you a discount. About four hundred. Five if you want the ceiling done."

That's a discount? Forget babysitting, I should become a painter.

"Okay, sounds good," I said, though I sounded like I'd hoped for a larger discount. More weight on my credit cards, which were already groaning and sagging from so much weight. Anger at Arial for her defacing of the wall flared hotly then retreated as I once more reminded myself that this uncharacteristic behavior must be a bizarre symptom of her trauma.

But why did it have to be so expensive?

"Oh, and just because Jordy isn't here doesn't mean we can't meet up. If you're up for it." Salem flicked me his business card through the window. "Give me a shout."

He gunned the engine and rumbled down the hill.

Chapter Thirteen

"You're not going to believe who I saw."

"Salem Collins," Debbie said.

I turned and gaped at her.

We were sitting on a bench at the same playground in the center of town where we'd met before. This time, Arial and Nashua were climbing all over a jungle gym set.

I was keeping a keen eye on Arial but, so far, she hadn't come near to Nashua. She was much more nimble than he was, and had effortlessly swung herself up to the top of the monkey bars while he stood below, staring up at her as if she was an exotic bird in a tree.

She flew round and round.

"How did you know?" I asked.

"He's friends with Jack and told him. Said, and I quote, you looked as smoking as in high school."

I couldn't help but smile at the compliment. It had been a long time since anyone had called me "smoking"

—in fact, I don't think anyone ever had. At least that I knew about.

I'd forgotten what it was like being in a small town. Everyone knew each other, and everyone knew everything. While I'd assured myself that this was the sort of thing I wanted more of— that I preferred everyone being in my business to the soulless anonymity of the city—now that I was having difficulties with Arial, I wasn't sure I wanted it.

Had Salem also told Debbie's husband what he'd read on my kid's wall? Debbie was showing no sign that she was aware of it. If she did know, I wondered if she'd still allow her son to play with my daughter. Between that, and the possibility that Arial had shoved Nashua off a table, my kid wasn't coming across like a suitable playmate for anyone.

I was already having a few misgivings about whether to enroll her in the local middle-school in the fall. Would I have to hire a special teacher for her? Homeschool her?

The number of valuable items I'd seen in the local Goodwill indicated there might be people in the area who needed an organizer. I'd been researching starting my own business. But how could I hold down a job if I couldn't leave Arial in school? How was I supposed to teach her math, something she was already better at than I was?

I dreaded that she was on her way to becoming the town pariah. That would negate a big reason I'd moved here—wanting a closer-knit community. Wanting more support. Wanting *any* support.

"He's all grown up now," I said of Salem.

"He sure is." Debbie smirked in a way that let me know she too thought Salem had grown up impressively well. "You know he had a big crush on you, right?"

"No. Come on."

"He did too. Remember we'd be in the backyard in Jordy's tree fort, and he'd be on the patio, spying from behind those big potted plants? It was you he was staring at."

"It wasn't."

"Okay, whatever," she laughed. "Half the guys in school had a crush on you."

"That's ridiculous."

Maybe they had. Junior year, I'd been voted "Nicest to Look At." (Senior year a friend of mine, Leah, had taken over the title.)

But because of everything going on with Jed—secretly meeting up with him, getting pregnant near the end of senior year—I'd felt so removed from the high school boys. They were no more than irritants to me. I had no interest in their partying, their jabbering on about football or basketball.

Jed would talk to me about serious things, about how he wanted to change the world. About inequalities. About injustices. Things I'd never considered.

Looking back, I realized he was using those "big ideas" to get into my pants but at the time, that thought hadn't occurred to me.

"All seems forgiven between those two," Debbie noted, jutting her chin towards Arial and Nashua.

Arial had her legs slung over the monkey bars, at

least six feet above Nashua. He'd stopped staring at her and was doing a funny hopscotch dance back and forth under the bars.

"How is she doing, anyway?" Debbie asked.

I couldn't tell whether this question meant she knew what had been written on the bedroom wall—whether Salem had told Jack what he'd seen, and Jack had informed Debbie. I hoped that, like a therapist, a painter had to respect the privacy of his clients and keep the things he saw in their homes under wraps.

"She's fine," I lied. "Thanks for recommending Nora. I had a session with her."

"You going to keep seeing her?"

"I think so. I haven't quite decided. Arial doesn't seem like she wants therapy and I don't want to push her into it."

I didn't add that Nora was pretty adamant that I do something I really didn't want to do yet—tell Arial the truth of her paternity.

"I wanted to run something by you," I said, watching Arial swing down from the monkey bars in one fluid motion. Nashua jumped up and down and clapped, apparently impressed with her maneuver.

"I got a surprise visit from the district attorney prosecuting Kevin's case," I said. "Maybe I'm reading into things but he seemed to be implying... well, he seemed to want me to say that the guy who attacked Kevin did it because Kevin was half-Asian."

"*That's* why he got attacked?"

"I don't think so. But... the DA kept asking if I remembered the guy saying anything about Kevin's ethnicity. He worries the guy will plead insanity. But if he killed Kevin because of his race, then it's a hate crime."

I sighed and wriggled uncomfortably on the bench, squinting into the pearly, marigold afternoon light.

"I think the DA wants me to lie."

"What?" Debbie spat. "Wow. And these guys are there to uphold the law."

"I know. I don't want to do it. But I'm really nervous the killer might get a slap on the wrist and be out soon. Maybe kill someone else."

I watched Arial prance from one end of the monkey bars to the other as Nashua tried to keep pace, attempting to imitate the bold flinging of her legs. I still had wrenchingly painful thoughts about what would have happened to her if the man had killed me, too. Would Jed have stepped up to claim her as his own? I doubted it. Doing so would have destroyed his chances of becoming mayor. It hurt my heart to know the reality: that his ambition was more important than his daughter.

"What would you do?" I asked Debbie.

She said nothing for a while, considering the question. Then she turned to me and said, evenly, "To be honest, I'd probably say what I needed to say to keep that guy off the street. I couldn't live with myself if he did it to someone else."

She returned her attention to Arial and Nashua, who now had their heads together. They were examining something small and dark that Arial had picked up off the ground. Hard to tell what it was from here but probably a pine cone. Arial collected pine cones, would gather them up for painting and glittering. There was already a basketful of them at home.

Thank God, she and Nashua were getting along and there hadn't been any incidents… yet. I couldn't deny that a constant low-grade edginess about her had burrowed under my skin.

I felt I had to monitor her every movement, something I hadn't experienced since she was a toddler and would try to climb up the CD tower or pull the flatscreen TV onto her head.

I'd gone around our small apartment taping down wires, padding the sharp corners of furniture, removing anything heavy from tables, and installing child-proof bars on the windows. "Arial-proofing," I'd called it. Yet another thing Jed hadn't helped with or even asked about.

"Yeah, I guess I'd say what I had to," Debbie affirmed. "I mean, what if that guy kills a kid next time? Not that an adult isn't bad enough. It is. But a child? And thinking I might have prevented it? I couldn't survive that."

"No," I said. "I couldn't either."

Arial suddenly turned and began running towards me, Nashua barreling his way after her, trying to keep up. She had the pine cone in her hands and a curious, expectant look on her face, as if she was about to show it off to me. Perhaps it was larger than usual or had silvery colors in it. I leaned forward, ready to give praise at her find when I realized the dark thing in her hand wasn't a pine cone.

"Mom, look!" she cried exuberantly. "A bird!"

"Honey, honey, put that down!" I scolded, standing and pointing to the ground. I didn't want to touch it and was surprised Arial had scooped it up as if it was a pleasant thing to hold. "Now! Put it down! It has germs!"

I reached into my tote bag for the antiseptic wipes I brought everywhere with me.

Arial reluctantly let the bird tumble out of her grasp.

It was dead.

Chapter Fourteen

*I*t was my first time being in the Methodist church since I'd left town. The church had been a vital part of my grandparents' lives.

My grandmother had played the gargantuan pipe organ during services. It stretched almost to the alpine ceiling, with its oscillating, vibrating drone, melancholy and otherworldly, as it played along to centuries-old hymns.

We hadn't gone every Sunday for worship, but we had been there for every big occasion—Easter, Christmas Eve, Christmas Day, various weddings and funerals. My grandparents' major wedding anniversaries.

They'd also been married there, and so had my parents. It was a beautiful old white church with one spire, a bell, and red-and-blue-hued stained-glass windows. Inside were long wooden pews and a pulpit. Downstairs, a basement and kitchen, where all kinds of festivities were held.

Today was the strawberry supper. This, more than even Christmas, was *the* church gathering. Everyone in town came. Even people from out of town. The more active members spent all day washing and slicing strawberries, making the juicy strawberry concoction, the homemade whipped cream, and baking the fluffy biscuits over which the strawberries would be ladled.

The dinner was potluck and everyone brought something. My grandmother would usually make her "famous" clam chowder with broth base. Every year, the church published a cookbook of members' recipes. My grandmother's clam chowder was the first dish listed.

I'd seriously considered making the chowder myself as I had a copy of the church cookbook, but after timidly examining the directions, I'd decided against it. The part about "removing the black stomach" creeped me out.

I decided to prepare something I wouldn't screw up, and wouldn't disgust me, so I baked the vegetarian lasagna that Arial loved.

All of the dishes were arranged on long folding tables around the perimeter of the room. People filled up their plates, then sat at more long tables in the middle of the room.

It was like being in high school again, trying to find a place to sit where you'd feel comfortable. I'd hoped Debbie and her family would come so I'd know someone, but she had other plans.

I reassured myself it was better that it was just Arial and me. This would force me to talk to new people. But as I inspected the crowd and realized most of the attendees were thirty or forty years older than I was, I started to feel pretty awkward.

But it was worth it. Arial was goggle-eyed at the varieties of food and was piling her plate with fare I wasn't sure she'd like, such as fried chicken and baked ham with pineapple slices.

"Are you sure you want that, hon?" I asked, watching her grip a drumstick with tongs. A couple of years ago, she'd informed me she didn't want to eat animals, so I'd been diligent about keeping her meals vegetarian.

"Yeah, Mom," she confirmed, layering a few slices of pink, fatty ham next to the drumstick. Perhaps she was just excited to see so many unfamiliar dishes and felt compelled to load up on them but wouldn't really eat them. I'd have to have a talk with her later about wasting food.

I randomly chose one of the long tables. While some of the faces looked familiar to me, the embarrassing reality was I didn't remember anyone's names. I had not only left Orchard shortly after graduating high school, I also had a pathetic memory for names.

"Hello, Neely," greeted an older woman across the table. She said it so confidently, I felt she must be a friend of my grandparents. She had short, dark, permed hair, and was wearing a blue dress stitched with bright flowers, and a red-jeweled broach, circular with long, thin spikes and sparkling rhinestones. She appeared somewhere in her eighties, but a well-preserved eighties. Perfume hung heavy in the air from the older women.

Now I'd have to admit I had no idea who she was.

But she saved me with, "I'm your great-aunt, Pearl. Earl's brother's wife."

"Oh! Hello! Forgive me, I'm bad with names."

Though I definitely remembered "Aunt Pearl." She would send me birthday and Christmas gifts every year and my grandmother would make me hand write thank you cards to her and everyone else. I was also sure I'd seen her at church gatherings. I now noted that her left pupil was slightly askew, something that made her more unforgettable, even to a forgetter like me.

"No worries." She turned her attention to Arial, who was already biting into her drumstick, her lips greasy with its juice. I was amazed but at least she wasn't wasting it.

"This is my daughter, Arial." When Arial didn't look up, I said, "Arial, what do we say when people say hello?"

"Hi," she said. On top of being an uncharacteristic carnivore, she was being uncharacteristically impolite. But Pearl continued to smile at her as if Arial had done a charming little tap dance for her.

"Arial, this is your—what? Great-great-aunt?"

Pearl shrugged. "Something like that."

"What's that?" Arial said, pointing at Pearl's broach.

"This belonged to my mother," Pearl said, caressing it.

"It's pretty."

"Thank you, young lady."

"Is it a spider?!" She was very enthused with this prospect.

"It's a flower," Pearl said. "But it's called a spider lily

because it looks like a spider. So, you're not far off. My mother loved them because they were so unusual."

Arial grinned then said, "Mom, can I have more chicken?"

I was confounded to see she'd finished off the drumstick and its greasy bones were scattered on her plate. Sitting untouched next to them was the vegetarian lasagna she normally scarfed down.

"Of course, boo. Can you get it yourself or do you want me to?"

"I can." She hopped up and was gone with her plate in hand.

"Normally she's a vegetarian," I said, shrugging at Pearl.

"New place, new tastes," she said. "Are you visiting?"

"Oh, no. I actually bought my old house. We're here to stay."

"Isn't that something," Pearl said. "You bought Earl's old place?"

"Yep. I really wanted my childhood home back."

"Good for you," she said. "I'm sure Earl and Lillian would be so pleased."

It occurred to me that Pearl, being a relative, probably knew all about the bank foreclosure on the house.

Soon Arial was back with three more hunks of chicken on her plate. And they were the dark meat pieces. This was so unusual that I started to wonder if she was feeling alright. But I told myself to relax. She was eating heartily, so she must be fine. I couldn't explain her sudden change in dietary preferences but the important thing was that she had an appetite.

I began to pick up pieces of the chatter around me. Somebody's granddaughter had been admitted to Harvard. A farm that was being sold and fears that a condo developer would buy it. Taxes going up again. The new traffic circle in the center that everyone hated. None of the topics arrested my attention but I tried to seem engaged. In Brooklyn, it would have been all about jobs, who'd had a book published, real estate, how challenging dating was, and a sprinkling of politics.

Volunteers appeared from the kitchen area and began picking up the emptied plates, replacing them with shallow bowls. Then came big bowls full of the strawberries swimming in their own juice, the freshly-made whipped cream, and wicker baskets of fluffy biscuits. Some people applauded.

"Here's the strawberries, Arial," I said, getting a thrill out of watching her follow the bowls with big, attentive eyes.

"They came from Scott's Orchard this year," Pearl said. "You remember Scott's?"

"Sure do. I worked there one summer."

I didn't mention how grumpy the owner, Scott Something, had been to me all summer. So much so that I never even shopped there again. I tried to put that out of my mind so I could enjoy the strawberries.

Everyone used tongs to pluck biscuits from the large baskets, then around came the ceramic bowls of strawberries and bowls with whipped cream. I made a plate for Arial, and proudly presented it to her.

"I don't want whipped cream," she said.

"Since when?"

"I'm full."

"Fine, but it's homemade and delicious," I said, giving myself the plate. "I can remember the taste of this whipped cream from when I was a kid. That's how good it is."

"Lorraine Daily made it," Pearl informed me.

I nodded and smiled, acting like I remembered who Lorraine Daily was, though the name sounded familiar. Then I made a plate for Arial, minus the whipped cream.

"I hope you can both come over for dinner one night," Pearl said.

"We'd love that," I said genuinely. The idea of sitting down to dinner with a relative, albeit a distant one, gave me a little charge, as besides Arial, she was the only relative I currently knew. Hopefully, more would come out of the woodwork.

I didn't know much, if anything, about my extended family. In fact, I didn't even know my grandfather's brother's name and was too embarrassed to ask Pearl what it was.

I assumed that he, like my grandfather, was dead. But perhaps he was home, too old and infirm to make it to the supper.

"Won't that be fun, Arial?" I said to her.

She'd taken a few tentative bites of her strawberry dessert but was mostly staring at it as if she didn't like it. Which was strange, because she loved fruit, all fruit. She'd probably eaten too much food.

"No," she said.

"I'm sorry, no what, boo?"

"No, it won't be fun."

I was appalled. Recognizing that one of her little episodes was about to begin, I should have swiftly turned my attention to Pearl and changed the topic. But I was so caught off-guard that I said, "How can you say that, Arial?"

"Listen, cock-eyed old bat," Arial said, staring hard at Pearl. "No one wants to go to your piss-smelling house. No one wants to eat your shit."

Then she reached into her shallow bowl, squeezed a handful of strawberry slop, and smeared it all over her mouth and chin.

The look on Pearl's face. Frozen.

The look on the faces of the other people at the table.

Equally as frozen.

I had to say, to do, something. But I was paralyzed, couldn't move or speak. I stared at Arial, the lower portion of her face blood-red and dripping. The strawberry juice was pooling on the dress we'd picked out for the occasion—her favorite cotton summer dress, light green and stitched with a ladybug design.

"Arial," I said breathlessly, my limbs regaining their ability to function. I grabbed my cloth napkin and vigorously scrubbed her face. I wanted to wipe her mouth right off. "It's time to go."

"Whhyyyyyy???" she whined.

"It's late. Time to go."

I apologetically glanced at Pearl, who'd regained her composure and seemed remarkably unfazed. But the people around Pearl, all one or two generations older than I, still appeared stunned. Many of them had their mouths wide open. More than a few faces showed distinct disapproval.

"I'm so sorry," I told Pearl, forcing Arial to stand with me. "She hasn't been well. I shouldn't have brought her but thought she was feeling better."

"Moooom," she squealed. "What are you doing? I haven't finished!"

I couldn't remember ever gripping her so forcefully, muscling her to do something. But I was afraid she'd say something even worse if I didn't get her out of the door immediately.

"Don't you worry about it," Pearl said. "I hope she feels better."

Pearl had a benign smile on her lined face, gazing at my daughter as if Arial had done something a tad mischievous rather than spit out that crude profanity. And that she'd made an unbearably unacceptable comment about Pearl's wandering eye.

Cock-eyed.

How would she even know what that meant?

As I literally pulled her from the room, my cheeks burned in a way I didn't ever remember them burning. I looked like a horrible mother, physically dragging my child out of the church. Most of the people at the surrounding tables wouldn't know what she'd said. Excruciating humiliation poured hotly into my chest. I could feel all eyes on me and Arial. I was about to become a major topic of town gossip.

You remember Neely Pfau, don't you? Earl's granddaughter? Got knocked up at sixteen. Did you see what happened at the strawberry supper? Her child wiped her face with the strawberries! I guess that's what happens when you're too young to be a good mother, you end up with a brat like that.

We should have stayed in the anonymity of New York.

Chapter Fifteen

*a*t home, I removed Arial's wet, stained dress, then led her into her bedroom and instructed her to occupy herself. When she pleaded to have her favorite book read to her, I told her I wasn't feeling well from all the food. I found the book she wanted me to read on her bookshelf, handed it to her, and left.

I was slowly but assuredly becoming more fearful than embarrassed. Nothing that had erupted from my daughter's mouth—especially the words *cock-eyed* and *piss-smelling*—sounded remotely like her.

Not to mention she showed no memory of what she'd said and done, repeatedly asking me why we'd left the supper. She also kept looking down at the large, dark stain on her dress, confusion apparent on her face.

Something abhorrent was happening. I began to dimly suspect that her behavior went deeper than trauma, wider than the capillary waves of what she'd witnessed that horrific night. A loathsome idea was taking shape in my mind.

Could Arial have a brain tumor? Could it be pressing against the bulb in her brain that controlled impulses, that controlled language? Could this tumor be forcing her into actions, into utterances, that were so unlike her?

I glanced all around the living and open kitchen areas. At the gray walls. At the popcorn ceiling with its swirly concentric circles. Could there be something in the house that had caused a tumor to grow in my little girl's head? Some kind of poison leaking into the yard? Something toxic in the walls or water? Could I have moved my daughter into a house that gave her cancer? Beckett had said the little girl who'd lived here before us had cancer. Had she gotten it from the house, too?

Yet I'd grown up in this house and was fine. And Arial and I had only been here a few weeks. How could a mere few weeks' time cause something as serious as a brain tumor? Especially one large enough to trigger such extreme behavior changes?

I paced between the kitchen and the living room, biting a knuckle. I craved a drink but had no alcohol in the house. Would it be wrong if I sneaked out to the liquor store that was only a ten-minute drive away, leaving her alone in her bedroom? This was the safe, quiet country, wasn't it? I'd be right back.

But no. I wouldn't be able to stop at one. I'd get obliterated, hammered. I couldn't have Arial seeing that, seeing her mother out of control, feeling as if her mother was checking out. I needed to face this, stare down this monster.

I'd have to find a pediatrician. Someone who took

our inadequate insurance. I thought of Jed. He had excellent health insurance, paid for by the New York taxpayers. Paid for by *me*. His other daughters must have it as well. But not Arial. Not the "second-class" daughter.

I went outside, walked all the way down the sloping backyard to the rim of the woods, and took out the flip phone that Jed and I used to communicate. These days, I knew to only call him in emergencies. He'd made clear that while running for mayor, he'd constantly be surrounded by people, and many of them would be seeking any opportunity to derail his campaign.

But I considered this an emergency. Although he'd never shown much fatherly interest in Arial, a stubborn and rather delusional part of myself not only held out slim hope he'd develop it but also felt that, as her father, he should simply be informed of her alarming behavior.

"Jed, it's me," I said after the automated voice that only repeated his phone number. "I assume you're back from Rome. You need to call. There's something wrong with Arial. It's very important you call. Do *not* ignore this message. Do *not* make me call again."

Chapter Sixteen

"Can you walk from one end of the room to the other in a straight line, Arial?" the doctor asked.

I watched, my heart beating jagged in my throat, as Arial flitted with supreme grace from one end of the examination room to the other, did a little twirl, and returned.

"Superb," the doctor said. "You a dancer?"

"Gymnastics," Arial answered proudly.

It had taken me three days to get an appointment with the doctor Debbie had recommended, Dr. Miranda Weir.

The last name was a common one in town. There were Weirs everywhere. I'd gone to school with several of them, including, I was fairly certain, the doctor's younger sister. But I didn't bring that up.

I was nervous that the doctor would forget the direction I'd given her before allowing Arial to enter the room. That under no circumstances could she utter the words "brain tumor." As far as my child was concerned, we were simply here for a regular check-up as it had been a while since she'd had one.

The doctor indicated that Arial should sit on the examination table, which was lowered for children. She shined a pen light into Arial's eyes, directing her to look up, then down, then right to left and back again.

"Any headaches?" the doctor asked her. "Any pain in your head? At all? Even a small amount?"

"No," Arial said, shaking her head.

The doctor looked inside Arial's ears with an otoscope, then listened to her heart, then her back, thumping on it with her knuckle and directing Arial's breathing. Then she got out a chart with lines on it and asked Arial if any of them looked wavy.

"No," she said.

"Does your vision ever go blurry? Kind of out of focus?"

"Nope."

The doctor finally directed Arial to go get a lollipop from the receptionist. She hopped off the table and practically sprinted out the door. I didn't stop her even though she normally wasn't allowed candy except on special occasions.

"Everything seems normal," Dr. Weir said, closing the door behind her. "Better than normal. She's in perfect shape. We could run a blood panel to be on the safe side."

"What could be causing the things happening?" I asked.

I'd given the receptionist a brief rundown of Arial's

symptoms, divulging how she was using "adult words" she shouldn't know, and how she'd smeared strawberries on her face in public.

Once spoken aloud to a busy, distracted receptionist, these behavioral changes didn't sound that irregular. Parents were probably always calling, thinking their children had brain tumors when they acted bratty.

"She's acting out in strange ways," I continued to Dr. Weir even though she already knew this. "Using words I've never heard from her."

"Kids are masters at picking things up," Dr. Weir said indulgently. "I have a four-year-old. Know what he said last week? Penis head. Hadn't heard that one before."

I stared at her, fighting the urge to lash out. Kids said *penis head*. Kids did not say *piss-smelling house*. *Penis head* was funny. *Cock-eyed old bat* was not. *Eat your shit* was not.

But I didn't want to make an enemy of one of the only pediatricians in town. This wasn't Brooklyn, where you could hop from one doctor to another and go years before you ran out of them. Nor did I want to tell her *exactly* what ugly things Arial had said. I had a feeling she'd think I was exaggerating.

Sometimes I wondered if there was any way I'd misheard her. If the problem was actually me. Only remembering the shocked, disapproving faces of the older people at the church table convinced me that it had all happened.

"Then what?" I asked. "What could be causing it?"

"You both just moved here, right? It could be stress. Losing her friends and familiar places."

"I know she's been under stress. I do know that. She had something terrible happen to her. That's why we moved back. I know she's traumatized. She is. But the things she's saying… It doesn't sound like her at all. Not even close."

Despite my acute embarrassment, I decided to reveal what she'd written on the wall. I needed to impress on the doctor how serious this was, that this wasn't ordinary rebellious-child behavior.

"She wrote 'die you slut' on her bedroom wall, okay? In red paint. What ten-year-old does that?"

The doctor folded her arms over her white lab coat. For the first time, her expression betrayed that she was slightly stumped. "Well, that is atypical. But you'd be surprised. Some children are very disturbed."

"But mine isn't! Not until recently. And it's been so sudden."

"You said something terrible happened to her. Can you share what?"

"It—she saw someone die. Murdered."

The doctor looked stricken. "That will do it alright," she said somberly. "Is she seeing a therapist?"

"We just started," I lied.

"My only advice is to keep doing what you're doing. Getting her mental health support. Keep her on a consistent routine. Make sure she's getting plenty of sleep and eating healthy. Spend lots of quality—"

"I'd like an MRI. I'd really like an MRI. Just to rule out anything physical."

"I'm afraid I couldn't recommend an MRI unless I had good reason to believe—"

"Dr. Weir," I growled, thrusting a finger at her. "I want an MRI for my daughter. I demand one."

"I'm sorry," the doctor said, sweetly. "I'm going to have to ask you to leave."

* * *

AT HOME I checked the "Jed phone," which I kept hidden in my bedside table drawer. I'd missed a call from him. Arial was in her room occupied with an art project. I'd taken the paints from her but she had plenty of markers, crayons, and felt-tip pens.

I wasn't sure why I'd bothered to seize the paints as she had more than enough tools to draw on the wall again, if she was so inclined. I'd tacked up an Indian-patterned tapestry over the offending words until Salem could blot them out.

"You said it was important," Jed said as I stood staring into the woods in the backyard. "Something wrong with Arial?"

"Yes, and it took you three days to call."

"I'm sorry. I haven't been able to get a minute alone."

"Whatever. Listen to me. I need you to work your magic, pull whatever strings you need to pull. I want Arial to get an MRI. The pediatrician here won't give me a referral."

"An MRI? Woah. What's wrong?"

"She's not acting right."

"She wouldn't after what happened to you both."

"It goes beyond that. I know my daughter. I'm not going to argue with you. Get her a specialist. I want her checked for a brain tumor."

"Brain tumor? Christ, Neely. What makes you think—"

"Do you know her favorite book?"

"Her—what?"

"Exactly. I'm not one of your voters and I don't have time for this charade. Just get her an appointment."

Although I'd been the one to initiate conversation, and my first instinct had been to have a discussion with him about what was happening, the fact that he'd waited three days to return such a desperate-sounding message had again kicked my expectations in the teeth. I stopped hoping he'd give something he couldn't—concern and love—and only wanted him to give something he could: connections.

"Okay, I'll get Becks on it. He knows people at Mayo."

"That's too far. I can't put her on a plane and freak her out. It needs to be around here. I need to tell her it's only routine."

"I'll do what I can. But, Neely, tell me what's happening."

"Jed, please. Stop. If you cared at all, you'd come here and *see* her."

"I'm in the middle of campaigning."

"You had no problem bringing your other kids to Rome in the middle of campaigning. But you can't take one day and come here? You took Gia halfway around the world for her birthday. Where were you on Arial's? You didn't even bring over her bike, you sent it."

He said nothing.

"There's something wrong with her. You haven't done anything for her for her entire life, so I need you to do this. Get her a specialist. And get it soon. Don't test me, Jed. If you want to be mayor, don't fucking test me."

I hung up the phone.

Chapter Seventeen

For three days, Arial's favorite sundress with the ladybug design had been sitting atop the washing machine, its dark strawberry juice stain soaking in Out Spot.

I'd meant to do the laundry before now but had gotten sidetracked with finding an in-network pediatrician and doing research on brain tumors. The symptoms I read about online—wobbly walking, headaches, blurry vision, the same ones the doctor checked for— didn't match up to the symptoms I was seeing in Arial, but I wouldn't stop pursuing an MRI until I was able to eliminate that possibility.

The washing and drying machines were out of sight downstairs in the basement, which had also put the dress out of my mind. A narrow, almost perpendicular staircase led to the musty basement, which smelled exactly as it did when I'd lived here: damp and subterranean. But, also, somehow clean and invigorating. I'd always liked the smell.

The staircase had concerned me, especially as my grandparents got older. They'd managed to avoid falling down it, but now I worried Arial might, so she was forbidden to come down here without my permission. The door had an outside hook-latch that was up high enough that I was confident she couldn't reach it.

The washer and dryer were also the same ones as when I'd lived here, the family apparently having decided not to replace them with newer ones. The machines must have easily been twenty years old, made back before "planned obsolescence."

I poured laundry detergent directly onto the strawberry juice stain, then put a capful into the washing machine and dumped in the rest of the laundry. There was a long metal cabinet to the side of the dryer that looked old enough that I was almost certain it had been here when I'd lived here.

It had survived the passing of the house to the bank and then to the new family—probably for the same reason the washer and dryer had—because it was very large and it would have been an incredible challenge to get up those narrow, nearly-perpendicular stairs. How the cabinet had managed to get down here in the first place was a mystery. Perhaps my grandfather had built the basement right around it. It needed a good cleaning. The cabinet would be the perfect place to store detergent, softener, a laundry basket, and the like.

Bending, I slid back the front door, which stuck a little. Inside were a bunch of dust-encrusted cardboard boxes. I pulled them out and went through the first one, which contained several manila envelopes.

Opening one of them, out came dozens of photographs. Most of the photographs were in black and white, and the hairstyles, clothing, and vehicles all pointed to the photographs being extremely old—turn-of-the-nineteenth century old. Or even older. There were people standing with horses and carriages.

I was dumbfounded. Was this something the family who'd lived here had left behind or did these things belong to my grandparents? The layers of dust inside the cabinet spoke to everything having been in there for many years—which pointed towards these pictures belonging to my family.

It was too dark in the basement to investigate further, so I carried the cardboard box upstairs. In the bright light of the kitchen, I slid the photos back out. Many of them contained no information—no dates, no identification, nothing written on them. But others had handwriting on the backs of the photos—handwriting I didn't recognize.

In one of the sepia-tinted photos was a dour-looking but strikingly handsome brunette woman in a black Victorian-era dress. Handwritten on the back of the photo was:

Viola Dutton Hubbard, 1876

There were several pictures of her. In one, she was in a wedding dress, holding a bouquet of flowers, and a man in a bow tie stood next to her. The back read: Viola and Hermann Hubbard, Wedding, 1875.

I was giddy with excitement. This had to be a treasure trove of family photos. All this time hidden in the house. The morbid thought occurred to me that if

Kevin hadn't been killed, I never would have lobbied Jed to buy the house back. I never would have seen these.

Other than Arial and Pearl, I knew of no family.

But here, all of a sudden, was family.

Chapter Eighteen

*N*ora came out of her office with Arial. In the attached sitting room, I stood up off the couch, examining Arial's face to gauge her mood. She looked normal, as if her and the doctor had been chatting about mundane things. Perhaps they had. I'd told Nora not to push her to talk about Kevin if she seemed reluctant.

"How'd it go, boo?" I asked.

"Good," she said noncommittally.

"Can you sit down over there? I'd like to talk with Nora for a minute."

"Okay, Mom."

Nora waved me into her office and shut the door.

"How did it go?" I asked, anxiously.

"She's definitely suffering some trauma," Nora said. "But she's also a great kid—bright, sensitive. She seems to like it here."

"Did you discuss Kevin at all?"

"We had some play therapy." The doctor pointed to

a plastic doll house with several small dolls on the floor. They were about three-inches long, with plastic clothing molded around their stiff little bodies. "I asked her to make a family. She put you, her, and Kevin in the doll house."

"What does that mean?" I asked, stricken.

"It means her brain is having some difficulty processing what happened to Kevin."

"I'm concerned there's more going on here than trauma," I said, moving on from the doll conversation. None of the dolls remotely resembled me or Kevin. I refrained from suggesting to Nora that she ethnically diversify her doll collection. Nor did I understand what my daughter was supposed to do with the dolls—put Kevin in a pretend coffin? "Some of the ways she's behaving are so not like her. I'm trying to get her an MRI to see if... well, if maybe there's a tumor."

The therapist's expression darkened with concern. "If that would give you peace of mind, then it's not a bad idea."

"But maybe it's something else," I said. "I was doing research. Could she have Tourette's?"

"Tourette's?" The doctor put her finger to her mouth. "Unlikely. I was with her for nearly an hour and didn't observe any outbursts. And Tourette's tics are repetitive. From what you've told me, it sounds like the things she says are different every time."

I indicated that the doctor should walk with me farther away from the door. I was concerned that Arial might overhear me, even though the dark wood door looked extremely thick.

"What about split personality?" I asked. I knew this sounded like I was jumping to the worst-case scenario but I didn't care. I wanted to consider every conceivable possibility, even if outlandish. "She never remembers what she says and does. I read that's part of having multiple personality."

"Dissociative identity disorder?" With her mouth twisted down at the corners, Nora adjusted her beaded eyeglass chain. "Genuine cases are extremely rare."

"But something as traumatic as what happened to Arial... it could cause that, right?"

"Yes, it could. But typically, the disorder is an emotional defense mechanism brought on by severe, long-term trauma. Abuse."

"Oh." I went quiet. The last thing I wanted to plant in anyone's mind was that I might be abusing my daughter.

"One thing we may want to consider," Nora went on, "is a phenomenon called cryptomnesia. This means that everything Arial has said were latent memories. She'd heard all these words somewhere, stored them in her subconscious, then retrieved them. She may not have heard them from you, but from anywhere. People passing by on the street. A radio playing in the background in a mall. There's some evidence that we even store sights and sounds experienced in infancy."

"Uh, maybe," I said reluctantly. While I'd never heard the term cryptomnesia, I had to admit there had been times that odd bits of trivia had surged to the forefront of my mind. When I'd looked the trivia up, I'd found my mental musings had been accurate, though I had no recollection of ever learning them.

"If that's what's happening," I asked, "why is everything she's saying so... nasty? Why would she only retrieve profanity and insults?"

"Well, this is what we'll try to figure out."

I sighed, chewing on the tip of my thumbnail. This theory sounded fantastical but definitely was preferable to a brain tumor.

"Neely," Nora said, gently, her gaze brimming with empathy. "You're a good mother. You're doing everything you can."

She subtly began herding me towards the door; she must have another appointment.

"It's natural to be concerned. But from what I saw today, your daughter is a well-adjusted child who had an extremely traumatic thing happen to her. What you've described is typical PTSD reactions. But she'll get through it; you'll get through it together. Have you thought more about what we discussed? Telling her the truth about her father?"

"Yes. I'm trying to think of a good time for it."

I sounded like I was making up excuses. But this woman had no idea the things I'd witnessed from Arial. Even though I'd described them to her, there was no way to convey the true strangeness of it—how even the last time she'd spouted such shocking things, her voice had been slightly altered, lower and grittier. As if she'd smoked a pack of cigarettes before speaking.

Given all that was happening, I had no idea how to tell Arial something so life-altering—that her father wasn't buried in Greenwood Cemetery, but was very much alive. That he was the man who'd pop up every few months bearing gifts but otherwise had no interest in her. That he had an entire other family he preferred to be with.

Every Father's Day, he was with his other daughters. He spent holidays and birthdays with them. He appeared to be a good, present father to them but couldn't be bothered with Arial. What kind of thing was this to let a child in on?

And given that her aberrant behavior could be caused by trauma, was it really the time to be heaping more of it on her?

"Would you like to tell her here, with me?" Nora asked.

"Please," I begged. "I need time to think. If you saw how she behaves sometimes, you'd understand better. I don't think she can handle anything else right now."

"Neely, there's the possibility that she already knows, subconsciously. Perhaps that's contributing to her behavior."

"There's no way. No way."

"It's been ten years," she challenged. "Plenty of time for a stray word or look between you and Jed to tip her off. I often have parents who think their conversations are private but it turns out the child knows everything."

Intensely paranoid that Arial may have heard what the doctor had said, I only nodded, wanting to end the discussion. The idea that my daughter had been stealthily absorbing and storing all my interactions with

Jed from the time she came out of the womb was too much to fathom.

"Another thing we can consider is anti-anxiety medication," Nora added.

"Medication? For a ten-year-old?"

"It would be low dose. And temporary."

"I don't know."

I loathed the idea of my kid on drugs. I tended to be of the mindset that Americans jumped too quickly to pharmacological solutions.

"Tell you what," Nora said. "I'll call in the prescription to the pharmacy on Main Street. You can fill it or not. You've got three months."

"Okay, sure," I said dismissively.

I had no intention of filling the prescription.

Chapter Nineteen

There was a black pickup truck parked in the turnaround drive. It took me several moments to realize that sitting inside was Salem Collins. I'd forgotten that he was scheduled to paint Arial's walls today.

"Ugh, Salem," I said, as he hopped down from his truck and Arial and I got out of the car. "I'm so sorry. I completely forgot about today. Have you been here long?"

"Only about ten minutes. Thought I'd wait to see if you showed."

"Please forgive me. Things have been so busy. This is my daughter, Arial."

"Hello there, Arial," he said, smiling and coming around to shake her hand.

"Hi," she said, shyly. "Mom, can I go play outside?"

"Of course," I said, elated to hear those words. "That's why we moved here, isn't it? Just don't go anywhere else."

"Like where?" she said, rolling her eyes. She flashed a giggly smile at Salem, then ran off around the side of the house towards the jungle gym.

* * *

A COUPLE HOURS LATER, Salem came out of Arial's room.

"The blocker and primer are on. I want to let those dry overnight. You look at the samples?"

"Yep," I said, holding up the yellow spectrum swatch and tapping on a shade called Vintage Sunshine. I'd since softened my stance that Arial was not allowed to choose her own room color. This was the one she'd picked.

I followed Salem into her bedroom. The lurid red DIE YOU SLUT on the wall was invisible. Though it would remain permanently visible in my memory.

"Great," I said, getting a couple inches from the wall and staring into where the writing had been. This close, I could faintly detect small portions of the letters underneath the layers of stain blocker and primer. "Will that come out completely?" I asked.

"Yep. Going to do a coat of emulsion paint. Won't see a thing."

In the driveway, I watched him load his paints, brushes, and trays into the flatbed of his truck, then close the tailgate. "I'll leave the drop cloth if that's okay," he said. "I have a dedicated sink at home to clean everything."

"No problem. Can Arial sleep in there tonight?"

"Should be fine. What I used is zero VOC. That means it's not toxic. Just leave the window open till she's ready for bed. Try not to touch the walls overnight."

I nodded and we stood awkwardly. He didn't appear to want to leave. "So, Neely," he said, with utmost confidence. "You up for that drink tonight?"

"Sure, if my babysitter is available."

I paused to watch his reaction. It was something I did with men—throwing up the childcare roadblock—to test if they were going to have any issues with my having another human being to worry about, one who would always come first.

Not that I'd put many men to the test. I'd hardly dated since Arial's birth. If I'd managed to get any kind of time to date, then there was the babysitter expense, and all the issues with men who wanted to come back to my place and dive into bed.

Until I'd met Kevin randomly in a coffee shop, I'd given up on the idea of dating. The complex strategizing was too energy-draining.

"Bring her along," Salem said, without hesitation. "The more the merrier."

He'd passed the test. A-plus for him. I supposed I was sniffing him out as a romantic prospect. I wasn't really ready for romance but couldn't help thinking about the potential of it anyway. Because Salem was handsome, seemed very kind, and, mostly, because I felt safe with him as I already knew him. And because I was human and it had been months since a man had looked at me for more than five seconds.

"I'd actually love some adult time." I smiled. "But if the sitter isn't available, I'll bring her along."

"How about The Diamond? Seven?"

The Diamond was a combined restaurant and pub in town that had been there since I was a child. I told him that sounded perfect and waved him off. Then I went inside to call Amara, fiercely hoping she was available.

I really needed a couple hours of adult time.

Chapter Twenty

"I never saw you as a painter," I told Salem, as we sat at a table outside at The Diamond. Our drinks had been delivered—a glass of white wine for me and a Guinness for him—and we awaited our meals. "Weren't you a kind of geeky, science-type guy back in school?"

I hoped the lilt in my voice sounded more curious than critical. Though my teenage memories of him were vague, there was a clear one: Entering Salem's house from the backyard to use the bathroom, I'd passed him as he sat on the patio with glass beakers, pouring a smoking chemical from one to the other. I remembered hoping he didn't blow up the house.

"Yep," he said. "I painted during the summers. Got a degree in engineering. Had trouble finding a job, believe it or not. Or at least one that wouldn't make me move to Seattle or somewhere. But I kept getting more referrals for painting and other handyman stuff. Was bringing in good money. Decided I liked the freedom of having my own business, making my own hours."

"Seattle sounds kind of cool. Never had the desire to leave town?"

"Leave all this?" he said, sweeping his arm towards Main Street. All around were charming historical buildings housing local businesses. "Besides, why would I give up being the only black person in town? I feel so special."

I almost spit out a mouthful of wine. "You are not the only one."

"Let's see… there's Kyle Caldwell." He put on a mock pensive face. "Me and Kyle. That's about it."

"I'll have you know my babysitter is black. Very nice high school girl, Amara."

"So, me, Kyle, and Amara. Three."

"Stop," I said. Though he likely wasn't far off.

"But no," he continued. "Never thought about leaving. Got everything I need right here. I know everyone and everyone knows me. I got friends, I got family, I got a business doing so well I can't keep up, and Buddy's Bar has a tab with my name on it that goes back to 2005."

"Were you legal drinking age in 2005?"

"No, but don't tell Buddy."

I laughed.

"And look. You left, and here you are, came crawling back. Couldn't stay away, could ya?"

He fluttered his thick-lashed eyes insinuatingly.

I waved as if to dismiss the topic. I wasn't inclined to bring up tragedy at the moment. "You're not married yet? No kids?"

Despite his flirtatious demeanor, I figured I better do my due diligence.

"You think I'd be sitting here with a hot blonde if I was married with kids?"

I laughed again. This was the first time I'd laughed this much since that horrific night.

Soon the waitress brought our orders—the chef salad for me and a turkey burger for him. The portions were enormous. I'd also chugged quickly through my wine so I ordered another. I deserved it. But I asked the waitress to only fill the glass half way. I didn't want to risk a strong buzz while driving. One of the downfalls of being out of the city, returning to a car-dependent way of life.

"I've been meaning to ask you something," I said.

He leaned forward with exaggerated intensity. "Am I single? Why, yes, Neely Pfau, I am. Thank you for asking. Or maybe you want to know how someone as clearly desirable as myself could still be unattached. It's luck, really."

I smiled. "Your name. Now I get why Jordy would call you a witch. How'd you end up with the name Salem?" I felt so comfortable with him that, without thinking, I plucked a few French fries off his plate.

"Thank my mother for that. She grew up in Salem, Mass. She was—" He hooked his fingers into air quotes. "—reclaiming the name."

"I might as well tell you—my daughter wrote that on the wall." I wasn't sure why I'd admitted this except I strongly suspected he knew anyway. And the wine was doing a bit of the talking.

"Yeah, I figured. What possessed her to do that?"

The waitress deposited our check on the table and Salem snatched the holder. "On me," he said.

I thanked him, debating how much to reveal. It was mentally taxing, having to go through this with every person. Because after someone heard about the murder, they wouldn't know how to treat me. I'd stop being a normal person and instead become a "trauma person." A person who had a well of pain so expansive, yet hidden under the surface, that even the most considerate, the most circumspect could blunder right into it, knee deep.

"She's been through a lot." I went quiet, pinching one thumb, steeling myself to hear it. "We were walking through the park with a guy I'd been dating when he was attacked by a stranger. He died."

Salem's mouth hung open a little and he murmured, "I'm so sorry."

"Since then, she's been having these small antisocial episodes. Including painting that on her wall. I've got her in therapy. Me too. I'm also working on getting her an MRI, to rule out anything physical."

"And her father?" he asked so softly I could hardly hear him over the plentiful traffic whizzing by on Main Street. In the decade since I'd left, Orchard had become popular. "He in the picture?"

"No, and that's another thing. Could be an additional reason she's acting up."

I decided not to elaborate, including my lie to Arial about who her father was. I'd hit Salem with enough for one evening. Not to mention that particular detail made me sound unhinged.

He tapped his lower lip several times, then mused, "Maybe she needs a guy in her life. An older brother figure. Someone who can introduce her to—" He lowered his voice an octave. "—smelly socks, muddy boots, snails, and other manly things."

"Sure, but who would have all this manly knowledge?"

"Hello?" He twisted around exaggeratedly as if looking for someone. "Is there a man sitting at the table? Are my socks not smelly enough for you? I promise they are."

"I'm sure you've got better things to do than hang out with a ten-year-old."

"As a matter of fact," he said as we prepared to leave. "I don't."

AMARA CAME out of the inside door as I opened the outside screen. "You didn't get my message?" she asked hurriedly, slipping past me.

"No, I'm sorry. What message? Amara?"

"I called you. I'm sorry, Ms. Pfau. But I can't watch Arial again."

She rushed up the crumbling pathway to the turn-around drive, where her car was parked in front of mine. I quickly followed.

"Amara! What happened?"

She submerged into the dark and ten seconds later, I

heard her car start. The car pulled out of the drive and vanished down the hill.

I figured I better get inside and find out for myself what was going on. The living room was empty. "Arial!" I called out, hurrying down the hallway. Her bedroom door was closed. If she'd vandalized the newly-primed walls, I was going to be furious.

When I opened the door, she was sitting in her bed, propped up against her headboard, reading. Several dolls were piled around her, resting on her legs.

"Mom!" she cried, smiling at me. It was her usual exuberant *you're home* greeting. Normally, it gave me a fuzzy, squishy feeling in the heart but this time I was too busy sweeping my gaze around the walls. They were pristine.

"Why did Amara run out of here?" I asked.

"She did?"

"Yes, it seemed like something happened."

Arial pushed her lower lip out in a contemplative pout. "I dunno."

"Arial, did you say anything to her?"

"Like what?"

"I don't know. I'm just trying to figure out why she left here so fast."

"Mom, I don't knooooow. Can you read to me? Please?" She held up her book.

"Let me get settled, boo."

I walked back into the kitchen, bewildered, my stomach in a knot. Then I went to the screened-in porch, closed the door, and called Amara. When I got her voicemail, I said in a trying-to-remain-calm voice,

"Hi, Amara. I don't know what happened. Arial seems fine, so I'm confused. Would you be willing to speak with me?"

* * *

THE NEXT DAY, I watched as the high school across the street spilled out a dozen or so students. I was standing at the edge of the nearby playground, where I had a pretty good view of whoever came out the front of the school. Despite my teasing of Salem, the truth was that Orchard wasn't a hugely diverse town by any means. Amara should be easy to spot.

When I saw a pretty black girl with a pile of curls, I quickly crossed the street and planted myself on the sidewalk. "Amara!" I called, holding up my hand.

Even though she had texted last night and agreed to speak with me after rehearsal for the summer play, it was obvious she was reluctant to approach me. She said goodbye to some other teens, then slowly made her way to me. I suggested we head to the park.

"What play are you putting on?" I asked as we made our way to the crosswalk.

"*Grease.*"

"No! I remember that from when I was a kid."

"I'm Rizzo."

"Well, darn, that's the best role."

She shrugged and smiled a little, avoiding eye contact.

When we got to the park and sat down on a bench, she said, "Ms. Pfau…"

"Neely."

"Neely, it's just that…" She was twisting her backpack strap in her fingers, still not looking at me. "I don't want to tell you what happened."

"Why not?"

"Because…" She redirected her skittish fiddling to the silver keychain hanging on her backpack. "I don't think you're going to believe me."

"Amara," I said, using a serious tone. I leaned forward a little, trying to draw her gaze. "I will believe you. Trust me."

She sighed, still avoiding eye contact, and kept silent for several long moments. I didn't want to press her. I didn't even want to know what had happened, because I knew it was going to be bad. But I had to know. I had to bring anything new to Nora and maybe even Dr. Weir.

"Everything was going fine," Amara finally began. "We created a book. She likes to make books. It was about a bird. That was going well but then, I dunno, it got a little strange. She drew the bird falling off a tree branch and breaking its neck."

"Okay," I whispered.

"We watched a little TV. Some comedy with kids who talk really loud."

"iCarly?"

"Yeah, that's it. Then it was time for her to get ready for bed."

She stopped fiddling with the keychain and began kneading her backpack. "She was very good, brushed her teeth and put on her nightgown with no arguments. We were lying in bed, reading. She was snuggled up next to me, it was so cute…" Her voice started to hitch, her breath coming shallow. "Um. Then she… she looked up at me, and it was like…" Amara slowly began shaking her head as if she couldn't continue.

"Like?" I gently prodded. "You can tell me."

"Well, she said… Neely, do you mind bad language?"

"No."

"She said… well, she said, 'Your parents won't like you fucking your boyfriend, will they, you cheap little whore?'"

She buried her face in her hands and I thought she might be crying. I sat absolutely catatonic, my hand over my mouth. This was the first indication I'd ever had that Arial knew what sex was. Not just sex but *fucking*.

But no. I remembered the "bad dream" she'd had shortly after we'd arrived in town. How she'd said, "cheating son-of-a-bitch." *Cheating*.

This was inconceivable. This was not right. This was irrefutable evidence that something was going on that was much more than trauma. More than PTSD. But I didn't know *what* was going on, as physically, she seemed fine. Playing and eating well; her balance, dexterity, and vision all normal.

I felt Amara needed comforting and validation, so I touched her shoulder. It took some effort to pry my hand off my mouth.

"I believe you, Amara," I said.

"I was so shocked. So shocked." Amara wasn't crying but was extremely shaken. "I got off the bed. Quick as I could. I was… To be honest, I was scared of her. I went to the living room and left you a message but you didn't call back. I—I didn't want to stay there."

"I don't blame you."

"It's that… um…." She jostled around as if sitting on the bench was causing her physical discomfort. "I just started, um, sleeping with my boyfriend. So it was, uh, really odd she said that. It really freaked me out. And if my parents knew... I, ah, we're, ah, being very careful. But, um, they'd *kill* me."

Finally, she turned and looked right at me with an imploring expression.

"I have no intention of saying anything," I reassured her. "Arial would never meet your parents."

"But maybe… we all run into each other somewhere. Maybe she blurts that out. I don't know."

"I promise you if we ever see you with your parents, I'll make sure we don't approach."

She nodded, seeming relieved. But still shaken.

"Amara, I want to tell you something… my daughter had a horrible tragedy happen to her right before we left New York. She's been out-of-sorts. Sometimes she says bizarre things, then doesn't remember them."

"Oh," Amara said, seeming unconvinced.

"I'm very sorry she said that to you. I'm sorry I didn't warn you. Because you two had gotten along so well the first time you sat for her, I didn't think anything would happen. It's unpredictable. I don't even know where she's getting this language. I assure you it isn't coming from me, and we've hardly seen anyone else in the past six months."

Amara hiked her backpack over one shoulder, as if

she wanted to depart and get back to her normal life. I knew that, again, I sounded like I was making excuses for a disturbed child or one who was just a brat.

"Thank you for telling me," I said, standing. "I won't take up any more of your time."

She stood as well and we began walking. When we reached the parking area, near my car, I turned to her.

"Can I drive you anywhere?" I asked.

"Uh, no, thanks." She smiled weakly. "My boyfriend should be here any minute."

"Thanks again for telling me, Amara. And again, I'm so sorry."

"It's the 'cheap' part that got me," she said, and thrust out a sour laugh. I found myself joining her. It felt like we had to cling to any humor we could find in the situation, no matter how slight.

Then she looked like she was wrestling with whether she should say something else. I waited, a premonition telling me there was more, and worse, coming.

"See, when she said that, when she looked at me…" Amara stared out past the parking lot towards a scrim of trees and appeared to shudder even though it was quite warm out. "Her eyes. Her eyes were… ah… they looked…"

"Yes?" I prodded.

"They looked… glowing. Like there was a red light in the room shining on them. Or coming through the window. But, um, Ms. Pfau? The shades were down."

Chapter Twenty-One

*B*ack at the house, I moved apprehensively through the hallway. The sound of Arial interrogating Salem as he painted her walls floated to me.

"What's that for?"

"That's a roller."

"Why don't you use a brush?"

"Because a roller is easier for large areas."

"Is that your ladder?"

"Yes."

"Where did you get it?"

"The hardware store."

Arial could be like this when she felt comfortable with someone—a thousand questions. When she was little, she'd run out of questions about the outside world and eventually turn to topics about herself, asking something like, "Why am I talking?"

I'd always found it charming and comical. That's what she sounded like now—that funny little girl gushing with questions. Not the girl who'd said that appalling thing to Amara. Not the girl who stared at Amara with—red eyes?

Occasionally, cars came into our driveway to turn around. The head or tail lights from one must have flashed into the window at the most inopportune time, as Arial was having one of her episodes. Amara had said the window shades were down, but I knew streaks of light could flit past the edges.

I stood in the doorway. Arial was gazing up at Salem, who was on the ladder, rolling Vintage Sunshine over the primer. Most of Arial's things were piled in the middle of the room but I'd done so much decluttering before we moved that it wasn't too much stuff.

"Everything going okay?" I asked.

"Mom!" she shouted, bolting to me. As she flung herself at my waist, I put my arm around her and glanced up at Salem. Studied his expression. Had she said anything awful to him? If so, he wasn't showing it.

Everything must have gone okay. There is no way a child says those kinds of vulgar, offensive things to people and then they don't react. Salem would have been scurrying out of here as Amara had.

"Anyone want lemonade?" I asked.

"Yeah!" Arial yelped, throwing her arms up triumphantly and twirling.

"How about you help me? You can get out the nutmeg. Grandma always used nutmeg."

"I don't want nutmeg," she pouted.

"Fine, but help me anyway."

"But then can I come back and help Salem?"

I shared a quick, bemused look with Salem.

"If you're not bothering him."

"Am I bothering youuuuuuu?" she sing-songed, planting her legs apart and doing a near backbend.

"Not at all," Salem said. "You're keeping me on my toes."

He winked at me and my heart fluttered a little. He was really flirting with me. For some reason, I had a difficult time believing it. As if, after Kevin's murder, no man would ever find me attractive again. As if the price for dating me would be death.

About twenty minutes later, Salem took a break and I walked him onto the porch. Arial had finished her drink and run outside to the jungle gym. I handed him a tall glass of lemonade.

This was the kind of thing I'd wanted so badly. To renew these little traditions that I'd grown up with—lemonade on the porch, admiring the dense, birch tree-filled woods behind the house, listening to the birds musically cawing and trilling. And Arial outside getting exercise in the fresh air as I'd once done.

It seemed grossly unfair that things were so good and yet so abnormal at the same time. Hadn't we suffered enough?

"What was it like growing up with your grandparents, Neely?" Salem asked.

It was an unexpected question though it shouldn't have been. His sister, Jordy, had been over multiple times during high school, so Salem must have known my parents weren't around. I'd never been ashamed of the fact that I lived with old people, and often invited friends over.

"To be honest, I wouldn't have had it any other way," I said. "Of course, it's a tragedy my parents died when I was a toddler. They were on vacation. From me." I laughed uneasily. "They needed a break. I was a tough kid, always crying. So they dropped me off here and drove to a campground in Vermont for some peace and quiet. They were hit by a truck."

My grandmother had never told me this story. In my teens, I'd found my mother's diary. The day before my parents had left, she had an entry describing why they were taking a short camping break.

Neely cries all the time. So sensitive! I haven't slept in three nights. NEED some time alone or this Mama will go crazy.

I'm sure my grandmother had always left that part out because she didn't want me to feel guilty.

"That's terrible," Salem said.

"My grandparents didn't expect their babysitting gig to last forever. They were in their sixties at the time so it couldn't have been easy. But they always acted like it was exactly the way things were supposed to be. It's definitely made me different from people my age, but that's okay. I mean, I write thank you cards. Handwrite."

"That's different, alright," he smiled.

"They were pretty shocked when I got pregnant so young. But they stepped up for that too. I wish we'd stayed here instead of moving into the city. But, at the time, I thought something would change with her father, that he and I would end up together. That was a delusion."

"She's a great kid," Salem said, diplomatically side-stepping the topic of Jed.

Normally, I would have enthusiastically agreed with him, but with her antisocial behavior so fresh in my mind, and especially with what she'd said to Amara, a little cynical puff of air escaped my chest, sounding like *humph.*

"She hasn't said anything unusual to you, has she?" I asked.

Deep down, I was worried that, given how crudely sophisticated her outbursts had been, she might say something unforgivable to Salem.

"She asked me five billion questions about my painting career. Why I'm a painter, why I like painting, when I learned to paint, where I learned to paint... I see CIA agent in her future."

I laughed. "Yeah, that sounds like her. She must like you to ask so many questions."

I took a couple sips of lemonade and forced myself to confront my worst fear head-on.

"Salem, I want to get ahead of this. She has something going on—some kind of psychological issue. It's probably trauma from what happened in the city. But I'm also trying to get her an MRI to rule out anything physiological."

"I'm really sorry to hear that, Neely." He looked concerned but also bewildered, because no doubt the child he'd spent an hour with seemed perfectly normal.

"If, um, well, if she says anything insulting to you, I want to apologize in advance."

"Insulting?" He sounded baffled.

"It's just that she goes into these trances—and things come out of her mouth that are, uh… they're very unchildlike, and uh…"

I couldn't bring myself to straight out admit what I feared—that in her dissociative state, she might say something that could halt my budding friendship with Salem, something despicable.

But now he had no problem reading the look in my eyes.

"Are you implying she might… maybe I'm getting this wrong… but are you thinking she might say something racist to me?"

I made a cringe face. I couldn't help it.

"I don't think so," I said, grasping my throat. I couldn't believe this was a discussion I was actually having. "She's never said anything of the sort. But… I might as well tell you that she scared off Amara. My babysitter. Last night, she said something awful to her. Nothing racial. But bad enough. It's like she not only knows words she shouldn't know, but concepts too."

I glanced out the windows. Arial was coming down the slide. She looked so childish and innocent. If I hadn't heard with my own ears what she'd spit out at Pearl, I would have absolutely thought that Amara had mental issues. That there was no way my daughter could have said anything remotely like what Amara claimed.

"I didn't bring it up with her because she never remembers what she says," I continued. "I have no idea where she's getting this stuff. She doesn't have access to the Internet and her television time is supervised. It's completely not her usual personality. For me to have to worry about what might come out of her mouth, I can't even describe how stressful this is."

Salem finished his lemonade and I took the glass from him. "You think it's trauma?" he asked.

"I have no other explanation. I'm praying it's not a brain tumor but I'm going to get that checked out."

We both looked out the window, watched as Arial clambered back up the ladder for another dip down the slide.

I'd always felt so lucky she was generally bubbly and easygoing. She was the kid I'd have picked out if you could go to a store and pick these things out. Even as a baby, she was always smiling. She'd cry if she were sick but otherwise was sweet and joyful. Unlike me, who'd cried so much I'd pushed my parents into a mini-vacation that would kill them.

Given how young and clueless I'd been when I'd given birth, it was a miracle she'd turned out so terrific. So, to be telling a man that my kid might call him a name I could barely conjure up in my mind was surreal. It was horrifying.

"Listen," Salem said, standing by my side as we continued to watch her out of the windows. "She's a little kid. If she's got something going on, then she's got something going on. Whatever might come out of her mouth, I won't take it personally. But I'm glad you warned me."

Relief surged through me. I turned and wanted to hug him but stopped myself. For one, he had some fresh paint streaks on his overalls. For another, though we were striking up a friendship, he was still here in a professional capacity.

"Thanks for understanding," I said, working to hold back tears. "Just please let me know if you witness any unusual behavior from her."

"Will do," he said, saluting.

About an hour later, Salem had finished the first coat. I walked around Arial's room admiring the walls. They looked so smooth and sunny that I was almost glad Arial had defaced them. And it didn't hurt that the debacle had reconnected me with Salem.

At the door, I touched his arm. "Can I ask you a question? It—it's another awkward one."

"More awkward than everything you told me before?"

"About as awkward."

"Hit me up. I love awkward conversations, especially about race. I mean, who doesn't?"

"Let's say something happened to you. Someone attacked you."

"Okaaaay," he said, warily.

"In one scenario, the person attacks you because… well, just because. Maybe the person is insane. Or evil. Or who knows. In the other scenario, the person attacks you because of the way you look."

"You mean because I'm black."

"Yes."

"These are two not-optimal scenarios," he said.

Poor man. First, he gets the "my child might say something racist" talk and now this. I'd be surprised if he returned to finish the paint job.

"No, they aren't," I said. "But would you want one scenario punished more harshly than the other scenario?"

He put his hand to his chin, in mock hard-concentration, then wagged a finger at me. "Neely Pfau, you owe me another dinner date for all this."

"Was that first dinner a date?"

"Ouch," he said, grabbing his heart.

I smiled. I hope the smile conveyed I was kidding.

"Let me see," he mused. "Would I want someone punished more harshly if they attack me because I'm black as opposed to attacking me just because? I'd need to think about that one."

"That's fine. Gah! I'm sorry I have so much weird stuff going on." I opened the door for him. "You sure you want to go out again?"

"Strangely, I am. Very sure."

He winked and loped off down the pathway.

SHORTLY AFTER SALEM LEFT, I noticed I had a missed call that said "No ID."

There was no message but it had to have been either the police or the district attorney's office. I made the call outside even though it looked like it could start raining any minute. Arial had returned to her room and I didn't want her hearing the conversation.

"District Attorney," a gruff voice said.

"Mr. Acosta? It's Neely Pfau. Did you call me?"

There was a pause on the other end but I heard the

murmur of people in the background. The sound faded. I got the impression he'd moved into another room.

"You thought more about what we discussed?" he asked.

"Well, I'm thinking about it. I've been very distracted. My daughter is having some health issues."

The DA had already told me that, because of her young age, Arial wouldn't be expected to testify at trial. The statement she'd given to the police the night we'd sat inside the station for hours was enough.

"I'm sorry to hear that," he said.

"Yes, so... I haven't been thinking too much about that night. It's too painful to think about."

"I'm sure it is. But I've got some info that they're planning to change the plea from not guilty. We want justice for Kevin. He deserves that."

My stomach curled with a dull soreness. Of course, he deserved that. I resented the insinuation that if I wasn't willing to lie, that meant I thought Kevin didn't deserve justice.

And what was I supposed to claim the killer had said? It's not as if I had racist insults tickering across my brain. I couldn't risk doing a Google search and leaving behind a digital trail.

What exactly was Acosta risking? He could always deny he'd told me to lie, as he hadn't really told me that, just hinted broadly at it. But if I got caught in the lie, I could go to prison for perjury. I had no idea how I'd get caught but anything was possible.

Then who would take care of Arial? Acosta wasn't going to do it. Her father wasn't going to do it. And what if this ever came out, what kind of example was I setting for Arial? Wasn't I always telling her not to lie?

"I need to think more," I said.

"Don't wait too long, Miss Pfau," he replied, tersely. "He's a dangerous guy. We don't want him going free."

Chapter Twenty-Two

$\mathcal{I}$ hadn't been to see my grandparents' graves since I'd arrived, and it was time I visited. The cemetery was fairly large and although I knew where they were buried, especially given I'd been the one to oversee my grandmother's burial and graveside service, it still took me a good fifteen minutes to locate their stones.

The staff did a good job of keeping the brush around the headstones trimmed but both graves were speckled with grayish-green lichen. I'd have to research how to clean them without ruining the stones. I was glad I could now regularly visit the cemetery and honor the two people who'd raised me.

It was a clear June day. The sky was an immaculate, solid blue with gossamer ribbons of cloud dangling on the horizon. On my knees, I rested the bouquet I'd bought at the grocery store between their headstones and began to talk to them as I normally did.

"Grandma, Grandpa, you've probably seen some

things going on with Arial. Please keep watch over her. Please send her all your love and wisdom. I don't know what's happening with her but it's scaring me. And there's something else. I don't know what to do about Kevin's trial. The DA wants me to say something not true. If I lie, it means Kevin has a better chance at getting justice. I'm so conflicted. I know you've always told me to tell the truth about things but you can probably see that this is a complicated one. Can you please send me some guidance?"

I clutched my hands in a little prayer gesture, then stood back. I wasn't a big believer in the afterlife but I was so unmoored with what was happening with Arial that I figured it couldn't hurt to have a chat with the only people, besides her, who'd truly loved me. Perhaps it would bring some clarity.

When I turned, a short woman in a dark dress was staring at me. I hadn't expected to see anyone so close by and her presence startled me with a little jump.

"I didn't want to interrupt you," the woman said, walking closer.

I realized it was Pearl, my great-aunt.

"Pearl," I said, clutching my chest as my heart was still spasming. "Surprised to see you."

"I visit Henry nearly every day."

"Henry?"

"Henry Pfau. My late husband." She pointed to a nearby grave. "Your great-uncle."

I slowly walked over and stared at Henry's headstone. How had I never noticed that there were relatives so close by? Looking at the dates, I saw Henry had died rather early, at forty.

"He was so young," I said quietly.

"Yes, it's unfortunate. Henry had a drinking problem. It did him in."

"Oh, I'm sorry."

Although I knew my grandfather had had two brothers, I couldn't ever remember him discussing them. Maybe it had been too painful. Or maybe it was too difficult to say to a young person such as myself, "By the way, I had a brother who died of alcoholism." Not to mention a drunk driver would take his only son, my father.

My grandfather also came from a different era, one where people tended to be more stoic and didn't gauge the depth of their trauma by how many other people knew about it.

"And there's another brother, right?" I asked.

"Yes, Arno. He died even younger. In the war. They buried him overseas. I know Henry was always trying to get to visit but couldn't and that affected him. Arno had no children. Henry and I have a daughter. She lives out in California. I suppose I should move out there with her at some point." She sighed and shrugged as if to say *but this is where I belong*.

"I wish I could have met them. I vaguely knew he had siblings but my grandfather never talked about them that I recall."

We solemnly gazed at Henry's grave. I felt the silence between us was pulsing with the unspoken—

what had happened with Arial at the strawberry supper. Like it or not, I needed to acknowledge it.

"Pearl, I want to apologize for my daughter's behavior at church. She's not normally like that. We've had a rough time lately."

Again, I sounded like one of those parents. The ones who can't admit their child misbehaves, are in denial that their precious kid can be a little jerk sometimes.

"Yes, I found articles about what happened to you in the city," Pearl said. "I hope it's okay that I looked around."

While normally this would have felt like a breach of privacy, this time it didn't, because Pearl knowing our past backed up my defense of Arial. "So, you can see..." I pressed. "She's been through a lot. That doesn't excuse what she said. But most kids don't ever have to see what she saw."

Pearl smiled an understanding little smile. Then she blew a kiss at Henry's gravestone. When she turned back to me, I noticed her eyes were glowing cerulean blue in the late morning sunshine. With those bright blue eyes, her pert nose, and high cheekbones, she must have been a stunner back in the day. Even the slightly off-center eye gave her a unique, appealing look.

"Do you have time for tea?" she asked. "My house is only up the street. I feel—well, I think there's something you ought to know."

Chapter Twenty-Three

*P*earl served us Earl Grey tea in what she called her parlor. It was small, decorated with layers of antiques, and overlooked a long, tidy front yard.

I used to drive by this house regularly on my way to one of the local watering holes—the same area where Debbie had told me about the man we'd gone to high school with becoming paralyzed after leaping off a high rock wall—but I never knew a relative lived inside of it.

"Did you ever come to visit us?" I asked her, taking the tea she'd poured into an elaborately-painted china cup. "I don't remember you but, in all honesty, my memory isn't fabulous."

"A few times," she said, sitting in an armchair across from me. "You were only a child. But as Henry died so young, I faded off into my own life, and Earl and Lillian faded into theirs. I would see you all at church gatherings though."

"It's so strange to think my grandfather had two

brothers. I never thought to ask him about his childhood. By the time you want to know these things, it's too late."

"Did Earl ever mention his mother?"

"Mm. Not that I remember."

"She'd be your great-grandmother. I suppose you haven't heard about her mother. Your great-great-grandmother."

"No."

I noticed Pearl's hand, the one holding her teacup, was shaking a little. I didn't know if that was a consequence of her age or a health condition—or was it because she was nervous?

"But it's interesting you say that," I went on. "Last week, I found old photos in a cabinet in the basement. One of them said 'Viola Dutton Hubbard' on the back. And a wedding photo that said 'Viola and Hermann.' The pictures were from the 1800s. I haven't had a chance to go through the rest."

"Yes, Viola Hubbard is your great-great-grandmother."

"Oh, wow! It's a miracle those pictures were down there the entire time and never thrown out."

While I was sharply intrigued with the idea of hearing more family history from Pearl, my mind was also on Arial. I'd left her at the house with Debbie and Nashua. These days, my mind was almost always on Arial, and how she might be behaving. But Debbie hadn't called so I figured things must be okay. Just to make certain, I glanced at my phone again but the home screen still mercifully showed no missed calls.

I was also wary about whatever it was that Pearl was going to impart that she thought I should know, the reason she'd invited me over. *Something you ought to know* is the sort of opener that people typically use to preface negative news.

"I can see why your grandparents never mentioned her," Pearl said. "I believe the family wanted to forget everything."

"Oh?" A ripple of foreboding slithered through my abdomen and I rested my teacup on my lap.

"Yes, I didn't even know when I married Henry. I wish I had."

She looked around, her eyes falling on a black-and-white framed wedding photograph. The couple were coming down cement steps, the woman smiling widely, dressed all in white. The man in a black tuxedo and bow tie, a carnation in his lapel, held her arm. The steps looked like the ones at the top of the Methodist church, as did the stone wall behind them.

The parlor was cluttered with objects so I hadn't noticed it before. I leaned forward, trying to get a better look at the photo. True to my theory that Pearl had been striking in her youth, there she was: Quite the beauty. Her groom was equally as good-looking.

"Yes, I wish I'd known," Pearl continued. "Because Henry could never shake the way his mother was."

"His mother was Viola?"

"No, no. That's his grandmother. His mother was Viola's daughter, Maybelle. Maybelle Pfau."

I smiled but was already lost. Family trees could be

confusing. "And there's something you wanted me to know?" I prodded. "Something specific?"

"Your great-great-grandmother. Viola Hubbard. Definitely not ringing any bells?"

"Afraid not."

"She owned an inn on the outskirts of town. Back when traveling long distances was arduous. There were inns everywhere. Travelers would come, stay the night, leave in the morning."

"Do you know the name of the inn?"

"I believe it was the Hubbard Inn but don't quote me on that. This was the 1870s. Viola had two daughters. Maybelle, who'd go on to have your grandfather and his brothers. And Maybelle's younger sister, Carrie. She was mentally disabled."

"I never knew about any of them."

Pearl rested her teacup on an end table and gave a shuddery, doleful sigh. Her blue eyes were watery. Whether they were glistening with emotion or this was their natural state, I couldn't tell.

"Viola's husband died of yellow fever. She was left with two girls to support. Then the railroad came and people weren't stopping at inns like hers much anymore."

"That must have been hard."

"Yes. Very." She gazed out her large bay window for a long time, then resumed her thread. "At some point, people began disappearing. And someone figured out that the missing people had all last been seen at Viola's inn."

I said nothing. The import of what she'd uttered hadn't yet registered with me.

"There was an investigation… Dear, there's no pleasant way to put this. Viola was killing her guests, robbing them, and burying the bodies on the grounds of her inn."

"What?" I blurted, loudly.

"I know it's a shock, Neely. But I thought you should know."

"Okay, I—I guess, I—" I sputtered, trying to compose myself. "How was she doing this?" I asked, raising a brow. There was more than a smidge of skepticism in my tone.

"Poison. With arsenic-laced tea before they'd go to bed. Common method of killing at the time, long before there were tests for such things. Then she'd stab them once in the heart to make sure they weren't going to wake up, rob them, and bury them out back."

I sat with my mouth hanging open. Finally, I began to shake my head infinitesimally while making an array of facial expressions steeped in disgust and disbelief. The idea that my daughter and I shared DNA with a woman who could do something so ghastly was a profound punch to my psyche.

But I also couldn't dismiss the possibility that Pearl was suffering the beginnings of dementia or an emotional disorder of some kind, and that none of this was true. I used to have a coworker who fabricated all kinds of extraordinary stories. It had taken me awhile to figure out that, while she was a nice person, much of what she said was suspect. Maybe Pearl had a similar problem.

"So, Viola was hanged," she went on. "Public hangings had been banned a few decades before, but they got around that by moving them to the sheriff's grounds. As far as I know, she was the last woman hanged in this state."

"Oh… my…. God," I finally groaned. Something as fact-checkable as Viola being the last woman hanged in the state didn't sound fabricated.

"All the family knew," Pearl continued. "And much of the town—or at least the old guard. But you didn't. I thought you should."

"Thanks, I guess?" I laughed, edgily.

"The sad thing is that, back then, people went to hangings as entertainment. They'd even sell tickets. No one cared too much about a little girl who watched her mother's execution. For Maybelle—your great-grandmother—always said she saw it. After the hanging, the sisters went to an orphanage. Carrie, being disabled, lived there her entire life. Maybelle was adopted out as a teen to work on a farm, essentially as forced labor. She married the family's son, William Pfau. They had three sons—Arno, Henry, and the youngest, your grandfather."

I sat quiet, blinking rapidly, trying to take all of this in. And yet… I still couldn't allow myself to believe it. There had to be some explanation for what Pearl was telling me. This could be family lore. Highly inaccurate, highly exaggerated, highly just-plain-old false family lore. But wasn't family lore usually an upsell over the reality? Your great-great-grandmother is a countess type of thing?

Seemingly able to read my thoughts, Pearl added, "The historical society has information on it. In case you wanted to do any research."

"Oh," I said, dully.

"You see, Maybelle was so traumatized from watching her mother die, and learning what her mother had done, that she herself was never a decent mother." Animus seeped into Pearl's tone. "Arno signed up for the Navy the second he could. Henry drank himself into an early grave. Your grandfather is the only one who fared alright. I think because he met Lillian, who was such a lovely, solid woman. Without her, he may have ended up like his brothers."

"I'm not sure what to say," I said, still partly disbelieving. "Is there any reason you thought I should know all this?"

I didn't tell her that I could have happily lived the rest of my life without knowing I was (supposedly) directly descended from a serial killer.

"When I first married Henry, we lived with his mother. Maybelle," Pearl said. "It was only for a couple of years. We were saving up money to build our own place." She opened her arms to indicate this was the place they'd built. "But it was the worst two years of my life. It affected me so badly that I could never be a good wife after that. I resented Henry for putting me through it."

She pinched her teacup up from a doily on the end table, stared into it, then *tap-tap-tapped* on the side with one clear-polished fingernail. Finally, her watery cerulean eyes focused back on me.

"The reason I felt I should mention it is… Well, when your little girl said those things to me at the supper…" She paused. "It was as if Maybelle was in the room."

Chapter Twenty-Four

I was glad the ride home was a short one because I was so distracted. The roads were hilly and twisty and I drove extra slowly so I'd get back alive. Once your parents die instantly from a truck swerving around a blind corner, you don't take curves lightly.

I didn't know what to think about Pearl claiming that Arial sounded like Maybelle. I only had Pearl's word about any of this and for all I knew the woman—who looked to be in her eighties at the least—was suffering mental decline.

Was she suggesting Arial had inherited Maybelle's nasty disposition? That everything going on with my child wasn't PTSD, wasn't a brain tumor, but was, in fact, genetics?

After she'd shared her contention that my daughter's outburst at the supper had sounded like Maybelle, I'd stammered, "Well, that *is* something!"

Then I told her I needed to get back home.

At the door, Pearl had said, with a pitying tone, "I know this is all a surprise to you." She encouraged me to look through the material I'd found in the basement. "Might be more information in there," she'd said. "And the historical society. Last I knew, they had quite a bit on Viola."

"Pearl, this inn…" I'd asked with dread. "It wasn't where the house is, was it? There aren't bodies in my backyard, are there?"

Viola's inn was supposed to be on the *outskirts of town* but perhaps Pearl had been trying to spare me from the truth. If, indeed, *any* of this was true.

"Oh no, dear, no," she'd said, patting my arm. "Earl bought that property from a tobacco farmer. You should be able to find records in the town hall. I didn't mean to scare you that way."

I'd nodded and then walked down her driveway in a daze.

Both hands tightly clutching the steering wheel, I kept up a steady, low chant of profanity until I was parked behind Debbie's van in my drive. For some reason, cursing helped release tension.

I was actually kind of angry at my great-aunt. Couldn't she see that I had enough going on? She knew what had happened with Kevin. She knew I was having trouble with Arial. Yet she thought I also needed to know about my great-great-grandmother, the serial killer?

And to know that my soft-spoken, pure-hearted grandfather had been raised by a mother so emotionally embattled that her parenting style had sent two of her sons to an early death?

No wonder my grandfather never talked about his family.

My mind zinged around, touching on one belief, then flitting off to land on another. Pearl's grasp on reality may have eroded to the point where she fabricated stories (though she seemed perfectly lucid?). Or she may genuinely but mistakenly believe in overblown family lore.

Or... it was all true.

Debbie was on the porch. As I poked my head around the doorway, I saw she was reading. "How's it going?" I asked.

Arial and Nashua were on different levels of the jungle gym—Arial atop the platform, and Nashua digging his way down the slide with both feet. I was a tad irked that Debbie didn't have her eye on them but I'd been gone for a couple of hours. I couldn't realistically expect a human being to keep her eyes focused on nothing but two children for that long. Debbie was also accustomed to letting Nashua romp in woodsy yards and playgrounds with the barest of supervision.

"Fine," she said, lifting her book towards them. "No incidents. You get your alone time with your grandparents?"

"Yes, thanks."

I knew as soon as Arial saw me, she'd run over. But now she had her eyes intently focused on Nashua, who'd reached the bottom of the slide. My daughter moved to the top of it. Something about the way she was walking was unusual but I couldn't pinpoint how exactly.

Holding her hands up, she whizzed down the slide.

"I also went to my great-aunt's house," I told Debbie. "I'll have to tell you that story over drinks. It's too much sober."

Debbie's big, toothy grin came out, her eyes sparkling with intrigue. "Not even a hint?"

"Trust me. Drinks are in order for this one. Besides, Arial sees me and here she comes…"

Arial was walking at a leisurely pace towards the porch. This was also uncharacteristic, because normally if I'd been away for any length of time, she'd sprint at me. Nashua traipsed several feet behind her. Both of them had slow, draggy body language.

"Hi, boo," I said opening the screen door.

"Mom?" she said. Her expression was worried.

"What is it?" I asked.

She held out her palms to me. I saw blood.

"Oh my God!" I yelled. I grabbed her wrists.

"What happened? What happened?" Debbie blurted from behind me.

"Come on, come on," I said, hurrying Arial through the porch and kitchen, down the hallway, and into the bathroom. I threw on the tap, quickly adjusted the water to warm, and pulled her hands under it. The damn playset must have something jagged on it, pieces of metal or splintered wood sticking out somewhere. I expected to see gashes on her hands but when the blood washed away, her palms were unblemished.

"What's going on?" Debbie asked anxiously from the

doorway. "What can I do? I didn't see anything. Arial, what happened?"

"Is Nash okay?" I asked her.

"He looks fine."

I patted Arial's hands dry, then began examining all her skin that I could see—her legs, arms, neck, and even her face, though I already saw she had no injuries there. Something, somewhere, was eluding me.

"Check him!" I commanded. My fear startlingly crystallized into Arial having done something to Nashua. Injured him in some fashion. Just a couple of weeks ago, I never would have seriously entertained the idea that my daughter could hurt another child—at least not enough to draw blood. But this suspicion had chillingly grasped hold of me.

"I did," Debbie insisted.

"Check him again. This blood came from somewhere!"

"Nash, come here," she said firmly.

Nashua jammed one finger in his mouth and reluctantly toddled to his mother. She crouched and pulled up his t-shirt, running her fingers over his small, protruding belly. Then she turned him around, drawing her thumb down the curvature of his little back, staring at the expanse of his flesh as if reading a detailed map.

"Nash, are you hurt?" she asked, her voice tremulous.

"No!"

He was pouting in such a way that I intuitively felt he was hiding something.

"Arial, why were your hands bloody?" I used my *Don't even think of lying to me* tone.

"I don't know, Mom."

"What do you mean you don't *know*? It came from somewhere."

I stared hard into Debbie's eyes. "Please take every inch of clothing off him and check him out thoroughly. Everywhere."

"Neely, he's fine."

"Please! Bring him into a bedroom. Check everywhere."

Debbie started to look a little scared. "Come on, Mr. Nash," she said gently, herding him into the nearest bedroom, the spare room that I planned to use for an office if I could ever get a career going. She shut the door.

"I don't understand," I said urgently to Arial as I squirted liquid soap on her hands and lathered them up. "Was there blood on something? Did you stick your hands on something bloody?"

"Mom, I don't *know*."

"Arial. You must tell me. You won't get into trouble."

"Mom," she huffed, exasperated, staring up at me with her biggest, widest eyes. "I don't know how it happened. I looked down at my hands and there it was, all the blood. Then I heard your voice. I knew you'd be mad at me but I didn't know what to do."

"I'm not *mad* at you. I'm concerned."

Debbie opened the bedroom door. "He's fine. I'm sorry I wasn't watching them more closely, but neither one seems hurt."

"Yeah, I—I guess that's what matters."

After Debbie and Nashua left, I walked all around the playset, testing its edges, dragging my hands along its underside, bending and inspecting its underbelly. The only blood was dark streaks of it on the ladder handles, where Arial had climbed to the top of the platform with her already-bloody hands.

I sprayed the handles with disinfectant and wiped the stains away.

Chapter Twenty-Five

I lay in bed with Arial, reading one of her favorite books. When the book was over, she launched into her usual routine of asking me to read it again. But I was exhausted.

Too much was crowding my mind. Everything Pearl had told me about my ancestor. Then coming home to find a mysteriously-bloodied child. I only wanted to get into bed, read a little of the paperback I hadn't even cracked yet, and drift into sleep. If I was lucky, I wouldn't dream about Kevin.

"Boo, I can't," I said. "I'm starting to get one of my headaches." This wasn't true but it was one of the only excuses I could use with her where she wouldn't continue to pester me.

"Okay," she said with concern. "I'm sorry you have a headache, Mommy."

"Did you have fun with Nash this afternoon?" I asked warily.

"Yeah. He's fun."

"And no idea how you got that stuff on your hands, huh?"

"You've asked me so many times, Mom," she sighed, rolling her eyes. "We went into the woods. Maybe there was something on a tree."

"You went into the *woods*?" I was aghast. Hadn't Debbie been watching them at all?

"Just a little bit. Not far in, I swear it."

"Why didn't you tell me this before, Arial?"

"I forgot about it."

She blinked innocently at me. I supposed it was possible an injured deer or some other animal had wiped against a tree and Arial had then pressed her hands on the same spot. I supposed the last few instances of Arial acting strangely had turned my mind towards a more sinister scenario.

But deep down, I had a revolting feeling. It sat heavily, morosely in my abdomen. There had been too much blood. The blood had appeared too fresh, not at all like something that had first been wiped on tree bark.

The doorbell jarred the silence. I jumped a little. It was almost nine o'clock. Too late for a casual visit from Salem. Had Debbie forgotten something? My phone was elsewhere in the house, perhaps she'd called and I'd missed it.

"Stay here, boo," I said, getting up.

I shut her door and moved down the hallway, considering for a moment dipping into the kitchen to grab a knife. But that was absurd. This was my childhood small town. Safe as could be.

The entire time I'd lived here, I only remembered

one murder, and that had been a telemovie-worthy drama involving a young high school couple who'd turned on the girl's mother when she tried to put an end to their relationship. There had never been, as far as I knew, someone who'd walked up to a house and randomly killed the person who answered the door. If I was going to carry a weapon everywhere, I might as well have stayed in the city and enjoyed its many benefits, which included having to buzz someone into the lobby before they could manage to get all the way to your door.

I flicked on the outside light and stared through the peephole.

A man stood on the front steps. He was older, maybe in his eighties. I didn't know him, but as he looked so old, I didn't feel threatened and opened the inside wooden door, leaving the screen door closed.

"Hi," I said. I wondered if his car had broken down and he was going to ask to use my phone. But, wait, no. Even elderly people had cell phones. "Can I help you?"

"Hello, there," he said jocularly. "I'm Ben Weaver. Sorry to bother you this late. I live across the street." He pointed. It was dark so I couldn't see the house he was pointing at but I knew the one he meant. It was built below a wooded incline so you couldn't see it from the road. It hadn't been there when I was a child, but had been built in the past decade. I'd never met its owner. Until now.

Strange time for a neighbor to come introduce himself.

"I'm looking for my cat," he said, his jocular tone

swerving into a concerned one. "He's big, ginger, and very friendly. He always comes home for dinner, so I'm getting a little worried. Wondered if you happened to see him."

"No, I'm afraid…"

My stomach began a long, slow slide to the bottom of my ass. My throat went completely dry.

"I looked up and down the street." Ben held up a long metal flashlight that was turned off. "But couldn't find him. If you've got a garage, would you mind checking?"

"I… no garage."

"Oh. Shed? Anything like that?"

I shook my head even though I had a shed.

"Well, if you happen to see him, would you call me?" He reached into a pocket on his red-and-black flannel shirt and slipped out a card. I realized he expected me to open the door and take it from him, which I somehow did.

"Sure. I—I hope you find him."

"Me too. His name is Rascal, cause he's a bit of a rascal. He's a sweet boy. I'd hate to lose him."

I only nodded. I'd lost the ability to speak.

When I didn't say anything more, only continued to stare at him, Ben gave a wavering grin, turned, and retreated down the pathway.

* * *

"Who was it, Mom?"

I stood with Arial's door cracked open several

inches. She had her comforter up around her neck. I'd put her long hair into two braids and they rested over the top of it.

"A neighbor. Looking for his cat. You see a cat in the yard today?"

"Mmmm. Yeah! It was walking around the yard. Nice, big, orange kitty."

"Did you touch that cat?" In my mind, my tone was sharp, direct, parental. In reality, it came out thin and quavering.

"Mmmmm. I pet him."

"And what happened to him?"

"He walked away."

"He walked away? Are you sure?"

"Yes."

"Did he look hurt?"

She stared off over her comforter, towards her one closet. "I don't think so."

"Which way did he go?"

"Mmmmmm. Towards the woods, I think."

"What time was this?"

"Mmmmmm. Almost when you got home."

I nodded and shut the door. From behind it, I heard her calling goodnight.

In the backyard, I headed towards the playset, all the way to the edge of the woods, the flashlight illuminating the ground. I knew no one was going to lunge out of the woods with a knife and stab me or anyone I loved. But I didn't want to be out here. It was fucking creepy. I hadn't anticipated that even in my own backyard, even removed from so much humanity, I still wouldn't feel safe.

What is it Grandma used to say?

Wherever you go, there you are.

"Kitty, kitty…" The words hovered pathetically at the edge of my mouth and came out in a strange, strangled warble. "Kitty, kitty…"

I kept the flashlight's beam sweeping, stretching. My other hand held a can of stinky tuna. I'd waited until I got near the woods to peel the top back, hoping the sound would be familiar to the cat, that he'd come slinking out from wherever he might be, even if he was injured, to get this treat. Or maybe he'd meow, make a sound.

The bright beam sliced back and forth, busting through the thick, country darkness. Leaves and branches crackled and crunched under the suede boots I'd slipped onto my bare feet. Pure fear was sparkling through my veins. Fear for what I'd find. But if the cat was injured, I needed to locate him. I couldn't let him suffer and die out here alone, in pain.

"Come on, come on, Rascal," I breathed, again barely getting the words out, my voice puny and weak, my throat strung tight. Saliva had pooled deep in the back of my throat, almost choking me.

The house was fairly isolated. Behind it, woods. To one side, a long row of pines that used to be so low I could see the house next door, but that had grown tall enough that the house was hidden.

To the other side, half an acre of yard that sloped down to more woods until it hit the next house. That house, shabby and rambling, used to belong to good friends of my grandparents, but they'd since died. I had no idea who owned it now. That's the direction I kept in.

The blast of white light irradiated the grass in front of me. My pulse jerked as I saw something—a small dark mass, slightly higher than the ground around it. I slowed, my heart battering against my ribcage.

I didn't want to approach but knew I had to. This was one of those unholy times I was called upon to be the brave adult, though all I wanted to do was hurry back inside before I saw it, before the vision would be seared into my mind much as the vision of Kevin, life draining out of him, was stamped permanently onto my soul.

As I got closer, closer, the small dark mass began to resemble a stuffed toy discarded on its side, limp and useless. The flashlight beam grabbed a smattering of color on the mass, brighter than the surrounding night. A smaller part of the mass was separated from the rest, lying about a foot away.

The head.

I dropped the tuna can and raised my hand to my mouth to plug my scream.

Chapter Twenty-Six

*G*oddamn parking in the city. I'd been gone for only two months and had already forgotten how bad it was. I'd been circling the area for half an hour.

"As soon as I find parking, I'm going to talk to my friend Jed, remember him? But it will only be for a short time, very short. The doors and windows will be locked but don't engage with *anyone*, hear me?"

"Mom, what's 'engage'?"

"Don't talk to anyone."

"I know but I don't understand why I can't come with you."

"Because it's boring, adult stuff. You know Jed is running for mayor, right? It's about election things."

"I don't mind. I don't want to sit in the car. It's hot in here."

"You can run the AC. If you stay in the car, we can go to the Brooklyn Bridge Park afterward and get lunch."

"Can we go to Grimaldi's?"

"No, there will be an enormous tourist line like usual."

"Mom, he's pulling out!"

My daughter's sharp eyesight came in handy. I pulled to the side and waited for the car to leave, then did one of my least favorite things in the world: parallel parked.

The rally to halt the planned construction of a condominium whose shadow would block sunlight streaming into the Botanical Gardens was at Grand Army Plaza, about four blocks away. I'd seen on Jed's mayoral candidate website that he was planning to be there.

I didn't like leaving Arial in the car, even in child-lock mode, but didn't know what else to do. Debbie was working, and I hadn't yet found another babysitter—not that I wanted to leave her with one, anyway.

I had no idea if keeping a ten-year-old alone in a car was illegal. Hopefully, New Yorkers would do their usual thing and pay no attention to anything around them. We were on an elegant, leafy, brownstone-flanked block at eleven in the morning. Nothing bad would happen here. Of course, that's what I'd thought about Prospect Park at seven at night. But I had no choice. I needed to see Jed. And I needed to see him alone.

"Are you sure I can't come, Mom?"

"I'm sure."

She sighed dramatically. "Then why couldn't I stay home?"

"We've gone over this. There was no one to watch you."

"Why not Amara? What happened to her?"

"You tell me!" I snapped. The difficult drive and parking situation had frazzled my last nerve.

"She doesn't like me anymore."

As her little face crumpled, I guiltily swabbed her cheek with my thumb. "That's not true, boo. She got really busy with her play. I'm sorry I snapped at you. You know I hate driving in the city. This won't take long. Then we can go to Grimaldi's, though we'll wait in line for an hour." I retrieved one of her books from the floor at her feet and placed it on her lap. "Now read, enjoy the view. I'll be back in fifteen minutes, twenty tops. Then Grimaldi's."

"I'm getting a calzone," she said excitedly.

"Perfect. Whatever you want."

"Then we can go see Dad!"

"No, boo. Not today. We have to beat the traffic back. But I promise you we'll return soon, okay? Now read."

Chapter Twenty-Seven

*G*rand Army Plaza was ridiculously crowded. Not only from an impressive turnout for the rally against the new condo—people brandishing signs and placards, people handing out flyers— but also due to the Saturday morning farmers' market. I'd forgotten how much teeming humanity was shoved into Brooklyn.

"Have you seen Jed Thompkins? The guy running for mayor?" I resorted to asking strangers, all of whom stared blankly at me.

Acutely aware of Arial sitting in the locked car, I started to feel I should give up and return to her. But then I spotted him. Tan chinos, a white golfing shirt. A red baseball cap that read, "JED FOR MAYOR."

These days, he had a sausage-like paunch hugging his waistline. Between that and the frumpy outfit, it was difficult—make that impossible—to remember why I'd once found him so magnetic and attractive that I'd changed the entire trajectory of my life for him. Somehow, I'd have impress upon Arial that to choose a partner based primarily on sexual chemistry was the worst idea ever. But I knew that would be a losing battle.

Jed was handing out flyers at the entrance to the park, next to a pillar of a caped horseman and a winged angel. Nearby was a foldout table filled with glossy, colorful campaign paraphernalia. At the table sat Jed's wife, Willa. I recognized her instantly, even though she was wearing a floppy hat. She was brunette, in her early fifties, and had a wide, brittle *politician's wife* smile on.

I also noticed two young women, one appearing in her early twenties, the other looking in her teens, standing on either side of the table. I suspected these were Jed's daughters: Gia and Antonia, known as Toni. They both wore loose, white JED FOR MAYOR t-shirts. I hadn't bothered to look up their photos in years but the way they were enthusiastically thrusting flyers at passersby told me these were the daughters. Arial's half-siblings. The ones she didn't know existed.

I'd never seen them in person. I'd never shared real life space with Jed's family. I had no idea what his reaction would be when he saw me in his family sphere. He'd spent all these years keeping me rigidly apart from them, and here I was storming into their sacred circle.

It reminded me of the time a call had come in from one of Jed's daughters when he'd been with me. The name that popped up on the screen was "ThomFam4."

Thompkins Family Four.

It was around that time I realized that he was never going to integrate Arial into his life. There was no room for a five.

I decided to say something before he saw me, to allow my voice and expression to communicate that while I hadn't necessarily come in peace, nor had I come to ruin his precious "ThomFam4."

"Hello, Mr. Thompkins," I said, stretching out my hand. "I'm the one who calls your office about the garbage cans."

He turned and glanced at me, at first with the "politician's smile," similar to his wife's—that *I love the public!* smile. But it quickly and almost comically deteriorated. He looked stunned and rather horrified that I was standing in front of him and he didn't return my handshake.

"I'm the one who wanted more garbage cans," I repeated, lowering my hand. "They keep disappearing. I hate litter."

He didn't say anything, but his smile reappeared, though it was the stiffest, most disingenuous smile you could imagine. One of his daughters—the oldest one, Toni—glanced over at us, then got distracted by a young, bushy-bearded man on a skateboard who approached her.

It sickeningly hit me that not only were his eldest daughter and I essentially the same age, but we looked similar. Unlike her parents, Toni was blonde. I also saw Arial in her. Arial in a decade.

"Can I show you where the garbage can was?" I persisted. "It was right over by the entrance. It's so odd that the sanitation department took it. I hope we can get it back."

He better not try to get out of coming with me. I

didn't have all day and needed to get back to Arial. If he messed with me, I'd say everything in front of his cherished ThomFam4.

"Sure," he said, gruffly. He didn't glance at anyone in his family before following me around the dramatic pillars of the archway that led into the park. It was the first time I'd been near the area since Kevin's murder and I could barely bring myself to glance at the trees.

In one of Jed's big hands was a stack of glossy, thick-board flyers. On them was the silhouette of a building with a red X stamped over it. The type read, "Don't Kill Our Garden." Absurdly, he handed me one and I took it.

"When's the MRI?" I said, shielding my eyes from the relentless sunshine with the flyer.

"I told you…" he said with gritted teeth. "I left a message."

"Yes, and I left *you* a message and didn't hear back. So you've forced me into this."

"Neely…" He kept his voice low and scanned the crowd as if someone might be sizing up our interaction for abnormalities. "I can't order up an MRI. I called a few places. They need a pediatrician's referral."

"I can't get one."

"Try another doctor."

"Listen, asshole," I said, pointing to the lawn as if showing him where the errant garbage can used to be located. "They're all going to say the same thing. And it's not easy finding one that takes my shitty insurance."

"Then she probably doesn't have anything wrong."

"What would you know about it?" I tilted my head

at him as if discussing the mundane matters of garbage can removal. "You know nothing about her life. You've rejected your child in favor of these strangers who care nothing for you except what you can do for them."

I eyed the surrounding mob of people, a few of whom were hovering, waiting for the chance to speak to Jed. I shoved the flyer at him and he sheepishly rejoined it with the pile in his hand.

"Just remember one thing," I said, keeping my tone low and even. "The last thing that will go through your mind before you die is 'I was a bad father.' Now get her the damn MRI or I call a press conference."

Chapter Twenty-Eight

*A*rial and I got back to Orchard about six hours later. I stopped at the small shopping mall in the center of town to pick up a pizza. It would be our second time having Italian today but I didn't have the energy to cook and Arial could eat Italian food all day, every day. Fitting, considering that, through Jed, she was a quarter Italian. But who doesn't love Italian?

I sent her in to get the food while I went next store to the pharmacy and asked for her anti-anxiety medication. I'd called it in yesterday, the day after discovering the cat. I still hadn't decided to give it to her, nor did I know what I'd tell her about it if I did. I was nervous the medication might create an addiction in her, but was also fearful I might be withholding something that could benefit her.

At home, I set her up with pizza and apple juice on the porch, told her I'd be back in five minutes, and warned her not to go anywhere. She cast me a flinty-eyed stare as she picked up her first slice.

"Mom, you said living here would be like free-range. That I wouldn't be watched so much like I was in the city, but it's even worse here. Ten times worse. A hundred!"

"You've had a few little episodes where you've said and done things that you don't remember. So, I'm being extra cautious. That's all."

"Nothing's happening, Mom," she drawled before dragging a gooey sheet of cheese into her mouth.

* * *

WHEN BEN ANSWERED his door and saw me, his face lit up. He looked so hopeful that I was about to tell him I'd found his cat.

"Yessss?" he said eagerly.

"Mr. Weaver, I hate to be the one to tell you this…"

I watched as his face slowly fell. He knew he was about to receive bad news. I felt horrible.

"I found Rascal out in the road. It looked like he'd been hit. I didn't want you to see that so I buried him in my backyard."

Ben's hands began shaking, his eyes glistening. He was assuredly upset about the passing of his pet, but I couldn't gauge how he felt that I'd gone ahead and given the cat a burial.

There was no way I could have shown Ben the kitty as I'd found him. It had taken every ounce of willpower I possessed to retrieve a towel, lift the parts of the cat into a cardboard box, and walk deep into the woods where I pushed aside dirt and brush with my feet and covered him up as best I could with a layer of leaves and small branches. I knew that wild animals would soon dispose of him.

It was those wild animals my mind had turned to in order to settle blame. A fox, coyote, or fisher cat had done the poor cat in. After all, that had happened several times with our indoor-outdoor cats as a child. Arial must have discovered the kitty and touched the carcass, getting blood on her hands. She may have even been trying to help the poor thing. Then, she had one of her forgetting episodes…

It was too much blood, too much blood…

She said the cat walked away…

I refused to believe the other hypothesis knocking ominously at the back of my brain. Arial adored animals. Pretty much every t-shirt or dress she owned had to have an animal on it. She'd been begging me for a dog since she could speak. She routinely carried bugs outside rather than allow me to kill them. She also insisted if she didn't become a gymnast when she grew up, she'd be a veterinarian.

She would never harm an animal.

Besides, her hands were delicate and small. And, despite trying my best not to look at the remnants of the cat, the weight of it told me it was a large tom. There was no possibility that Arial's girlish hands had the strength or size to wrap around its neck and…

"You see," I stammered to Ben, "he wasn't, uh, he wasn't… well, it was a mess, Mr. Weaver," I finished as diplomatically as I could. "Trust me, you didn't want to see it. I put him in a box and gave him a nice burial. I can show you where if you want."

I figured if Ben showed up, I'd bring him to an area in the yard behind a bush where I'd buried all my childhood cats. There were still large flat rocks marking the spots.

I wouldn't tell him I'd carried his pet into the woods and layered brush over him because I didn't have a shovel. Nor could I risk burying the cat in the yard and having Arial bounding over to inquire what I was doing.

"No, no. Thank you." Ben shook his head. "He was so good about staying in the yard. If he did cross the street, he was so careful about it. But he was getting older... maybe he'd lost some of his senses."

"Those cars come up the hill quite fast."

"Yes, I guess they do. I shouldn't have let him outside but he'd howl and howl until I did."

"I'm so sorry, Mr. Weaver. If you ever want to see where I buried him, please come over. I have to get back to my daughter now."

He nodded, still appearing grieved by the news. I was halfway up his flagstone pathway when I heard him call, "Miss? Oh, Miss?"

I turned. "Neely Pfau. Sorry I didn't give you my name before."

"You mentioned a daughter. How old is she?"

"She's, um, she's ten."

"I see, I see..." He raised one shaky finger. "Does she have long, dark hair?"

"Yes." I smiled.

"See, my wife was at her fiftieth high school reunion

last night. In Colchester. We moved here a few years ago, but she grew up there. Fifty years, you believe that?"

"Congratulations," I said, wishing he'd get to the point.

"She didn't get home until something like 11:30 at night. She was coming up the hill and told me a little girl, with long, dark hair, was standing right there—" His trembling finger pointed to the street. "—in the middle of the road. Just next to your house. I sincerely hope it wasn't your daughter."

"Oh no," I said, firmly shaking my head. "No, no. My daughter is in bed by then."

But even as I said it my heart was contracting with foreboding.

"I wonder who it could be then. My wife almost hit her; she was real shaken up about it. Said it was the strangest thing—the girl was standing there, just staring at the car. My wife pulled into our drive, but couldn't see her anymore so she started to doubt her faculties because we don't know any children on this street. To be honest, I thought maybe she was imagining things, but when you said you have a daughter…"

"Thanks for letting me know. I'll talk to her but very much doubt it was her."

"Good, good. I hope it wasn't. My wife said it scared her half to death, seeing a little girl like that standing in the road in a pink nightgown."

Chapter Twenty-Nine

$\mathcal{O}$n Monday night, I held out the pill and cup of water for Arial. The bathroom was so small it was almost claustrophobic with two people in it, even if one of those people was more like half a person. Arial scowled at the pill. "I'm not anxious, Mom."

"I know. It's just that Nora—Dr. Bertussi—said it will help with these little episodes where you forget things."

"I'm not forgetting, *you're* forgetting!" she countered. "You think I wrote that on my wall, but I didn't!"

Then she snatched the pill out of my palm and defiantly swallowed it, scrunching her face up as if it tasted bitter.

I loathed drugging my child. But I kept telling myself that drugging her was better than her running around outside at night—if she'd done it. I kept telling myself millions of children all around the world were on drugs for one thing or another. We were lucky to live in a time when they were available.

Of course, I'd questioned her, asking more than once if she'd left the house after bedtime. She'd vociferously denied it. By now, she was plainly irritated with my random accusations of this and that. But it seemed too coincidental that the neighbor described a girl who not only looked like Arial and was right in front of the house, but who was also wearing a pink nightgown.

The idea of her slipping outside late at night—whether she was conscious of it or not—and standing in the middle of the road where two tons of speeding steel could have easily flattened her filled me with terror.

I was starting to feel our city apartment building had been safer, after all. The inside door had two locks and the lobby had two heavy glass doors that she could never fully open without help. But was I supposed to keep us in the city where we could never use the park? Where simply walking around our neighborhood would remind us of that dreadful night?

After I read her favorite book and kissed her goodnight, I shut her door and made a beeline to the fridge, grabbing the bottle of white wine I'd bought earlier. I poured myself a hefty glass. It wasn't only my child who needed drugging.

After a few long sips that mercifully unknotted my mind a little, I took my cell phone, headed out to the front yard, and pressed Salem's number.

"Well, hello, Miss Pfau," he said, cheerily, picking up on the second ring.

"Hi, just wanted to say I love the room. Arial does too."

"You didn't hire the best painter in town for nothing."

"You said you do handyman-type stuff as well, right?"

"Yep. Got something else you need?"

"Yeah, I—I think I do. My daughter, she—well, she may have started sleepwalking. I need to... I think I need to lock her in at night."

He was silent. No doubt wondering if I was crazy. Perhaps he'd even report me to authorities. Child protective services.

"Is that legal?" he asked quietly.

"I don't know what else to do, Salem. Our neighbor reported seeing her in the middle of the street, in the middle of the night. She was almost hit. I've got her on medication that hopefully will help but until then I've got to keep her in her room at night. I could put her in mine but she could still sneak out while I'm sleeping."

"What about hanging a bell around her neck? Like a cow?"

Despite myself, I burst out laughing. Everything was so absurd it was either laugh or cry. Once I could breathe again, I said, "She'll just remove it."

"Sure, I could put a lock on. What kind do you want? Slide latch, deadbolt, key knob, smart lock…"

"Something simple. Maybe not a slide latch. I wouldn't put it past her to figure out how to open that."

"When she's *asleep*?"

"How about a doorknob with a key that I can turn from the outside?"

"I can do that."

"Can you come tomorrow?"

"Welllll, I got some things going on but… I can tell you're buggin."

"Very much so."

"Hey, Neely, I was thinking about what you asked me. If I got attacked."

I stared up at the dark starry sky. I'd forgotten all about my question to him. I'd even forgotten all about Kevin's case and what the DA wanted me to do. I was too consumed with how to help my daughter.

I'd even stopped calling Rachel and other friends from the city, unable to bring myself to tell them about Arial's issues. No matter what comforting words they might offer, I had a feeling they'd think she wasn't adjusting to the country. That it had been my fault that, on top of the trauma inflicted on her that night, I'd then excised her support system: her friends, her teachers, the places she loved and was familiar with. Even her "Dad" in the cemetery.

"I was reading about what happened to you," Salem continued. "I saw the guy's name. Huang. So, I think I have an idea why you asked me that question."

I said nothing, sipping my wine, grateful that the alcohol was allowing me a brief respite from being wound tighter than a serpent ready to strike. I should be doing something healthier to relax—yoga, running, meditation—but right now I didn't give a crap about any of that. Anything that stopped me from tearing out my hair while running around the yard naked and screaming obscenities was a good thing.

Ditch, here I come.

"I guess my answer is I can't give you an answer," Salem said.

"Why not?"

"Because there's a lot of different variables. Besides, whatever I think is best for me wouldn't necessarily be best for you and that poor guy."

"Sounds like a copout, Salem."

"Maybe. But this isn't my story, it's yours."

"I'm sick of my stories," I grumbled. My tolerance for booze was so low that I was already slightly slurring. "I'm sick of me."

"You're having a tough time, no doubt about it," he said.

"I'm sick of being alone, sick of being a single parent, sick of her father doing nothing, and sick of whatever the fuck is going on with her and worrying about it."

"Neely," he said, softly. "I know we're trying to get to know each other under difficult circumstances. But so long as you give me some notice, I can watch her if you need it. I'm not scared of a little girl. I'm not scared of whatever crazy ass shit she might say to me. And if she *does* say some crazy ass shit to me, I'm gonna laugh at it, okay? Hahaha!"

"Oh my God, Salem," I said, feeling I was about to cry with gratitude. "I have to go to the historical society for a couple of hours, as soon as possible. Is there any way you can watch her while I do that? It's one thing to lock her in at night but during the day when I'm not here? I suspect the authorities would have issues with that one."

"I'm coming over to install the lock, anyway. Can I watch her at the same time?"

"Absolutely. If you can do that, I'd be forever grateful. I'd owe you big time."

"Then I'm going to hold you to a second date, Neely. And, yes, we did have a first one."

I smiled and stared up at the billions of stars twinkling peacefully in the velvet, moonless sky. For this moment, all was well.

Chapter Thirty

*T*he Orchard Historical Society was lodged in an old brick manor house on Main Street. The building was so unimposing that I'd hardly taken notice of it before. Outside was a plaque that read "Built in 1755."

I was a mixture of conflicting emotions as I pulled on the big wooden door handle to the brick house. On the one hand, I felt my ancestor's gruesome predilections had nothing to do with me and there was no reason that I shouldn't walk in with my head held high.

On the other, I was deeply ashamed in an atavistic way. My hands were trembling slightly and my stomach felt like it had taken an elbow. The idea that whomever I was going to ask for help might give me a judgmental look, might be able to infer my sordid family history, made me queasy.

"Hi," I said to the woman sitting at a small desk next to the entrance. I tried to sound cheerful and not like I was descended from a serial killer. "I'm here for a little research project. I was wondering if you had anything on Viola…" Suddenly, my throat was parched and I had to swallow. "Hubbard," I rasped.

The historian stood. She was tiny, not more than five feet tall, with short, graying hair in a shaggy cut. Somewhere in her sixties. A brown, formless dress. Exactly what you'd expect a historian to look like. Her badge had her name on it but the print was too small for me to read, which reminded me I still needed glasses if I could ever get the money for them.

"Oh, absolutely," she said. If I wasn't mistaken, pride galvanized her tone. "We have an exhibit on Viola Hubbard. The last woman in the state to be hanged."

The museum was small but had a back room. She walked me to it and over to a corner. There were several oversized, blown-up, black-and-white photographs on the walls. One of them was a woman in a black Victorian dress, appearing stoic and somewhat miserable, as people from that era tended to do.

She also looked remarkably like the photograph I had back at my house. Seeing her here blown up on a wall of a historical museum, I was struck by the level of her fame and that my family had gone so many years not even mentioning her. I also had a very odd and unexpected sensation of self-importance that back home were photographs that might be valuable.

"Anything in particular you're looking for?" the historian asked. She seemed eager to help. There was no one else in the museum and I guessed she didn't have much to do.

I crossed my arms and leaned into the photographs.

Recessed light from above was trained on them and each contained a side placard. I tried to read the print but was so preoccupied expecting the librarian to deduce that I was Viola's descendent that I only scanned the words.

"What—why was she hanged?" I needed to see if Pearl had the facts correct.

"She had an inn, the Hubbard Wayfarer, about ten miles from here in what used to be called only 'east of the river,'" the historian said. "Viola was accused of killing dozens of travelers to the inn and robbing them. She'd give them poisoned tea and, once they passed out, stab them through the heart."

Dozens. Dozens!

"Did—did she do it?"

"A trial said she did, but it's not as if there was forensic evidence back then. Doubtful she even had any kind of legal representation. According to reports at the time, bodies were dug up from the property." The historian pointed to various placards as she spoke. "She was convicted of highway robbery which was a capital offense. If you can believe it, at the time, that was a worse crime than murder."

"Did she have any children?" I tried to sound nonchalant, although it felt painfully obvious that Viola's killer DNA was staring out from my face.

"Yes, two." The woman pointed to a smaller black-and-white photo. I crouched forward and squinted. Two young girls. Both with dark hair like their mother.

"Carrie and Maybelle Hubbard," the historian said. "Probably about eight and ten in this photo. Maybelle went on to marry a local man, William Pfau, and the family stayed in town."

I startled a little at hearing my last name but hoped my expression remained impassive. Well, that settled it. Pearl had been correct. Unless the last name was a big coincidence, I was directly descended from a serial killer. I supposed my friends' and my complete lack of interest in the history of the town saved me from stumbling upon or being confronted with this information sooner. And the "old guard" that Pearl had mentioned were too classy to bring it up to me.

"A crowd of hundreds gathered to see the execution from the gallows," the historian continued, staring somberly at the photo of the sisters. "Rumor has it the girls were present at the execution."

The photo was a little blurry but the pair were standing so close together that it appeared they were holding hands. They too had that flat, haunted look of the era. I was drawn to the face of the older girl, Maybelle, whose dark, bottomless eyes spoke of misery and hardship. She especially pulled on my heartstrings as in the photo she was ten. The same age as Arial.

To think that the sisters, at such tender ages, had witnessed the hanging of their mother, watched a large crowd of supposedly better-knowing adults cheer it on, then were shipped off to an orphanage for who knew what other depravity.

To think that by the time Maybelle was my daughter's age, she'd already experienced the worst humanity had to offer. I supposed, in that way, she and Arial had something in common. They'd both seen a person they loved executed right in front of them. Early on, they learned that the world could be dangerous and cruel, with no protection anywhere.

"It's said that Viola gave a speech to the crowd declaring her innocence," the historian said.

"Was there any chance she *was* innocent?"

"Plenty of innocent people were put to death in those days. Anything is possible. But there were definitely bodies on the property. Did Viola have help or did someone else do it? Some say a male companion was the real culprit but I'm afraid we'll never know for sure. The male companion ended up dead, too."

The woman looked at me for so long that I offered her a side glance. I felt glowing with self-consciousness, though it was clear she didn't have any psychic insight about my ancestry and was only pleased to be sharing her knowledge.

"Legend has it," she went on, "that when Viola's plea of innocence failed and she realized she was about to be put to death, she screamed out, 'You think I'm the devil? Fine, you've got the devil. And you'll never rid yourself of him!' Then she jumped to her death before the trapdoor could be released."

I had to give Viola grudging respect that she preferred to take her own life rather than allow someone else to do it for her. At that point, it was the only control she had.

I was also struck by the strangely similar language that Viola and the man who'd killed Kevin had used.

I'm the devil.

Chapter Thirty-One

"Go Fish," I heard Arial say as I opened the door.

She and Salem were sitting on the living room floor, playing her favorite card game.

"Mommy!" she cried but didn't hop up and greet me like she normally did. She was too engrossed in the game. Salem smiled at me. I could tell from the winsome scene that nothing had gone wrong but couldn't help asking, "Everything okay?" with a hopeful quaver in my voice.

"I'm beating Salem," Arial announced.

"She's kicking my butt," he said, then covered his mouth and comically raised his brows at her. "Is that okay to say?" he asked me.

I laughed. "Who wants lemonade?"

"Me!" Arial screeched.

"Afraid I've got some work to do," Salem said, standing. "Love to take you up on it another time."

"Salem, don't leave!" Arial implored. It was the

same pleading tone she'd once used with Kevin, reserved for men she liked. Men she thought might step into the role of father.

"Sorry, kiddo," he said gently. "But we'll hang again soon."

I poured Arial some lemonade while Salem grabbed his bag of tools. Then I walked him to his pickup.

"I can't thank you enough. She behaved the whole time?"

"Yeah, she was cool. Didn't even have much to say about the new knob on the door." He handed me two small silver keys that locked the knob and I slipped them into the back pocket of my shorts. "There's an extra there," he said. "Don't want to lock her in and lose it."

"Yeah, I guess not." I couldn't believe this was something I'd just done.

"I don't think she realizes it can be locked and I didn't volunteer the information," he said.

"I didn't tell her that part. Just said the knob was sticking and needed to be replaced. What do I owe you?"

"How about dinner?"

I grinned. "I meant money-wise."

"I know what you meant and how about dinner? Both of you."

"I'd love that."

"Great, I'll be in touch." He turned to get into his truck but then something occurred to him. "Oh, I almost forgot. Hate to say this but looks like shingles might be coming loose on your roof on the other side." Squinting, he pointed past me.

"Is that bad?"

"Could mean the whole roof is due for a replacement."

"Oh God," I groaned. Here it was. One of the myriad reasons I'd feared owning a house—all of the maintenance. This was nothing the inspector that Beckett hired had even mentioned.

"Don't panic," Salem said. He had a very comforting voice. I wished I could record it and play it back whenever I started to do exactly that. "I'll bring my roofing ladder and check out the situation. If anything needs to be replaced, you gotta do it before winter. Snow sets on that roof, it might start to leak."

With his campaign in high gear, Jed had been even more difficult to reach. Despite my threat about calling a press conference, he still hadn't contacted me about an MRI. I had no idea how I'd get money out of him to fix a roof. Being involved in such a high-profile campaign had likely made him extra cautious about tapping into whatever he was using to get me funds. If he thought he could get away with it, there was no doubt he'd set us adrift to fend for ourselves.

I needed a job so I wouldn't be financially dependent on him but how was I supposed to get a decent-paying, full-time job with Arial's issues? How could I leave her in someone's care?

Seeing what must have been despair on my face, Salem rested a hand on my arm. "These are things that happen with old houses. They're fixable. Don't worry about the money, okay?"

"I have to worry."

"I've got a roofer pal. He'll give you a deal. And you don't have to have dinner with me to get me to check out the roof."

"But I want to." I smiled.

"Then I'll stop by in a few days and take a look at it. Now get in there and have some fun with that awesome kiddo of yours."

Chapter Thirty-Two

"*M*ommy, why are you locking me in?" Arial asked.

I had put her to bed, read her a book, read her another book, kissed her, stroked her hair back from her forehead, and was almost out of the door, my hand on the dimmer dial.

I turned to look at her. There was no mistaking it. She was glaring at me. I had absolutely no idea how she'd figured out what I'd planned to do after she fell asleep.

"Boo," I said, my voice sounding nothing like a parent but more like a small child who'd been caught in something naughty, "it's just to keep you safe."

"Safe from what? I thought you said we were safe here. That's why we moved."

I returned to her bed and perched on the edge. I reached out to take her hand but she rejected my overture, shoving her hands under the covers. Her eyes were still accusatory.

It was remarkable to me how she'd acted normal all evening, even taking her pill with no complaint, then sprang this on me at the last second. And how did she know? Salem wouldn't have told her. She was an extraordinarily astute child and must have figured out my plan based on the new knob having a keyhole, and how I'd lately been helicopter-parenting her every move.

"Hon, you're having little episodes where you forget things. That's why you take the medicine before bed." I didn't tell her what the neighbor had said about her appearing in the road—I didn't want to frighten her. "This is only to make certain that you stay safe in your room."

"What if I have to go pee?"

Now I knew she was manipulating me. Arial never went pee during the night. I often joked with her about her iron bladder. As someone who got up multiple times a night to pee, I envied it.

"Tomorrow I'll get a baby monitor and set it up. That way, if you have to go pee, you can call for me."

"I want a cell phone."

"Not now, boo. When you're older."

"Mom, I don't think you're allowed to lock me in my room."

"This is temporary, okay?"

I tried to wrest back control of the conversation. I was the parent and I'd make the decisions. If that meant locking my daughter in her room so she didn't get killed outside, then that's what I was going to do. I'd figure out the details as I went along.

"For tonight, if you need to get up, come knock on

the wall," I said, pointing to the rather thin wall that separated my room from hers. As a kid, I often fell asleep to the sound of the small black-and-white television that my grandparents kept on in their room. If I concentrated, I could still conjure up the bouncy opening melody of *Late Night with Johnny Carson*.

"If you knock on the wall, I promise I'll hear it."

I AWOKE when I began shivering. I'd folded into the fetal position, and my legs were shaking under the top sheet. Groggily, I pulled up the light comforter and tried to get back to sleep but it started to penetrate my mind that this wasn't right. It was far, far too cold.

The night-time temperature must have dropped precipitously. Very odd, for it was early July, but this was a rural area, and we were high atop a hill. I got up, arms tightened around my ribcage to still my shaking, went to the window, and closed it. It had only been open a few inches. The room was too chilly. It made no sense how chilly it was.

I decided I better go check Arial's room too. She tended to run hot and was always kicking off her blankets, but my bedroom was like a meat storage freezer. I wanted to make sure hers wasn't as well.

I turned on my overhead light and went to the mother-of-pearl lacquered jewelry box where I kept the limited amount of jewelry I owned, and into the top drawer where I'd placed the two knob keys. I took one out, my hand trembling from the cold.

At Arial's door, I struggled to get the key in the hole. It took three or four tries before it slid in and I was able to turn the knob. When I opened the door, a blast of ice-cold slapped me. It was the type of cold that only comes from outdoor air and I quickly saw that both her bedroom windows were wide open.

I was shocked that she'd gotten both windows up. They were old and heavy, sticky. I turned the dial of the dimmer light about a quarter of the way. I didn't want to wake her but I needed to see better so I could cross the room without stepping on her various toys and shut the windows.

This is when I saw her bed was empty, her sheet and blanket bunched up at the end of the mattress. For several sickening seconds, I could do and say nothing. I only wanted this scene to explain itself. For Arial to come out of her closet and laugh at me.

But the reality of what had happened swiftly punched me in the face. Arial had opened both windows, crawled out, and left the house.

"Oh my God," I breathed, unable to get my voice to project. It was as if my throat was being tightly held by a strong hand. At the window next to Arial's bed, I leaned out and frantically peered around the moonlit yard.

"Arial!" I screamed. My voice was blasting out at full volume now. My neighbors weren't close but I wouldn't be surprised if they heard me. "Arial!"

"Oh my God, oh my God, oh my God," I chanted as I ran from her bedroom, down the hallway, and into the living room. My hands were shaking so badly from the deep cold and my raw panic that it was difficult to unlock both front doors. Barefoot, dressed only in my usual sleepwear—a long t-shirt and underwear—I stumbled around the front, side, and back yards, hysterically calling out my daughter's name.

Realizing this wasn't the way to go about finding her, I hurried back into the house and went to the kitchen. On the counter was the big metal flashlight. When I flicked the lever, the light was dim and weak. I shook it, hearing the batteries rattle inside, and the light went out entirely.

"No!" I cried.

I was now hysterical and bawling. I should call the police but was afraid that once they found Arial—and I was sure she was in the yard somewhere—she'd inform them that she'd gone out the window because I'd locked her inside her room. She'd say she needed to use the bathroom, had knocked on our shared wall, and I hadn't woken up.

What kind of mother locks a child into her bedroom? I didn't think my explaining that she'd sleepwalked outside a couple of nights ago would excuse what I'd done. My little girl would be put into a foster home. I did the only thing I could think to do in my scattered, panicked, terrified state. I called Salem.

* * *

By the time Salem arrived, which was only about fifteen minutes later but felt like fifteen hours, I'd wandered through the ballpark across the street and walked up the sidewalk until it ended several houses away. The whole time I was shivering, crying, and calling for her.

Salem had brought flashlights as I'd requested.

"Don't worry," he said, handing me one. "We'll find her."

I tried to speak but could hardly form words. "I shuh-shuh call—call puh-police. But I-I scuh-scared. I-I luh-locked her in." I was shuddering so hard I didn't know if Salem understood anything I'd said.

"We'll find her," he repeated.

We searched through the yards, him on one side of the house, me on the other. Both of us calling, calling, calling.

"Let's drive around," he said. "In case she went down the street."

I was so disoriented that he had to grip me by the shoulders and direct me to his truck, then help me get into the passenger seat as if I were elderly. Inside, I broke down again, great, gusting sobs exploding from my throat. I began to wail her name over and over, as if this would bring her back.

"Neely!" Salem boomed authoritatively, trying to snap me out of my useless emotional state. "We'll drive to the end of Chestnut Hill and back. If we don't find her, we've got to call the police."

"Yuh-yes," I wailed. My little girl was going to be taken from me. I was going to be put into prison.

"Please, Neely, I know this is hard, but pull it together. You've got to keep a lookout so my eyes can stay on the road."

This worked to somewhat rein in my delirium. He

was right. I needed to pull it together. Being in hysterics was not going to find her.

As he drove down the long hill, I kept the window open, calling for her, keenly focusing in on every single shadow and flash of light that passed by. Streetlights became, for a moment, her. Trees became, for a moment, her. Mailboxes. Street signs. All for one, brief, hopeful moment, were my baby.

In about two minutes, we reached the bottom of the hill. To the right was an entrance to a pond, where I'd spent every summer of my youth lounging on the small beach, tanning myself with no regard for skin cancer, getting ice cream when the truck arrived playing its familiar jingle, flirting with the lifeguard, and gossiping with my friends.

Senior year, it's also where I'd secretly meet up with Jed. He'd arrive in his Mercedes near dark and we'd park at the very end of the driveway, where there was a picnic table and a sandbar that separated the swimming pond from a fishing-only one. That area was where Arial had been conceived.

"Go in here!" I yelled, pointing to the pond's entrance.

Salem swerved in and parked in the small parking lot. I jumped out, calling and waving the flashlight around, its beam hitting the changing station, the bathroom, the sandy beach, and a few benches. She was nowhere.

I heard something, a dull thumping noise. I followed the sound with the beam of the flashlight. The light splashed on the long, L-shaped metal dock that stretched from the shoreline into the middle of the water. This is where I'd learned to swim, clinging to the dock and paddling my feet as the instructor called to a string of children to kick harder, kick faster.

This is also where, as a teen, I came to understand that I was attractive. As I stood on the dock in my red bikini, all the men along the shoreline were focused on me. And as I slipped into the water with a smooth dive, their gazes would follow me until I reached the shore and came out wringing my hair, pretending I didn't notice their hungry stares.

The dock bounced up and down in the water. I recognized the dull thudding and creaking as the sounds the dock made when someone walked on it. I caught sight of her pink nightgown. Arial was headed down the dock towards the deep end.

"Arial!" I screamed.

Salem's deep voice boomed right after mine. "Arial! Stop!"

She walked to the edge of the dock, then turned and looked out towards us. I couldn't tell if she saw or heard us. My mind was so scrambled with panic that I could hardly take in what was happening. I heard a small splash and she was no longer on the dock.

I tossed the flashlight, waded quickly up to my knees, then dove. I wasn't the best swimmer in the world, I never did master the crawl stroke, so I held my breath and glided underwater, flapping forward as fast as I could through the cold, pitch-dark water towards where I'd seen her jump. When I came up for air, I screamed her name again.

I barely registered loud pounding on the dock but would later realize that Salem had run up the length of it and plunged in directly behind Arial.

"I got her!" I heard him yell. "I got her!"

I kept calling her name, and water surged into my mouth, sending me into a choking fit. If I didn't get back to shore, I was going to drown. Sputtering and coughing, I side-stroked jaggedly back towards the shoreline as fast as I was able, replaying Salem's words in my head. Forcing myself to trust that he would keep her safe.

He's got her, he's got her, he's got her…

Chapter Thirty-Three

*a*t home, I carried her to the bathroom like she was a baby, stripped off her clinging soaked nightgown, toweled her dry, and slipped a warm nightgown over her head.

The entire time, I kept asking her if she could breathe okay, kept asking her things like what her name was, how old she was, who I was.

"Mommy," she said, shivering and sounding very tired. "You're Mommy. I'm Arial. I'm ten."

I assumed Salem had left. Or, really, I hadn't given him any thought at all. I only wanted to get my daughter out of her wet nightgown and make sure she was okay.

Thank God starting from six years old I'd insisted on her taking swimming lessons at the local Brooklyn Y. The lessons weren't cheap and many times I'd wondered why I was spending money on that when we lived in the city. But having grown up in the country and around water, I felt it would be irresponsible of me if she didn't learn to swim. It was a matter of safety.

Still, when she and I traveled to the nearby city beaches—Coney Island, Brighton Beach, Far Rockaway —I made her stay on the shore unless I was with her. But the lessons had paid off with saving her life. That, and Salem being so fast.

I sat her on the toilet and blow-dried her hair until it was nearly stick-dry. This is when I saw Salem, standing hesitantly in the hallway, just outside the bathroom. I realized he must have been in the house the entire time. He was soaked and I hadn't even thanked him.

I staggered over and threw my arms around him. I tried not to cry, as I didn't want Arial to get scared, so I buried my face in his wet t-shirt, shaking and snuffling. "Thank you," I managed to choke out. "Thank you."

I pulled back, wiping my face. I was still drenched, my t-shirt sticking so completely to my body that it had ridden all the way past my underwear. But I didn't care.

"I'm glad I could help," he said. "You guys alright? I should get home and change unless you want me to stay."

"No, no, you should go. You'll catch the flu. Your flashlight is still at the pond."

He laughed a little. "That's fine, I have plenty of them."

"Salem, can you stay?"

We both turned. Arial was standing next to the toilet, her long hair snarled all around her shoulders. Her eyes were big, glassy, and full of innocence. As if she didn't remember anything that had happened.

"Not tonight, kiddo," he said, indicating his clothes. "Gotta go get into something dry."

I hugged him again. Then I watched him turn and head down the hallway. I heard the wooden door open, and the squeaking and scraping of the screen door.

"Okay, boo—" I said, tiredly, turning towards her.

I had no idea what to tell her about what had happened. And, so far, she hadn't asked. I'd worry about it tomorrow. Right now, I was only liquified with gratitude that she was alive, that she was home. There was no way she was sleeping in her room tonight. She'd be sleeping in my bed and I didn't care if she put up a fuss about it.

But when I saw her, my words stopped in my throat. The look on her face was hard and full of malice. Her brown eyes had grown darker, almost black.

She looked like my child, but another version of my child—a version I'd seen glimpses of, but which now stood fully extant, metamorphosed from child into Other.

Her face was the same but not the same. It was more angular, more mature, the baby fat on her cheeks thinned away. Her stance was different, taller somehow, and wire-tense as if she was ready to strike or bolt by me. She stared with hostility that was born of the kind of loss of hope and innocence that only comes from life's crushing disappointments. A look that could not be in a child's eyes—or at least *my* child's eyes.

"You think you can control me, bitch?" she—or the thing in the bathroom—said. She bared her teeth at me, like a cat backed into a corner. Like the cat I was suddenly completely certain she'd killed by twisting its head off. "You can't control me, stinking, cunt whore. Next time, I'll drag her down to the depths and shove her deep into the slime where she belongs."

Whatever was in the bathroom, I didn't want to touch it any more than one would touch a wild animal; a primal instinct for self-preservation, one so profound that it overrode even the maternal instinct, forced me into the hallway. I backed into the wall. My arm shot out defensively to hold the thing off from getting near me.

"Arial," I shouted, absurdly, because this wasn't my child. "Let's get you to bed."

"Bitch!" the thing shrieked. It rolled its black eyes up, up, up towards the ceiling, until I could only see the hazy, milky white membrane of its sclera. Then it deflated and crumpled to the bathroom tile.

Chapter Thirty-Four

*P*earl answered the doorbell wearing a flower-patterned dress of autumnal hues with an empire waist, her short, permed hair neatly layered, and no makeup except a touch of mascara that brought out the extreme blue of her eyes.

For a moment, her expression was joyful and welcoming but quickly morphed into deep bewilderment. My skin was bloated, my eyes splotchy red from crying most of the night. I'd had to do so silently as I'd kept Arial in bed with me even though, like Amara, I'd developed a fear of her. Encasing her thin, familiar body with my arms, the feeling was akin to snuggling an orphaned bear or tiger cub. The little animal might look cute and harmless but also might decide to sink pointy teeth into my flesh.

"Can I come in?" I asked. "Arial's in the car so I can't stay long."

Pearl peered around me towards her driveway. I looked with her, mostly to make certain that in the thirty seconds it had taken me to walk to Pearl's door, Arial hadn't escaped the locked car.

"Of course," she said. She didn't ask why Arial had to remain in the car. Between that and my swollen face, she must have deduced that something bad was happening.

She ushered me to the parlor. Its windows overlooked the driveway so I could keep an eye on the car. Arial had her head down, as she'd brought a couple of the *Benny and Belinda* series books.

But not the one Kevin had given her. That one, she'd slept with for weeks after his murder, never cracking it open, but wanting it near her. Then, one day, she'd relegated it to a wooden memento trunk, where she retired her toys and dolls that she couldn't part with but no longer actively used.

"What is it, Neely?" Pearl asked, her voice weighty with concern.

"Remember how you said that when Arial spoke at the strawberry supper, it was like Maybelle was in the room? What did you mean by that?"

Pearl took a deep breath and began caressing a medium-sized diamond ring on her finger. I presumed the jewel was from her late husband, Henry.

"I'm not sure I can fully explain it," she said haltingly, staring at her red and blue Oriental rug. "She... used similar language, spoke to me in a similar manner." She stopped staring at her rug and looked up. "I shouldn't have said that."

"Pearl, there is something deeply wrong with my daughter," I said, voice clogged with emotion. "It started soon after my boyfriend was murdered. One time, she wet the bed. Sometimes, she wouldn't speak for hours. She'd sit there and stare out the window, even though our window overlooked another building's wall. But that seemed understandable for a child who'd gone through something horrific.

But now… since we arrived here, it's beyond all that. Far beyond. Last night, she left the house in the middle of the night, went to the pond, and jumped in."

Pearl's hand, the one with the diamond on it, flew to her mouth.

"Then, back at the house, she spoke to me in a way that wasn't her. She didn't look the same or sound the same. She called me a whore, okay? The same way she spoke to you. That wasn't her either. I know I'm coming across like one of those parents who refuses to believe their kid can be anything but an angel. But there's something terrible, *terrible* going on. Her voice, it—wasn't *her*. This goes beyond trauma. It goes beyond anything physical. It's not stress, it's not crypto—whatever it is. It goes into areas I don't understand."

I pointed out the window, towards the car, where Arial sat reading.

"Because that was not my little girl. I know it with every ounce of my being. I *know* it, and that's the end of it. Would you talk to her? You know what Maybelle sounds like. You'd know if Maybelle got inside her somehow. Please, please, talk to her. I'm begging you. Please!"

I had my hands clasped in a pleading gesture. At first, Pearl said nothing. Then, with some difficulty, as if she had pains in her hips and knees, she stood and hobbled to a china hutch against one wall.

She took down a framed photo of a young couple—it must have been her and Henry—and stared at it for several long moments, then returned it to its place on the hutch. She seemed dreamy and far away, contemplative.

Impatience climbed like a ragged vine from my gut to my throat. This was no time for her to glide around gazing at photos. I needed help and I needed it now. I needed her to respond to me. Only clenching my hands as tight as I could prevented me from snapping at her.

"What you're asking could be dangerous," she finally said. "If Maybelle has entered your daughter, to engage her in discussion might only empower her."

"Oh, God!" I erupted, falling into the nearest chair and burying my face in my hands. I realized that, despite my speech, despite telling Pearl what I knew with every ounce of my being—that my daughter had somehow been possessed—I'd hoped that Pearl would tell me I was crazy. That she'd demand I take Arial back to the psychiatrist or even drive her to the nearest emergency room.

Instead, she was confirming my wildest, most frightening, most outlandish suspicion—that the disturbed spirit of Maybelle had entered my child. Pearl believed it. And, therefore, I was required to believe it.

I felt cool, tender flesh on my hands and glanced up. Pearl was standing over me.

"I don't want to do anything that could make this

worse," she said. "I don't have any experience. But I know someone. A spiritist. She lives an hour away."

I'd never heard of the term "spiritist," but knew there were people who claimed to commune with ghosts. In the city, you couldn't go five blocks without seeing a sign for a psychic who'd offer a phone line to the beyond.

"But those people are cranks, Pearl," I choked out despondently. "For ten dollars, they'll pretend they're talking to your dead uncle or Jim Morrison." I hoped she knew who Jim Morrison was. I didn't feel like explaining.

Pearl let go of my hands and slowly made her way back to her chair. I shot a glance out of the bay window and noted Arial's head still down, reading.

"I'm with you," she said. "But this lady came highly recommended through a friend. She was far more expensive than anyone else I researched but I decided to try. You see, Neely, I'd felt so bad that my husband Henry had had such a tormented life. I was young and didn't know nothing would make him happy, that his mother had ruined him. But I spent much of the marriage berating him, pleading with him, threatening him."

She slumped her head, her shoulders heaving a little. Her voice grew so quiet it was difficult to hear everything she was saying.

"I even had an affair and threw it in his face. I thought, wrongly, that these things would make him stop drinking. I didn't realize he was drinking to forget. I stood no chance against a potion that allowed him to forget."

She dragged in a deep breath and dabbed the corner of one eye with a knuckle. Then looked at me, blue eyes shimmering.

"Just when I began to think I needed to stop haranguing and be more understanding... I found him dead in our bed. His liver had given out. When I got older and learned how alcoholism works, I felt terribly guilty. I began dreaming of him every night. After years of this, a friend suggested I visit a spiritist. She recommended Jacinda. I was as skeptical as you are.

We had two sessions. On each, she held Henry's photo and was quiet for a long time. When she finally spoke, she told me she'd contacted Henry. She said that he forgave me, and he apologized for his part in things, too. I wasn't sure I believed it as it was happening but then... the dreams stopped. Well, no. I still have dreams about him. But instead of sad dreams that make me cry, in these, he's surrounded by white light and is so happy. He's finally at peace. Because he and I needed to have a chat, you understand?"

"Pearl," I said, carefully. I didn't want to offend her. After all, I was the one who'd charged in here with the theory that my daughter was possessed by the spirit of our ancestor. "I'm so glad she helped you. But just because she said she contacted Henry doesn't mean she *did*. I'm sure you were relieved to hear he forgave you, and that helped your guilt. And that's wonderful. Truly, it is. But Arial doesn't even know this is happening. I don't know how someone who claims she can talk to ghosts can help anything."

"I didn't tell you the whole story, Neely. There were, well, there were things Jacinda said to me—things she said were coming from Henry—that—there's no earthly way she could have known them."

"Pearl," I stressed, "they're trained in that. I don't know how they do it but they do it."

"I told her nothing about him," she said with a firm insistence. "Nothing. She didn't ask a thing. And everything she said was completely correct. It *was* Henry. She contacted him. I'm sure of it. Of course, I can't guarantee anything. But Neely, isn't it worth a try?"

Chapter Thirty-Five

"*W*hat if there's a fire, Mom?!"

Arial was staring out of her bedroom window, wide-eyed, as I hammered one large nail through the lower frame and into the side of the house.

"There's not going to be a fire," I said, projecting through the sturdy, closed pane of glass.

"But what if there *is*?"

I ignored her, got another nail from the box on the lawn, and hammered it through the opposite side of the frame. I'd been taught how to nail in a high school woodworking class, which I'd taken in favor of home economics—solely so I could hang out with boys.

I remembered none of the class except how to hammer a nail—hit firmly but not too hard. Hit straight on the head. Then *bang, bang, bang* quickly to drive it in. Don't hesitate, don't second guess yourself.

"Mom!" Arial shouted, her voice slightly muffled through the glass. "What if it gets hot?!"

"I'll get you another fan, hon."

"This isn't free range!"

I didn't respond. I no longer felt I needed to explain or justify myself to her. This was war. Something was fighting for control of my daughter and I was going to fight back. If that meant locking her inside of a bedroom-sized box until I'd won the war, then that's what I'd do. And make no mistake, I was going to win.

Once both nails had been driven in up to their heads, I tried to open the window. It didn't budge.

"What about fresh air, Mom?!" Arial hollered as I headed to her second window, on a different side of the house, overlooking the woods.

My phone jangled. Caller ID showed it was Beckett. I moved away from the house so I could take the call with privacy. Jed must have managed to secure an MRI. Despite my near-full conviction that my daughter was possessed, I still planned to get her examined. I would do anything and everything.

If only Beckett could see me now—nailing my daughter's windows shut. If he knew what was happening, I wondered if he'd report it to Jed. And if something this preposterous would make Jed take some interest in his offspring.

"Hey, Becks," I said, careful to sound casual and not like I was in the middle of imprisoning my daughter.

"Hey, Neely." His voice was unusually subdued. I stopped in my tracks, foreboding slithering through me. "I'm afraid I have some news for you. It's Jed. He's in the hospital."

"What happened?"

"He had a stroke. It's pretty bad. Happened last night and he's been unconscious ever since." He paused. "They don't know if he'll make it. I'm going to do everything possible to keep getting you income but things are about to get tricky. Willa will be taking over everything, including his finances."

I had my hand smushed up against my mouth, unable to speak.

So much was pouring through my mind—and not only practical matters, such as how I was going to pay for everything. I also remembered my last words to him —how full of anger they'd been.

And Arial. Did this mean there was no chance of her ever having a father-daughter relationship? A small, stubborn part of myself had always clung to that unlikely possibility.

Memories even surged forth of the days when I used to long for him, used to take so much keen pleasure in his lustful looks, his sweet words and promises, our long conversations, his expert hands on me in the dark backseat of his car. Things I hadn't dwelled on in ages, not since I'd finally accepted what he was really like.

As if only the idea that I'd never see or talk to him again was drastic enough to allow these early positive memories to seep through the density of the negative ones.

"You there, Neely?"

"Yes. I'm just—this is a shock."

"I know. And, like I said, I'm going to do what I can for you. Right now, it's touch and go. I'm not sure from one hour to the next exactly what's happening with him."

"Okay, Becks. I understand. Will you keep me informed?"

"I will."

Chapter Thirty-Six

*J*acinda lived in a dollhouse. It was a canary yellow cottage with a wraparound porch edged with a white picket fence, gingerbread detailing, a turret, and one eight-pointed window on the gabled roof.

"Pretty," Arial cooed as we approached.

When we reached the porch, we stopped and waited for Pearl, who was moving slower. I'd told Arial we would be visiting a woman who could contact people who'd gone to heaven.

I'd assumed she'd ask to speak to her "father." The name on the gravestone was Michael H. Overman but I always just called him her "father." This idea gave me some trepidation, for if the spiritist really could communicate with the dead, there was a good chance Arial's "father" would inform her he had no idea who I was.

When Arial had looked slightly intimidated at my offer, I'd told her it would be a game, a really fun game.

I'd also lied, telling her Debbie and Nashua had also visited the woman and loved it.

"Mmm, okay," she'd said, perking up. "Can we talk to Billy?"

The name Billy ignited my memories. Starting at age two, he was an imaginary friend of Arial's. He didn't go fully away until she was about six. Sometimes, she'd describe him as a mouse. Other times, as a dog. A few times, as a goat. And by the end of his tenure, he'd morphed into a little boy. She'd point to her window at night and tell me Billy had flown to the top of it.

She flew round and round...

"Sure, we can talk to Billy," I'd said.

Pearl told me she'd filled Jacinda in on what we were hoping to achieve—which was admittedly vague—but I'd given Pearl strict instructions that Jacinda should not even hint to Arial that she might be possessed by some kind of ghost.

I had no idea how the spiritist would manage to draw out this ghost while not alerting Arial to what was happening, but that was up to her to figure out. I was paying enough for it.

I came to the house with three hundred dollars in cash, basically all I had in my account. And given what Beckett had told me about Jed's finances, I had no idea when or even if more money would be coming. But I was desperate and Pearl's unshakeable conviction that this woman had contacted Henry at least gave me something to cling to. Because I had no idea what else to do.

A woman answered the door. She looked to be in her late twenties. I'd assumed the spiritist would be an older woman and was taken aback. The woman standing before me with a big toothpaste-commercial-worthy smile was model-attractive with full lips, sleek, pulled-back jet-black hair, and small, gold hoop earrings. She had on a black velour track suit with gold stitching in the shape of a butterfly on the front.

Her youth needled me. How could someone so young have any real understanding of otherworldly things? I wanted a guide, an usher to an unknown world, not a young woman my age who was probably equally as muddling and blind-groping as I was.

The suspicion that this was a hoax—a very expensive one—deepened.

The feeling was further compounded when Pearl finally reached the porch and the three of us piled into Jacinda's narrow entryway. Even before introducing herself, the spiritist had her palm out.

"My policy is to ask for payment first," she said in a slight accent I couldn't identify (I'd eventually learn she was born and raised in Brazil). "Just so we don't have to worry about anything later."

You mean so I can't refuse to pay later when this turns out to be b.s., I thought sourly, handing her the white business envelope stuffed with cash. A momentary flash of disgust surged through me, feeling as if this woman was taking advantage of people at their worst, most vulnerable times.

"Please, sit down," she said. "Pearl will show you where."

Holding Arial's hand, I walked with Pearl into a room that couldn't have been more than fifty square feet. In one corner was a large chair covered with burgundy fabric, and an ornate, dark wood high back. Like a little throne.

"Arial, why don't you sit there?" Pearl said to her.

When my daughter showed no inclination to let go of my hand, I encouraged her by burbling, "Go on, boo. This will be so much fun."

Arial wiggled into the chair, her feet dangling inches above the floor. Pearl and I took the couch, which was equally as elaborately carved and covered with an intricately stitched, apricot fabric.

Jacinda returned without the envelope. I pictured her hustling to secure the cash in a wall safe. I was nauseous with the idea that I'd handed over that much food money for a little entertainment show.

At the window, Jacinda lit a stick of incense in a holder, then sat down in a chair a few feet away from Arial. The spicy odor of the incense caused a tickling sensation in my nostrils as if I was on the verge of sneezing.

"Arial, I'm Jacinda," the spiritist said, pleasantly. "Would you care to speak to anyone? Anyone who has moved on to a different realm?"

Arial looked at me as if to say, *What the heck is THAT?*

The baffled expression on my child's face made me seriously contemplate putting an end to this. I could (strongly) request my money back, apologize for wasting the spiritist's time, and get the hell out of here.

But then what? Nora and Dr. Weir were mired in realism. Nora would continue with her doll play and anxiety pills. Dr. Weir would ask Arial to walk around the room and listen to her breathing. None of it was helping. With Jed in the hospital, I was unlikely to get an MRI.

This thing that had grabbed hold of my child was not only getting worse, getting stronger, but could kill her. She'd already risked her life twice by leaving the house in the middle of the night. I had nothing to lose here. Except money.

Jacinda closed her eyes and grasped the arm of Arial's chair. I felt helpless to interrupt them—as if things were speeding along as they should.

"You'd like to speak to Billy?" Jacinda asked. "He's here."

My mouth popped open. Had I told Pearl about Billy? I must have.

"Okay," Arial said, smiling a little but also looking uncertain.

Jacinda breathed in deeply, held her breath for several seconds, then slowly hissed it back out. She stayed silent with her eyes closed for a long time—perhaps three minutes. Arial was fidgeting and glancing around the room at all the gilded decor, vintage furniture, and intricate-patterned wallpaper.

Finally, Jacinda spoke.

"Billy says he's sorry he hasn't come to visit but he lives with another little girl now. One who is much younger and needs him more than you do. But he wants you to know he's never forgotten you. That he loved you and will always love you."

"What a bunch of horse shit, cretin," came a rough voice. It took me a moment to grasp that Arial had stopped looking at the vintage décor and was glaring at Jacinda. "Nice con you've got going, crook."

I saw Arial's little mouth moving, but it was not quite her mouth. Her lips appeared bluish, and it was as if a remarkably life-like latex mask had slipped down over her face.

Jacinda calmly opened her eyes. "Who am I speaking with?" she asked.

"None of your business, bitch."

"Would this be Maybelle Hubbard?"

"What shit do you give who this is, trash? That's what your mother was, and your mother's mother, and you. Trash."

"What do you want with Arial?"

The thing kept staring at Jacinda, and a slow, sly smile creeped over its ghoulish face. "She let me in. She's a dumb pig like her mother." The voice was glottal and venomous, had grown its full bristling, coarse personality. No longer was there the remotest trace of the chime and softness of Arial's voice.

The thing in the chair shifted its gaze to me. It had Arial's eyes but not Arial's eyes—they were darker, larger, and contained depths and slickness that my daughter did not have. That no child had.

"She fucks married men then wants you to feel sorry for her," it said. "She lies to her daughter and tells her fairy tales about dead daddies." The thing slyly shook its sharp-edged face. "Daddy died in a terrorist attack? Daddy jumped out the window to keep from burning to death? What a thing to tell a little girl, heartless liar."

Jacinda stood. The youth that had made me dismissive of her now worked in her favor. She looked strong and imposing, not remotely intimidated by the devilish little thing in the chair spouting cruelty.

"You will leave this innocent girl," Jacinda stated firmly. "You will go back to where you came from."

Arial—the thing—spit at her. The small blob of saliva went directly into Jacinda's face.

Jacinda barely flinched. But I gasped, loudly. Pearl, sitting beside me, also gasped. I felt I should run over and grab the thing—the thing that was still at least partly my daughter. To put a stop to what was happening. But I couldn't move.

"This body is not yours," Jacinda said calmly, not moving to wipe her face. "You are cast out of this body in the name of the legion of good and holy spirits. You are cast out of this body in the name—"

The thing picked up something small, a tchotchke, from the end table and threw it at Jacinda. It hit her in the chest and again she didn't acknowledge this assault. I instinctively jumped up from the sofa. I started towards the thing but Jacinda thrust her arm in my direction.

"Stop!" she commanded. "Do not approach. I'm handling this."

"I'm handling this," the thing parroted in a whiny, mocking voice. The thing laughed, a bobbing, cackling laugh, and for a moment I saw what appeared to be tiny, sharp, rat's teeth in its mouth.

Then the thing stared directly at me. "The last words to go through the rapist's mind were, 'I'm a bad father.' As you wished."

"Speak not to her, malignant spirit. Speak to me," Jacinda ordered.

The thing leaned on the chair, as if ready to spring forward and attack. "The girl is descended from my loins. She belongs to me. You can't have her."

"She belongs to no one but herself. Leave this body, damaged spirit. You have no business here. Return from whence you came."

Jacinda walked closer to the thing. I was in awe at her courage. On the chair was a spiky, dangerous little monster that looked grotesquely like my child but wasn't my child. Even I wouldn't have wanted to touch it. Jacinda suddenly clamped her hand hard on the top of the thing's head.

"Leave this body!" she ordered.

The thing writhed and moaned under Jacinda's touch as if being branded with something hot.

"You are cast out! Out, I cast thee, plaguing spirit! You will leave this innocent girl who is protected by the legion of good and holy spirits. Leave now, I command you!"

* * *

ARIAL WAS asleep on Jacinda's sofa.

As Jacinda had kept her hand clamped on the thing's head, the thing—Arial but not Arial—had twisted, moaned, and grunted as if Jacinda's hand was a hot poker. Then it had gone limp, slumped down in the chair, and closed its eyes.

"I'll call 911!" I'd yelled, terrified at what had

happened to my daughter. But Jacinda assured me Arial was only asleep, that she'd been wrung exhausted from the possession.

Since Arial was breathing normally and appeared peaceful, I carried her to the couch and lay her down, then gently covered her with a nearby crocheted afghan, and pressed my lips to her forehead. She didn't have a fever.

Jacinda indicated that Pearl and I should follow her to the kitchen. She poured herself a glass of water, then sank into the nearest chair at the table. "If you'd like anything to drink, the glasses are in the cabinet above the sink," she said. "I have no energy to get them."

She sounded like she was thrusting the words out of her lungs—as if she'd run a marathon and was no longer panting but was still weak from the exertion. She wiped her face with a cloth napkin folded on the table.

"Is it gone?" I asked. "Is my baby cured?"

Jacinda said nothing for several long beats then regarded me wearily.

"That is a very strong spirit. Stronger than any I've ever known. She came on so fast. I didn't prepare well enough."

"But… you cast it out, right? You told it to go."

"I did but that doesn't mean she will listen."

Pearl shakily lowered into the chair next to me. She was ashen, her wrinkled cheeks white as paper. She was in her eighties and I wasn't sure she'd survive another encounter like this one. I put my hand over hers.

"Are you okay?"

"Oh, yes," she said faintly. "Don't worry about me."

"Was that Maybelle? Did you recognize her?"

"It certainly sounded like her. She's not someone you forget once you live with her for a couple of years."

"Jacinda, please," I pleaded, refocusing on her. "How could this have happened?"

Jacinda closed her eyes for so long that I thought she'd fallen asleep like Arial, but asleep sitting up. However, by now, I knew that she closed her eyes when she was deep into her communing.

Finally, she opened them and said, "Something happened. Something that put a giant hole in your daughter's soul. It was recent."

"Yes," I said, voice strangled. "Someone was killed. Someone she cared deeply about."

Jacinda nodded slowly. "Your daughter's trauma allowed the spirit in. It was a continuation, through many generations. Maybelle saw an opening, one big enough for her to squeeze through, and she did."

"It—she—knew so much. Secrets I haven't— Jacinda, she repeated something I told a man when I was alone with him. How could she know this?"

"What can't she know?" Jacinda asked, still sounding drained. "She's not like us, bound by earthly senses. She's everywhere and all things. She's the air, the soil, the clouds, the water. But if she wants to speak, she needs your daughter."

She's not like us, bound by earthly senses.

I thought of how Nashua had told his mother that Arial could fly. Was this something she could do under the possession of the spirit? Or something that Nashua, only six years from the spirit world himself if you believed in reincarnation, could see while the rest of us couldn't? Arial herself used to have a flying friend —Billy.

"Will Arial know what she's saying? Even subconsciously?" I asked.

So far, my daughter seemed to have no recollection of anything the deranged spirit had spouted out of Arial's lips but now that she'd hit so close to home, spewing things I was desperate to keep Arial from hearing, I was extremely anxious. I was also terrified that, on some level, Arial would feel or know what was happening, or that she was suffering in any way.

"I don't believe so. When Maybelle takes over, Arial goes into hibernation." Jacinda rallied some energy and smoothed the sides of her shiny black hair. "Spirits are like the living in that they have a deep need to communicate," she continued. "What Maybelle needs to communicate is her rage. Unspeakable things happened to her when she was too young to fight back or even understand them. Now everyone pays for it."

Jacinda straightened, sipped some water, and looked at me compassionately but with an unmistakable warning in her tone. "She's learning her way around your daughter, figuring out how to control her, even how to mimic her. That little girl is still mostly your child. But we need to move fast. Soon, she could be mostly Maybelle. Even all Maybelle. And if she chooses to pretend to be your daughter, you'll never even know the difference."

Chapter Thirty-Seven

*I*n the car, Arial was deep asleep in the backseat. It had been a long time since she'd been so fast asleep that I was able to carry her in my arms from one place to another without waking her.

I still worried that something was physically wrong with her. Only the inability to come up with a satisfactory explanation for why my child was in such a heavy sleep stopped me from driving her to the hospital.

I was also afraid that if anyone in a position of authority got wind of the things I was doing—nailing my daughter's bedroom windows shut, bringing her to an occultist, insisting she was possessed, my girl would be instantly taken from me and I'd be jailed.

I was concerned for Pearl, who seemed frailer since the encounter with Maybelle. No doubt the session had brought up a lot of bad memories for her. I hadn't asked her the details of what had happened to her in those two years she'd lived at Maybelle's house, but the experience had obviously scarred her.

We were silent until I hit traffic on the perimeter of the capital. As we came to a crawl behind a line of cars, I initiated discussion. The fight-or-flight adrenaline of what we'd witnessed was still sizzling through my brain and limbs. I had to verbally process some of what had happened.

"Do you know how Jacinda does what she does?" I asked in a low voice not wanting to risk Arial overhearing, even in her stupefied state. I hoped Pearl's hearing was adequate.

"Interesting you should ask," she said. "I was so thankful with how she contacted Henry that I bought her a nice dinner. She told me she'd fallen through ice when she was a child. She was under the water for several minutes and died. She clearly remembered going to another realm and meeting many spirits. They told her she was chosen to return and be a conduit for them. I'll never forget one thing she said: 'Although we're all always dying, we're all also being reborn again.'"

"She certainly earned her three hundred," I said, chuckling nervously.

Jacinda had told me it would take a few more sessions to cast the spirit out of my daughter.

"Pearl, I need at least a thousand dollars to continue," I said. "I'm going to put it on my credit card but do you know anyone who needs work done? Errands run? Dogs walked? Decluttering? I used to work for a home organization company. I'll do anything."

"Decluttering," she said, glancing at me with a half-smile. "Now there's something to talk about. I have three generations' worth of stuff to figure out what to do with. A big reason I haven't joined my daughter out west, I suppose."

"Can I help you? I wouldn't charge much."

"Don't worry about the money, Neely. I was a teacher for forty years. It didn't pay a lot but I've lived frugally and have a pension. For all his drinking, Henry held onto his job at the paper mill. Have his pension, too. You need a thousand dollars to rid your daughter of my mother-in-law? I can't think of a better way for me to spend it."

Chapter Thirty-Eight

*T*he next session took place two days later. Jacinda didn't want to do the sessions back-to-back as they not only depleted Arial but herself. However, she didn't want to wait too long either, believing that too much time in between them would allow Maybelle to rejuvenate and resurge even stronger.

I had a difficult time convincing Arial we should return. She remembered none of what had happened after Jacinda passed along the message from Billy and was under the impression we'd only stayed for a few minutes. The long drive there didn't, in her mind, justify such speedy and banal interactions.

I resorted to the standby parental technique of bribery. I promised pizza, soda (which she was only allowed to have on special occasions), and yet another viewing of her favorite movie, which we'd seen a dozen times.

Pearl didn't accompany us. She offered but I could tell by her shaky voice on the phone that she wasn't up for it. I didn't want to be responsible for any health issues that might arise from her coming face-to-face with Maybelle again, so I urged her to stay home.

At Jacinda's cottage, she called me into another room and showed me a fleece wearable blanket, informing me of her intent to zipper Arial into it backward.

"We're not putting my child in a straightjacket," I snapped. Nailing her into her bedroom was bad enough.

"It's just a blanket," Jacinda said soothingly. "I'm sorry but last time she threw a figurine at me. I've cleared out the spirit room as best I can but I need to protect both of us as well as her."

"How am I supposed to get her to put this on?"

Jacinda shrugged as if to say *that isn't my job*.

It required more bribery: candy, which Arial was only allowed to eat on her birthday and Halloween. I promised we'd stop at a candy shop in town, one she didn't even know existed as I'd kept that information to myself.

With Arial on the throne, sheathed in a wearable blanket adorned with dancing penguins, the scene took on an aura of absurdity. It flashed through my mind that not only was Jacinda a malingerer, but my daughter was, too. They were both scheming, playing an elaborate hoax on me—the spiritist for money, and my daughter for attention.

But this impression retreated. There were so many things Arial couldn't have faked, unexplainable things. How she'd known my snipe to Jed about his deathbed thought: *I was a bad father.*

How she'd managed to open two old, heavy windows.

And the cat. By now, the squeamish edges of my consciousness had more or less accepted that Arial had been responsible for the death of Ben's pet.

None of this was my daughter. None of this was the gentle, happy, artistic soul who once carried a beetle in a jar down four flights of stairs so she could rehome it in the garden.

These occurrences were something else, something not my daughter, something not anything I knew or understood.

"Are you comfortable, Arial?" Jacinda asked, lighting the incense. I almost asked her to refrain as the peppery smell caused an itching sensation in my nostrils but decided against it. She should do whatever rituals she needed to do.

"I guess," Arial shrugged, clearly not thrilled with being shackled in a backward fleece blanket. I'd told her the blanket helped welcome the friendly ghosts. "Mom, you owe me."

"Lots of candy," I reminded her.

Jacinda closed her eyes. My stomach pitched because I knew this meant she was entering into the spirit world. I gripped the arm of the sofa and tried to stop my leg from jiggling. I didn't want Arial to see me full of nerves. When Jacinda finally opened her eyes, she stared at my daughter.

"Who is present?" she asked.

"Your stinking cunt."

I managed to stop my hand from flying to my mouth

and pressed my lips together to keep from gaping. My daughter's face had morphed into the slightly latex-y mask of the deranged Maybelle, her lips purplish-blue. Her voice was husky and distorted.

The physical change was more pronounced, more grotesque, than last time.

"Maybelle Hubbard," Jacinda said. "You are not welcome in the body of this innocent child. You are cast out for eternity in the name of the legion of good and holy spirits. They surround her and protect her. They guide her and shield her from harm."

"Baby killer," the thing said in a low growl. "Did you enjoy scraping your baby out of your dirty womb as she cried and begged and pleaded for her life?"

"You are cast out, disturbed spirit," Jacinda said. She pulled herself up off the chair and stood at her full height, towering over the thing. "Go back from whence you came, malignant spirit. You have lost your way."

"A baby girl. So pure and loving. No real woman would stomp out her own child like a bug."

"I cast you out for eternity, troubled spirit. You are forbidden to roost in the body of this innocent—"

"Your baby cries here in eternal burning pain, her limbs torn open and bloodied. You baby killer. You—"

Jacinda swiftly moved forward and clamped her hand down on the thing's head as if scruffing the neck of a hissing animal. The thing writhed, its mouth in a contorted grimace as if Jacinda's hand was scorching her. The thing kicked inside the blanket, trying to punch its hands around. As it did so, it slipped farther down the chair, all the while moaning, a deep, aggrieved moan, like a cow giving birth.

I fought the overpowering maternal impulse to claw my way between the two of them, to stop Jacinda from pressing my daughter's head so tightly. But I forced myself to stay where I was, gripping the couch for an anchor.

"Leave this earthly plain, tortured soul," Jacinda commanded, keeping her hand on the thing's head. "Go back from whence you came. This girl belongs not to you. I cast you out for eternity, cancerous spirit! In the name of all that is good and holy, you are cast out once and for all time!"

"Baby killerrrrrr!" the thing moaned from the depths of its soul before going completely limp.

Chapter Thirty-Nine

I lifted Arial and lay her down on the sofa, keeping the blanket jacket on her.

She was sound asleep, her face slack and ethereal, her flushed skin the tone of a ripe peach. I wanted to draw my fingers down her cheek, to reassure myself that the mask-like, almost undulating, skin I'd seen earlier was completely gone. But I didn't want to risk waking her.

Jacinda preceded me to the kitchen where she already had glasses of water waiting on the table. She drank thirstily. I was shaking, wiping tears with tissue from a box that Jacinda had prudently added to the table. This encounter had felt worse than the last one, as if the thing was amassing power, not losing it.

"Jacinda," I said once she seemed to regain a bit of strength and my shaking had subsided. "She was so brutal this time. Is—is she becoming stronger?"

I remembered how Pearl had said engaging the being in conversation could empower it.

"No. You see she didn't stay long. She's making last-ditch efforts to be in control."

Jacinda was drooped over, once more appearing as if she'd exerted great physical energy, running a marathon or up a flight of long stairs.

"I had an abortion when I was much younger," she said. "It was a very complex and difficult situation."

I hadn't wanted to probe her about anything the thing—I had a hard time thinking of the thing as a woman, even a dead woman—had said in the session but was once more stupefied at how it could know such intensely private information.

"You don't have to explain," I said. "I'm sorry she said all that."

"Never apologize for anything Maybelle says or does. That weakens you. She wants you weak."

I nodded but, even after all I'd seen and heard, it was complicated work teasing out my daughter from the thing that had parasitically attached to her.

Though the changes in her demeanor were shocking enough to make it clear that the thing was *not* my child, it still looked enough like her that instinctually I'd want to apologize for or direct its behavior.

"She'll say whatever she needs to say to weaken anyone protecting Arial," Jacinda explained. "She wants you distracted, doubtful, unsure. She only went after me today but don't think she's done with you. She'll use any ammunition she has, target where you're vulnerable. Never fall for it. Keep your mind on one thing only—getting her to leave. Now, trained as I am in spiritism, I believe that all spirits, even demonic ones, are on a journey to enlightenment and improvement. They all have the capacity to be pure, moral spirits. But I won't lie. This is one malevolent spirit. Her life must have been a nightmare for her to end up like this."

"But how long will this go on?" I asked pleadingly. "I feel like we made no progress today."

"Believe me, she's scared. She's like a dog backed into a corner, fur up and baring its teeth."

It could have been merely a symptom of her debilitation, but Jacinda didn't sound confident in her appraisal. I had the unnerving sensation that she also sensed Maybelle was gaining power. Perhaps she didn't want to voice this and have me fall into despair.

But perhaps she had another reason—she simply didn't know what to do about it.

Chapter Forty

$\mathcal{I}$'d been so consumed with what was happening with Arial that I'd ignored a couple of messages from Salem asking for a dinner date. This was no time to go out to a restaurant and try to pretend things were normal. Nor did I have the energy to come up with an explanation as to why I couldn't see him again.

But on his third try, he mentioned stopping by to check the roof. I remembered how he'd said work should be done before winter closed in and that snow piled on a defective roof could cause leaking. I had to make some kind of effort to keep the rest of my life together and a leaky roof in the middle of a freezing New England winter would not be that.

Besides, Arial was asking why all we were doing was traveling to see Jacinda. She was happy with the visit to the candy shop, where she loaded up a paper bag with sweet and sour gummies, but otherwise none of the things I'd promised her the country would offer—

picking blueberries, bicycle riding, swimming—had happened.

Debbie had called a couple of times to initiate a playdate but I'd told her Arial was sick and the virus was stubbornly clinging to her. Arial had met no new children. I'd confined her to the house and backyard, and was locking her in her bedroom at night.

I decided that the very least I could do was have Salem over for dinner. This would not only restore a modicum of normalcy for Arial but I owed him that at least, considering he'd saved her life at the pond. I didn't want to risk Arial having an episode in a restaurant, so I'd cook for him at home.

I prepared one of her favorite meals—fettuccine with Alfredo sauce, accompanied by a baguette of fresh bread procured at a local bakery, and a tossed salad with homemade dressing.

Salem showed up looking strikingly handsome, his paint-splattered jeans replaced with black dress pants, a form-fitting t-shirt, and a tan leather jacket.

Any other time, I would have been taken with the prospect of this good-looking and seemingly kind man and I getting to know each other better—the bonus being that we'd known each other since we were teens—but I could focus on nothing but what was going on with Arial. I ate and slept simply so I could keep up the strength to do what I needed to do to help her.

Arial assisted with food preparation and dinner plate-setting on the screened-in porch and kept up a steady dialogue with Salem, who had a gift for engaging her.

She told him how we'd gone to a woman's house who could talk to ghosts. Salem shot me a curious look but said nothing. After dinner, the two of them played a few rounds of Go Fish while I did the dishes. When Arial went to the bathroom, Salem came up behind me as I stood at the sink mindlessly scrubbing.

"You okay?" he asked.

The concern in his voice made tears threaten to bubble up my throat. It was so hard going through all of this alone and feeling as if I couldn't tell anyone—not even Debbie—what was happening. Only Pearl and Jacinda knew, and Pearl had retreated, probably for her sanity and safety.

"Things aren't that great," I murmured, turning to make certain that Arial was still down the hallway. "I'm trying to help her, that's all I can say. I can't offer details, I'm sorry."

"Anything I can do?"

I shook my head, trying not to leak tears as I knew my daughter would be back any moment. Salem put his hand on my shoulder comfortingly. I grabbed his wrist and squeezed it. "Not now but thank you. I'll definitely let you know if I need help."

He nodded and then Arial was back.

"Another game?" she asked him, spinning lithely in her bare feet on the kitchen floor's dull wood planks.

I'd asked her numerous times not to spin on the wood, worried she'd get a splinter, but she kept doing it. She'd been winning at the game—or Salem had been letting her win—and she wasn't going to want to stop playing as long as that was happening.

"Actually, kiddo, I should check the roof while it's still light out. But it shouldn't take long."

As Salem was outside pulling his ladder out of his flatbed and setting it up at the side of the house, I noticed a car turn into the drive. It was a green Sedan and looked familiar. But I didn't realize who was driving until I saw Jacinda step out. I was surprised to see her, as we'd made no plans for her to come to the house.

I rushed out to greet her. She was looking very summery and seventies, her white dress festooned with large pink polka dots.

"I tried to call you," she said. "But kept going straight to voice mail."

"Oh, sorry, yes. I'd turned off the ringer to have dinner." I pointed around the house. "My friend is here. Is there anything wrong? I mean, besides the usual?"

I couldn't help but smile a little. Sometimes I felt the only thing that kept me from going absolutely mad was the occasional joke.

"Can you go for a walk? Where's Arial?"

"She's in the house. I guess it's okay with my friend here but, um…" I trailed off, vague apprehension assembling in the corners of my mind. "Hold on."

Inside the house, I found Arial in her bedroom. She was at the little desk I'd set up for her, continuing an art project she'd started earlier—one with lots of sparkle glue and cotton balls representing snowflakes. She was excited for a country winter piled with snow, the exact thing that was sending Salem up to the roof. I can't say I was looking forward to it myself. I had many memories of my grandfather struggling to clear the small drive and pathway to the house, and me helping him with a smaller shovel, my fingers frozen numb even inside their thermal mittens.

I did, however, smile when I recalled that our shoveling session would usually end with a snowball fight.

"Hon," I said to her. "Jacinda came for a quick visit. I'll be right outside."

"Okay, Mom," she said distractedly.

I closed her door, went to my jewelry box, palmed the knob key, and as quietly as I could, turned the lock on her door.

I GUIDED Jacinda up the sidewalk that threaded along my street, past the homes of childhood friends who'd moved away. The walk was fringed with towering pines and littered with green needles and giant pinecones.

It was eight o'clock and dusk was encroaching, fireflies all around flaring then dissolving their lime-green lights. As a kid, I'd catch a few and keep them in a glass jar by my bedside until their glow dimmed and they died, something I looked back on with shame. Why did humans always feel the need to capture, and ultimately destroy, intense beauty? Why could we not stand the thought that we may not own it and control it?

"I've been doing more research," Jacinda said as we leisurely strolled. "I had a long communing, seeking guidance from the afterworld."

She spoke lowly but I was glad there was no one else

on the sidewalk. I could only imagine what my neighbors would think if they overheard this discussion.

"I've been trying to figure out why Maybelle has such a strong hold on your daughter. And what can be done to break it."

She stopped and I stopped with her. As she stared at me, and her big, dark eyes grew even more luminous in the gathering twilight.

"The power is coming from you," she said.

"Me?" My hand flew to my chest as if I'd been accused of something abominable. "What do you mean *me*?"

"It's not your fault," she said, trying to blunt her pronouncement. "But your anger, your trauma, is fueling the possession. It travels from generation to generation. It's especially strong between mother and daughter, as it was between Maybelle and her mother."

"My anger? Damn right I'm angry! A fucking demon has taken over my baby. Wouldn't *you* be angry?"

"I'm just telling you what's happening. I'm not judging it."

"How the hell am I not supposed to be angry?" The thought of that was making me angrier.

Jacinda began strolling again so I followed, pulling in deep funnels of balmy evening air to try and break up the tenseness in my chest. "Is there anything else going on?" she asked. "Besides this. I know something awful happened to you both. Someone died."

"Yes, my boyfriend was murdered in front of us. By a complete stranger. Over nothing. Am I not allowed to be angry about that?"

"Naturally, you can be angry. But unfortunately, that's feeding Maybelle. Your anger is passed down to Arial. It allowed a vengeful spirit to enter her body so it could express its own anger. And on it goes."

"You're saying this is my fault?"

We got to the end of this portion of the sidewalk, which was interrupted by a street. I was uncertain whether I wanted to continue. A large part of me wanted Jacinda to leave. How dare she come here and basically blame all of this on me?

"That's absolutely not what I'm saying, Neely."

We were facing each other but in the short time it had taken us to traverse the sidewalk, the atmosphere had darkened to the point where I could no longer read the look in her eyes.

"There's no fault here," she insisted. "Maybelle had horrific things happen to her and she became a terrible person because of them, and is now a terrible, restless spirit. She's like a soldier who won't accept the war is over. Your anger hasn't made you like her but it's created a trauma bond between you and Arial. Maybelle is feeding off that bond."

"Your spirits told you all this?" I asked skeptically. I sounded disrespectful to the only person trying to solve this unfathomable situation but I was appalled by the suggestion that I'd somehow, even indirectly, been the cause of it.

"Yes, they did," she said.

"What am I supposed to do? I'll do whatever it takes but I have no idea how to not be angry, not be traumatized."

257

We turned, heading back towards my house at a slow pace. My stomach was twisted into an aching knot. How was I supposed to not be furious at the unfair, unjust, and revolting things that had happened, not only Kevin's murder but everything before and after it?

Becoming impregnated by an older, married, chronically lying man while I was still basically a child, a man who'd then absolved himself of all parental responsibility.

A man who sent money but never knew when his child was sick, never knew when she had nightmares or was bullied on the playground, never spent a holiday with her, never once called and asked how she was doing, or simply inquired if she was dead or alive.

Jed had not given me a chance to decide if I was ready for the staggering responsibility of motherhood, for the pain and danger of childbirth, for the sleepless nights and anxiety-filled days. For the ever-present threat of poverty—one that seemed about to come true, as I doubt he'd made any provisions for his "second-class child" in case of his death.

As the rundown of his infractions unspooled in my mind, I realized I was even angrier at him than I'd known.

And then... my parents. Killed when I was so young, I never had the chance to know them. Killed by a drunk driver. Killed by someone who was so selfish that he'd had multiple drinks for his own pleasure, then got behind the wheel of his party planning company's truck, coming from one of the company's own parties. The business had immediately declared bankruptcy after the accident so there was no one to even sue, and the driver somehow never spent time in prison.

Kevin murdered. In front of me and my daughter. By a man he'd never seen or spoken to before. A man to whom Kevin had done nothing but try to calm down.

And then, as if that all wasn't enough, this atrocious thing happening to Arial—an ancestor so enraged with her own past mortal coil suffering that she didn't seem to understand that her suffering was over. So, she'd punched a hole in the afterlife and crawled back into the present in order to continue her reign of making people miserable.

I was supposed to be Zen about all this?

"Is there anyone you can forgive?" Jacinda asked.

"Forgive!" I stared at her like she was a lunatic. "Am I supposed to forgive Kevin's killer? We were only walking home! We did nothing to that man. You want me to hold hands with him and sing *All You Need Is Love*?"

"When I say 'forgive,' I don't mean act like you don't care or that you're okay with what happened. I mean loosen the resentment hardening your heart. Consider that these horrid things may have been sent to you for a bigger reason, a reason you may not even comprehend. Imagine that Maybelle is a hummingbird. Your anger is sugar water. It's attracting her and allowing her to thrive."

We reached my drive. The ranch house was warmly aglow with lights from the living room and kitchen. It looked as it did when I was a child returning home from a summer adventure—hanging with my friends at the pond, riding up and down the surrounding hills on my bike.

I'd so hoped my childhood home would be the place I could recreate this idyll for Arial but, instead, it had become her prison.

Chapter Forty-One

I heard moaning. A low, pained moan.

The sound sliced through me like a sharp object because I instantly knew it wasn't Arial suffering one of her episodes. It was a man's moan. My heartrate ticked up. I pushed my arm towards Jacinda to indicate she should stay quiet for I needed to hear the sound again, to pinpoint its origin.

I slow-jogged into the front yard, then around to the side yard. It was now completely dark, the front door light was off, and it was difficult to see anything. But the low timbre of the moan only meant one thing.

"Salem?" I called. "Salem!"

Around the side of the house, I saw the long silver ladder lying on its side. "Salem!" I yelled again, running.

He was on the ground, sprawled out in a broken, mangled position, like a string puppet dropped from a height. It was obvious that the ladder had crashed onto its back and Salem had gone with it. It was easily a twenty-foot drop.

"Oh my God!" I gasped. I sank to my knees in front of him. It was like a replay of Kevin's murder. Another man was critically injured in front of me, and I was helpless without a phone. I'd left mine inside the house.

"Call 911!" I shouted, hoping Jacinda was close behind me. "Call for help!"

* * *

THE AMBULANCE WAS THERE QUICKLY, perhaps ten minutes after Jacinda had called. She'd had to put the phone up to my mouth because she'd already forgotten my address.

Two paramedics carefully layered Salem onto a stretcher and carried him to the ambulance. I wanted to go with him but I couldn't leave Arial inside alone and I didn't dare leave her with Jacinda.

While on the ground with him, holding his hand and telling him he would be alright, that help was on the way, I'd repeatedly flicked my gaze up to Arial's bedroom windows. She must be hearing the commotion, yet her windows were nailed shut and her door locked, so she could do nothing. She may have even heard the ladder crash and Salem moaning and not been able to call for help.

Once he was safely inside the ambulance, I raced into the house. I hadn't even asked Jacinda to go check on Arial as I knew she couldn't. After locking my daughter inside her bedroom, I'd placed the key back inside my jewelry box because I was wearing a summer dress without pockets and didn't have the mental acuity to know how to describe to Jacinda exactly where the key was.

I retrieved the small key and, with a shaky hand, opened the bedroom door. Arial was sitting on her bed, her eyes wide.

"What happened, Mommy?" she asked as I ran in and swooped her into my arms.

"It was Salem, boo. He had an accident, but he'll be fine."

"Did his ladder fall?"

Now I knew she must have heard the accident as it happened, and may have even looked out the window and, while it was still light enough, seen him sprawled on the ground. I didn't feel I should lie to her.

"Yes. But he was breathing and awake. He's at the hospital where he'll get the best care."

"Mommy, I saw him go down," she said. "But I couldn't go outside to help him. You locked me in. Why do you keep locking me in? It wasn't bedtime."

There was no mistaking the scolding look and tone. If she'd been able to get out, she could have used my phone to call 911. I'd left it on the kitchen island where I normally put it, so she would have seen it. She knew how to call emergency services. We'd been practicing since she was old enough to recite her address. I always made her memorize her address, including this one. With her whip-sharp memory, she had no problem giving her location to people, and I had zero doubt she could have handled a 911 phone call.

How long had Salem been lying on the lawn? Was he going to die because I'd locked my daughter in her room?

She was still staring accusatorially at me. Waiting for an explanation. I had none.

Jacinda appeared in the doorway. "Everything alright?" she asked.

"Yes, everything's fine. I feel like I should call someone for him but I don't know who. He and I just started talking again. I know his sister but haven't spoken to her in years and don't have her number."

"Did he take his phone?"

"I have no idea. Boo," I said to Arial, who was still eyeing me with near-disdain. "I'm going to look for Salem's phone. You stay in here, okay?"

"Why? I can help."

"Just stay here!" I ordered in my *I'm-the-boss* tone.

I needed to concentrate on Salem and, these days, Arial was more of a burden than a helping hand. I couldn't risk her darting off somewhere. But I compromised by leaving her door unlocked as Jacinda and I hurried from her bedroom.

I searched on the porch where we'd had dinner. Nothing. Jacinda, meanwhile, was scouring the kitchen. Then we moved to the living room and scanned around the usual places one might leave a phone—table tops, the couch, the floor.

"He probably has it in his pocket," I said.

"Maybe it came out when he fell," Jacinda replied.

I went to the cabinet that held two new flashlights,

took out both, and handed one to Jacinda. "Let's go look."

Outside, I traced the bright white beam on the lawn around the area where Salem had been lying. The long, high ladder gleamed on its side. It was inconceivable that this had happened and I felt heavy guilt. Not only for locking Arial inside but for the entire disaster.

Why had I allowed him to go up and check my roof? Why hadn't I hired a professional? Why had I let him do this when darkness was rapidly encroaching? Why did I suspect that he didn't have much if any experience with roofing but was simply trying to impress me? I should have guessed this. I should have declined his offer. I should have—

I should have seen the danger. I should have yelled for us to run. I should have saved him. It's my fault he's dead.

The beam picked up something silver and metallic and, for a moment, I thought it was Salem's phone. But my brow furrowed. Buried inside blades of grass, nearly missable, was a nail. A long nail.

I must have dropped one when I'd hammered Arial's windows shut. I picked it up and stared at it. "Oh my God," I whispered.

My eyes traveled to Arial's window, which was only a few feet away. I walked up to it and shone the flashlight on the frame where I'd driven in two nails.

Both sides of the frame were splintered, the nails gone.

Chapter Forty-Two

"Jacinda," I whisper-shouted. When it appeared that she didn't hear me and was still searching for Salem's phone, I made my way over to her and put my hand on her arm to draw her attention.

I felt as if I was moving in slow motion, trying to wade through thigh-high water. I pressed my finger to my lips in a *sshh* gesture and indicated that she should follow me away from the house. Deep in the backyard, not far from the playset, I shone the flashlight on the nail, illuminating it for her.

"I'd nailed Arial's windows shut after she escaped one night," I said in a low voice. "She went down to a pond and jumped in. I didn't know what else to do. This is one of the nails. The other one is gone, too."

Jacinda touched the nail as the import of what I was telling her began to sink in. We stared into each other's eyes through the eerie pale beams of the flashlights.

"I think she opened the window," I stage-whispered.

"I think—oh, my God—she might have pushed the ladder over."

"She opened the window despite the nails," Jacinda said, sounding hushed and awed. "And that ladder is heavy. Superhuman strength is a classic sign of possession."

"Why did I leave them alone?" I cried in a strangled whisper. "She was fine all night. She's always liked him so much. I never thought—"

Jacinda gripped my wrist, hard. "Neely, it isn't *her* in there. Don't you understand that?"

"What do we do? What do we do?" Hyperventilation was climbing up my throat. I was close to letting it loose, letting it take over, allowing it to debilitate me completely. Then I could float away, mentally I could rise above this abhorrent scene.

"Listen to me," Jacinda said, sharply. "How strong are you right now?"

I shook my head. I was not strong at all.

"You need to get it together. Can you do that?"

"I—yes," I stammered, though I felt I couldn't save her. I didn't have the strength to save her.

Something in me, perhaps something evil, was urging me to run and never look back. To let someone else deal with all of this. To let authorities take her and lock her in some kind of institution where people were safe from her. Then I could live a life. This was no life. My girl was gone and whatever she was now, this devil baby, needed to be put away, held captive, contained and subdued.

But those shameful thoughts were engulfed and

deluged by my love for her. The Arial I'd had for a decade. The sweet, trusting girl I'd known for ten years. The girl who loved reading and gymnastics, who flitted and danced around like a carefree butterfly, who wanted me to make up stories for her before bed. No matter what lame tale I came up with, she was always enthralled. The little girl who said *Mommy, I love you* with such earnestness.

At about seven years old, she'd out-of-the-blue asked me if I'd jump off a cliff for her. I'd told her I would, unhesitatingly. Yet I wanted to flee and leave her to a thing that had grabbed hold of her and was strangling the good out of her?

My baby was in there fighting for herself. I wouldn't abandon her. Not like her father had. I would *never* abandon her, even if that meant death for me.

"What do we do?" I asked Jacinda. My voice was strong and firm, prepared for battle.

"We get in there and we save your child."

"How?"

"Do you happen to have anything that belongs to Maybelle's mother?"

"Viola?" I asked, perplexed. "I do. Pictures of her. In some envelopes I found in the basement."

"Good. Get one. I'll need one other thing."

"What?"

"Something to restrain your daughter."

Chapter Forty-Three

I had Arial swallow one-and-a-half of the anxiety pills, then checked on her in bed every five minutes until she appeared soundly asleep. I could hear her deep, rhythmic breathing. Then Jacinda and I worked together to bind her wrists and ankles.

For her wrists, we used a plastic jump rope Arial had on the porch, as I didn't want to use the rough rope that the movers had left behind. For her ankles, we used the rope but I was concerned it would cut into her skin. Jacinda urged me on, to bind her tightly.

"We have bigger things to worry about than rope burn," she whispered.

Then she went to her car and returned with incense, lighting one stick and placing it atop Arial's small desk. There was one chair in the bedroom, and Jacinda sat with the picture of Viola I'd given her, holding it reverently, tracing the image of Viola's dour face and high-necked Victorian dress.

Jacinda's eyes were closed, her lips moving slightly,

summoning Viola's spirit. I kept Arial's bedroom only faintly illuminated, could hear the thin, faraway ring of the dimmer at half-light.

Finally, a couple of hours after I'd put Arial to bed, Jacinda nodded at me and said, "Wake her."

I did so gently, not wanting to startle her. Right now, she still looked every inch my baby girl, her wavy chestnut hair straggled across her warm forehead, her soft cheeks pink and flushed.

I'd encouraged her to put on pajamas, rather than the nightgown she preferred, not knowing how physical the exorcism might get. I claimed the nightgown was dirty and needed washing. Sluggish from the medication, she hadn't put up an argument.

I felt as if I was readying my baby girl for a slaughter.

When she sleepily blinked open her eyes, they were the eyes I knew, my girl's beautiful brown eyes with hints of amber deep in their centers. She was bewildered, a little irritated, and not quite coherent.

"Maybelle Hubbard, come forth," Jacinda said.

Arial kept blinking, then stared up at the ceiling for several long moments. I watched as something came down inside her pupils, a dark curtain, transforming her gentle eyes into hard, glinting spheres. I began to back away.

There was something new, too. A thick sewage smell, strong and definitely emanating from her. She took in her restraints, then started to fiercely jerk her arms and legs against her straps.

"What have you done to me, witches?"

My little girl was gone. The voice was coarse and surly. The skin had the aged, slightly-stippled texture of a rubber mask.

"Maybelle Hubbard, there is someone who would like to speak with you," said Jacinda.

"Untie me, maggots!" The thing turned its rageful gaze on me. "The whore who couldn't keep her legs shut ties mine? Your grandmother cries all the time for how you ruined your life. You were supposed to be the smart one. The successful one. Instead, you forced her into poverty with your slutty ways. You broke her heart."

This momentarily gutted me but I forced myself to remember all the times when Arial was a baby and Grandma had held her, cooed to her, fell asleep with Arial on her chest.

I wanted to shout at the thing. To tell it that I knew my grandmother wasn't heartbroken and crying, that she'd loved me even though she'd been disappointed in my teenage pregnancy. And that Arial had given my grandmother much joy before she passed away.

But I wouldn't say this. Under no circumstances did I want to further agitate the thing that had control of my daughter's body. But it was the first evidence I had that the thing didn't necessarily always speak from supernatural omnipotence but rooted around your most vulnerable areas and threw out whatever it guessed would hurt you.

Jacinda closed her eyes for several long moments, then opened them and stood, holding one arm straight out.

"Maybelle," she said. Her voice too had changed. It

was raspier, grittier, and had the barest old-world accent, faintly British. "You will listen to me. You will do as I say, child."

The thing on the bed stopped thrashing, its rippled, gummy face turned towards us, its bluish lips puckered in surprise.

"Who is that?" it demanded.

"You know very well who this is."

"Liars!" the thing cried. "Witches!"

"You will obey me!" Jacinda ordered, moving closer. "You will do as I say! Leave here, release this young girl. She has nothing to do with us and cannot change the past."

"You won't fool me, cock-sucking maggots!"

Jacinda pointed her finger at the thing, who began cringing, pulling its legs up towards its stomach. It was the first time I'd seen the thing looking disempowered, looking... scared.

"You will leave this girl who has nothing to do with us! You will listen to me! Do you dare disobey me?"

"I saw you, Mother," the thing howled. "I saw you die. I saw your neck snapped. I saw you burning in hell."

"I did what I needed to do. I was left with no choice. I paid the price for it."

"*You* paid the price? You were shown mercy compared to what I went through! Where were you? Hanging from the gallows, spared it all. Carrie never spoke again. You abandoned us to be tortured by strangers. You're no mother. A roach is a better mother than you."

Jacinda walked even closer and grabbed the thing's ankle. "You will obey your mother and leave this girl!"

The thing suddenly flipped forward. I didn't know what had happened until I heard Jacinda emit an agonized scream. The thing had its teeth clamped on Jacinda's hand. I ran over and grabbed the thing's face, one hand cupped over its nose, trying to pry its small, brutish jaw off Jacinda's limb.

"Motherfucker!" Jacinda yelped.

The thing unlatched its jaw and began laughing with a wide-open mouth. Blood dripped off its teeth. "Stupid cunt," it spat.

I quickly steered Jacinda away, careful to close the bedroom door behind me. In the bathroom, I turned on the faucets and tried to get a warm temperature. As Jacinda shoved her hand under the tap, I squeezed by her and opened the small utility closet, scouring for antibiotic ointment. When I didn't see the tube right away, I returned and squirted liquid soap on her bloody hand.

"What happened?" I asked. "Did Viola take over your body?"

"No, no. She was only passing through me." Jacinda sucked in her breath, wincing in pain. "Spirits can't control me. And there were some things I refused to repeat. They had an extremely volatile but symbiotic relationship. I thought it was worth a chance to see if Maybelle would listen to her. But while she feared her mother, she knew it was my body."

I grabbed a hand towel on the rack and wrapped it around her hand, applying pressure.

"We need to get back in there," I said. "We can't leave her alone."

Jacinda took over, squeezing the terrycloth on her hand for a few more seconds. Then she nodded and discarded the blood-stained towel in the sink.

I carefully cracked the bedroom door open. The room was ice cold and smelled even more strongly of sewage, strong enough to cause a gag reflex. The thing was sitting up in bed, legs stretched out front, bound hands in its lap. It had a sickening, malicious, twisted grin on its viscid face.

"Sluts, sluts, sluts," it snarled in its rough, raspy voice. "The only power a woman has in this world is the juicy cunt between her legs. You both threw it away to the first men who wanted it. Weak, desperate, pathetic whores. At least I made the scum marry me."

Jacinda was like a boxer who's been bloodied but refused to leave the ring. She didn't hesitate to walk forward assuredly, stopping only a foot from the bed.

She raised her hand, the same one that had been bitten, and swiftly clamped it on the thing's head, as she'd done in the past. I was astonished that, despite being bitten, Jacinda was willing to get her hand on the thing again.

"You are cast out in the name of all that is good and holy! I cast you out of this innocent young girl. I cast you out for eternity!"

The thing whipped back and forth, bound feet scraping along the mattress. Jacinda refused to let go of its head.

"Return from whence you came, disturbed spirit! I

cast you out, malignant spirit! I cast you out for eternity, cancerous soul! I cast you out for all of time in the name of the legion of good and holy spirits. They surround and protect this innocent young girl."

Jacinda repeated the same chant, over and over and over, for what seemed at least ten minutes, all the while with her oozing, bloodied hand glued to the thing's head. It must have taken stupendous physical and emotional strength.

The thing thrashed, kicked, and screamed less and less and less until it finally, mercifully, went limp and silent on the bed.

"You are cast out," Jacinda said, her voice dwindling in volume and strength. "You have gone back from whence you came, and you will never return. You are at peace, spirit. You are home, spirit. You have no need to return and are forbidden to return to the body of this innocent girl. You will be at peace for all time, reconciled spirit. Sleep now, Maybelle Hubbard, and be at eternal peace. You suffer no more pain, no more fury, and you only rejoice in your forever, tranquil rest, reconciled spirit."

Jacinda's shoulders slumped, her voice was strained and weakened, and she looked ready to sink to the floor. I pulled the chair near her and she flopped into it, holding her wounded hand.

I crept closer to the bed. The thing no longer appeared to be there, the little pajama-clad body was Arial's and only Arial's.

"Mommy?" I heard.

The voice was definitely that of my baby. Her eyes

had flickered open and she sounded exhausted and bewildered. I moved towards her, the maternal urge to comfort her overruling all I'd just seen. But Jacinda came to life and snapped at me.

"Stop! Ask her something only Arial knows! Quickly!"

My mind went utterly blank. I didn't think I would come up with anything. Then it flashed on me, dropped into my brain. "What did Kevin give you for your birthday?" I asked.

After Kevin's death, Arial had spent weeks not wanting to be parted from his gift, requesting it stay on her bed where she could see it. But the gift seemed to become too painful for her to look at anymore. She'd relegated it to her wooden keepsake trunk, respectfully draping it atop her once-cherished toys and books. That's where it still was.

"*Benny and Belinda Go to Paris*," she murmured, with a slight smile on her face. Not the demonic, malicious smirk of the thing but the dreamy smile of an innocent child thinking of a book series she loved. A child who needed to be held by her mother.

I glanced back at Jacinda and nodded, confirming for her that this was the correct answer and silently asking if it was safe to approach.

"She's clear," Jacinda said, resting her head on the back of the chair. "She's clear."

Chapter Forty-Four

"*A*re you sure you want to drive home?" I asked.

I'd found the ointment and put that and Band-Aids on Jacinda's hand but it still looked a mess and must be painful. It was past two a.m. and I worried about her driving for so long after all she'd been through, but she'd already turned down my invite to sleep on the couch. Turned it down multiple times. I knew why. She didn't want to sleep in the same house as Arial and I couldn't blame her.

"I'll be fine," she said. "If I get tired, I'll pull into a motel or get some coffee. It's only an hour—less with no traffic."

"You definitely think it's gone now? Gone for good?"

She tapped her heart. "They tell me she's clear."

"Well, I can't thank you enough. I don't know what I would have done without you."

We stood awkwardly for several moments until

Jacinda smiled weakly, smoothed back her hair on one side, and got into her car. Her window glided down.

"I know my guides wouldn't mislead me. But Neely, if you see or hear anything… unusual… let me know immediately."

"I will."

I was about to let her drive off because I saw she was shattered with exhaustion, but I had to know one thing.

"But you did say that it—I mean, Maybelle—can mimic Arial. She told me Kevin's gift but wouldn't Maybelle know it too?"

"No," Jacinda said. "She only knows negative things. That's all she can see. All she allows herself to see."

Chapter Forty-Five

The room was dull beige with glaring fluorescent lights, and a striped curtain hanging from the ceiling to split it for another patient, but Salem had the room to himself.

The usual array of hospital equipment was near his bed: a white machine with a small screen which appeared to be monitoring his heart-rate, and an IV bag hanging on a tall metal pole.

He looked sleepy but was awake. Arial and I approached. I held her hand and we stepped gingerly, as if our very footsteps might cause him pain.

"How are you?" I asked.

"Okay, but hurting," he rasped. "Broke my collar-bone and left leg. They need to get some better pain relievers in here."

He tried to grin but it wilted. His gaze focused on Arial for a moment, then slipped away. Something about the way he looked at her made me tug her hand and lead her to the door.

"Boo, can you wait outside for one minute? Don't go anywhere, hear? Not anywhere."

I was trying not to use my *you're-in-trouble* voice, one I'd used so much with her lately through no fault of her own, but it was poking through nonetheless. I couldn't risk her wandering off and getting lost in a hospital.

"Okay, Mom," she sighed, drearily. She clearly didn't understand why she couldn't stay in the room. She'd been expressing a lot of concern for Salem and had wanted to visit him. I closed the door without shutting it all the way and proceeded back to Salem's bed.

I only looked at him. Silence ached between us for a long time, neither one of us knowing what to say or even if to say it. He stared back up at the soulless fluorescent ceiling. I decided it was my responsibility to voice the awful thing we were both obviously trying to avoid.

"Do you—do you know how—"

He turned his head very slowly and only a little bit. I could tell it pained him to do so.

"I know what happened," he said. "I also know it wasn't her. It couldn't have been. She had one hand out her window, one little hand. She's not that strong. A grown man wouldn't be that strong."

I slipped my hand into his.

"Salem," I said, lowly, careful that Arial shouldn't hear me, "she had this unbelievable thing happen to her. I can't even explain it. But it's over now. She's back to herself."

I curled my fingers around the tips of his, careful to be gentle as I didn't want to jostle his collarbone.

"I don't know what to say. I feel horrible. She'd been

acting so—*not her*—but I never, ever thought she'd hurt you. I had her locked inside her room. Her windows were even nailed shut. It never occurred to me she could get them open." I rested my head on his forearm, then glanced back at him. His pain-clotted expression tore me up. "I'm so sorry. It was such bad judgment on my part. This isn't an excuse, but I've hardly been sleeping at all, and I wasn't—"

"Neely," he said, hoarsely, cutting me off. "I don't know exactly what's gone on, but I know that little girl couldn't have done what she did. Not by herself. I'm trained as an engineer, remember? I understand the laws of physics." He tried to smile. "Do you read the Bible?"

"Um, not really." I laughed uneasily. "Maybe I should."

"I don't either, but I did have to go to church my entire childhood. I remember a line from it. Something about 'Forgive them, Father, for they know not what they do.'"

"Yes," I whispered. "I remember that."

"That's how I feel about it. She didn't know what she was doing."

I was so humbled and grateful for this tremendous grace on his part that I spontaneously kissed his hand. "Thank you, Salem, thank you."

"Doesn't a broken collarbone get me a real kiss?" he murmured.

I very carefully leaned over and obliged.

Chapter Forty-Six

That night I kept thinking about Salem. He could have so easily hated Arial for what she'd done to him, and by extension hated me for raising her. He could have thought what many would have—that she was an irredeemable brat, a devil child.

If he could extend that kind of grace and forgiveness to her, then what responsibility did I have to do the same for those who'd wronged me?

No, neither Jed nor Kevin's killer had been possessed by a vengeful spirit, at least that I was aware of, but perhaps they too did not know what they were doing. Who knew why—mental illness, pure obtuseness—but perhaps they too simply did not know what they were doing.

At any rate, Jacinda had admonished me about my anger drawing Maybelle into Arial, so I felt obligated to try and do what I could to tame it, to allow some forgiveness, or at least some small degree of understanding, to seep into my ossified heart.

As I listened to Arial chattering to her doll while in the bathtub, I retrieved my laptop and pulled up District Attorney Acosta's email. I wanted this on record.

Hi Mr. Acosta,

I'm so sorry I haven't been in touch earlier but I've had so many things happening. I just wanted to let you know that I've thought long and hard about what we discussed. I'm absolutely prepared to tell the full truth about Kevin's murder.

That night, I heard the man ask me what the hell I was looking at. He also said, "I'm the devil!" after he stabbed Kevin. Though he shouted something at us before the attack, neither I nor my daughter know what he said and I wouldn't want to speculate.

I sincerely hope that justice prevails for Kevin and his family. He was such a good, kind person, and deserves it. I truly appreciate your continued dedication to the case.

Let me know if you need anything else.

Warmly,

Neely Pfau

I had to trust that the justice system would work for Kevin. I couldn't risk a lie being discovered and getting charged with perjury, having to leave Arial for a stint in prison. Not to mention that a discovered lie about a hate crime could cast doubt on other hate crimes. Perhaps I'd unwittingly help weaken the legal apparatus that specifically punished those types of crimes. I didn't want that.

Then I went outside and called Beckett. I hadn't

heard from him since we'd last spoken. He usually answered when I called, no matter what he was doing, and this time was no different.

"Hey, Neely," he said. "Sorry I haven't been in touch. Things have been nonstop."

"I can only imagine."

"I assume you'd like an update."

"Is he alive?" I expected Beckett would have called me if Jed had passed away but this was the question that burst from my mouth.

"He's alive. But no one knows when or if he'll ever make any kind of a recovery. Neely, the doctors say he's brain dead."

"Oh my God," I breathed. "I can't believe it."

As much as Jed had inflamed my anger over the years, he was still Arial's father and I would always care about him for that reason only. I never wanted this for him. And despite my telling Arial her father was dead, now that he really was—at least technically—I felt a deep grief for her. I knew what it was to have no hope of ever having a father.

"He's obviously out of the race. Willa has taken his place. She's the party's candidate."

I had no idea what to say to that. Given that her party had ruled the city for two decades, Jed's wife was virtually guaranteed to be the next mayor.

"And Neely, we can talk about this more, but I think it's time you came forward. Even with the election. Willa had nothing to do with anything and it won't harm her campaign. Hell, it might even help it. And she's controlling the finances so Jed can't deposit anything into my account. For Arial's sake, you've got to lay a claim to his estate."

"Yes, I suppose I do."

"I can recommend a lawyer for you. He's a good friend of mine and would do it pro bono or cheaply."

"I'd really appreciate that."

"All this means I'll likely be resigning. It will take Willa about two seconds to figure out I've known about you for years. She's a good person but I have no idea how she's going to react to any of this."

"Becks, do you have access to Jed?"

"Access?"

"Yes, can you talk to him? Get to his bedside?"

"Sure. I go to see him every few days."

"Would you pass along a message to him from me?"

"Neely, there's no guarantee he hears anything. And, if he does, doubtful he'd understand it."

"I'll take that chance. Can you tell him that Neely says, 'You knew not what you did. I didn't like what you did, but you gave me the best thing that's ever happened to me. For that I thank you.'"

"Uhh, I should probably write that down." He chuckled a little.

Chapter Forty-Seven

*A*fter Arial's bath, she put on her favorite nightgown, her pink one. She thought it made her look like a princess and she was right. I figured it would only be another year or so before princesses lost their appeal.

I couldn't help sniffing at her, though I tried not to be obvious about it, in order to make certain that the noxious, excrement odor from the night before was completely eradicated. I'd spent a few hours cleaning her room, washing her bedding, mopping the floors, wiping down the walls, and doing everything I could to take away all evidence of what had gone on the night before.

I'd asked her if she'd like to change her room, either to mine or to the smaller room that I'd set up for an office, but she declined. She preferred overlooking the backyard, the playset, and the woods.

I didn't want to push her, to take away anything that was giving her pleasure, as I knew I'd already taken away so much. Besides, I doubted the room had anything to do with anything. As usual, she remembered none of what had happened when Maybelle had taken over.

I read her a long book about a good witch that guards a forest. It was a book I'd read to her dozens of times before, but now the innocent story seemed dark and disturbing to me—but she didn't mind it. All I wanted her to imbibe these days was rainbows and sunshine.

"Can you not lock me in?" she whispered as I was tucking her light comforter around her and kissing her forehead. She gave me her big, brown, irresistible, pleading eyes. "I don't like it. I'm not a baby."

"I know you're not a baby, hon," I said, stroking her cheek. Although Jacinda had assured me that my child was cleared, and I believed her, I had massive PTSD from the time she'd fled and gone down to the pond.

I hadn't re-nailed her windows shut. I supposed if she was going to escape, she could simply go out them again. But the idea of not locking her door scared the hell out of me. I'd already made the decision to withhold a pill. Leaving her door unlocked as well felt like too much freedom, too soon.

"Don't you trust me, Mom?" she asked. "Why do you always think I'm being bad?"

"I don't think you're being bad. Hey, maybe you can sleep with me tonight, would you like that?"

"No." She scrunched up her face. "You're treating me like a baby."

"What about me sleeping in here? On the floor."

"Whaaat?" She giggled. "Why?"

I hugged her and kissed her temple. "Because I miss you when I'm asleep."

"You're being so weird. Can I have a piece of candy?"

"Absolutely not. You just brushed your teeth."

I'd stuffed the bag of remaining gummies onto a high shelf in a kitchen cabinet but had recently caught her standing on a chair, door open, scrounging around for it. So, I'd hidden the bag inside the basement cabinet where I'd unearthed the family photos. She'd never find it there.

I wish I hadn't started her down the route of sweets outside of Halloween and birthdays, because now I had to deal with the near-constant requests for candy. Unlike me, she had a terrible sugar-tooth.

"As a reward for locking me in," she said playfully, grinning.

"I tell you what. A piece tomorrow after lunch. And I promise that next week, I won't lock the door. But let's take things a little slowly. It's only for your safety."

She rolled her eyes and pulled herself deeper under the comforter. "Whatever, Mom."

Chapter Forty-Eight

I settled myself onto the couch in the living room with a small tumbler of wine. My big plan for the evening was to relax with a book and get to bed early. I knew that with Arial's windows not nailed, and her not drugged from the pills, I may not get much sleep for worrying about her. Not to mention the zero sleep I'd gotten last night. The wine was my attempt to sand down the spiky edges of my anxiety.

I also knew there was one more person I had to forgive. The most important person.

I should have seen the danger. I should have yelled for us to run. I should have saved him. It's my fault he's dead.

My hands began trembling and I rested the book on my lap, bottom lip quivering.

"I—I—" I whispered. "For—for—" I couldn't finish the sentence as tears had clogged my nose and the back of my throat.

But I thought it. *I forgive you, Neely Pfau. It wasn't your fault. None of it was your fault. Please, please let go of this idea.*

It won't bring Kevin back, and it will give you no peace. To be the best mother you can be, the best HUMAN you can be, you must let go of this irrational notion that you should have, could have, saved him.

After a few minutes of silent tears, I felt a sudden and relaxing melt of relief enter my heart. Then I noticed a bright light sweeping along the far wall. This meant a car had come into the drive and was using it to turn around, something cars had always done. I had no idea why drivers, upon seeing the turnaround, suddenly realized they were going in the wrong direction.

However, the tunnel of light then shut off, didn't waver farther along the wall as it normally would have done for a turnaround. I crept to the large window that overlooked the front yard, pulling aside a portion of the curtain.

It was too dark to see anything. My heart began to beat jaggedly as a premonition snaked through me. I moved to the wooden door and turned the lock. About thirty seconds later, the doorbell jangled, causing me to startle and grasp my chest.

I worried the doorbell would awaken Arial, who'd only gone down about half an hour ago. But she tended to be a fast sleeper. I flicked the outdoor light on and pressed one eye up to the peephole.

On the steps was a woman. A middle-aged woman. Brunette. That's all I could determine. I cracked the door open and peeked out. The woman smiled.

"Hello, Neely," she said. "Sorry to interrupt you so late but I got a little lost."

The woman was Willa Thompkins.

* * *

I STOOD THUNDERSTRUCK, unable to speak. My brain refused to fully digest that Jed's wife was standing on my doorstep. And didn't look furious. Over the years, I'd occasionally imagined a scene of Willa confronting me. In my mind, she'd be screaming at me, hurling terrible but deserved insults my way.

I never pictured her looking as she did on my steps —smiling and relaxed. Even… friendly.

"Would you let me in so we can speak?" she asked through the screen. "It's rather important with what's happened to Jed."

I thought of Arial overhearing whatever Willa had come to say. I was still in deep shock that she knew who I was, and where I lived, and must know about my daughter. *Jed's* daughter. I found myself scanning her hands and clothing—a tan pantsuit—searching for signs of a weapon.

Reading the look on my face, she held up her palms. "I'm not here to hurt you, Neely," she said. "I've known about you for a long time. If I'd wanted to harm you, I could have done it long before. I'm about to become mayor of the largest city in the country. I'm not going to destroy that over a little domestic drama."

I reluctantly opened the door and escorted her towards the porch, where I thought it least likely Arial would hear us. I retrieved my tumbler of wine and, on the way through the kitchen, opened the refrigerator and snatched out the bottle.

"Wine?" I asked.

She waved dismissively. "I don't drink, but thank you."

Of course you don't, I almost said.

She didn't look the type who needed the boost of alcohol to handle a one-on-one with the mother of her husband's long-hidden child. She didn't seem as if she needed a crutch for anything life threw at her. The set of her face—confident, capable—and the squared shoulders and sure-footed walk made me suddenly hope she won the election. She might be here to read me the riot act but I had no doubt she'd be a kickass mayor.

I turned on the porch light and indicated a chair. Then I poured myself more wine even though the tumbler was almost full.

"I'm going to ask that you keep your voice down," I said, sitting opposite her. "My daughter is asleep and this is a small house." It was fortunate I'd had wine on hand. Otherwise, I probably would have shut the door in her face and hidden under my covers.

Her tanned fingers had several large, glittery rings on them, one wrist cradled by a thick, gold band. For so many years, I'd resented that Jed and his family were living in luxury while Arial and I eked it out in comparative poverty. But Willa's extreme-confidence, her ultra-assuredness, triggered my admiration. I wasn't sure I liked her, but I definitely admired her.

"Becks has told me you're aware of Jed's situation," she said.

"Yes."

"It's quite sad but, as his health care proxy and taking into account all he's directed me to do in the past, the family has made a conscientious decision not to continue with extreme care measures."

At my puzzled expression, she said, matter-of-factly, "We're pulling the plug."

"Oh," I whispered.

"So, I'm here for a couple of reasons—the first being that I wanted to know if you had any desire for Arial to see him before that happens."

A shock zipped through me that she'd used my daughter's name, though it shouldn't have. It was clear that Willa Thompkins knew all about my life. The tremendous secret I'd supposedly been living inside all these years had been no secret at all. At least when it came to the person for whom I'd most wanted to keep that secret.

It wasn't lost on me that while Jed's wife knew he was Arial's father, Arial herself did not. I decided not to get into that.

"I—I don't think so," I said, tremulously taking a sip of wine. "I appreciate the offer but I think that would be traumatic for her. She's been through enough lately. I'd like her to remember him the way he was."

I winced, not sure if I should have said that. Was Willa aware that her husband had visited his youngest daughter throughout the years? But she had no discernible reaction to this statement.

"That makes sense," she replied. "And now for the other reason I'm here. I know you must be concerned about finances."

I said nothing.

"The money will continue to come to you as it has in

the past. Neely, my husband was a city councilman. Do you know what they make? Not much. I'm the one who's been paying for you and Arial, not him."

My jaw slowly dropped open. And yet this wasn't a huge surprise. I knew city representatives didn't earn a lot, hence my long-held suspicion that the funds had been procured through some shady means. But I'd never suspected those shady means were Jed's wife.

"I come from decent money," she continued. "Not Rockefeller money, but enough to keep my husband's child from starving. Naturally, you're welcome to go the lawyer route. But you should know Jed has nothing. And my assets are protected with an iron-clad prenup."

She leaned forward, keeping her voice low as requested.

"We can draw up a contract so you don't have to worry about it. I'll support her until she's eighteen. It would have made sense to have it all out much earlier, so Jed and your daughter could have had a relationship. The problem was that you and he met when you were underage. You can see how that would throw a wrench into things. Jed swore you two didn't sleep together until it was legal, but even if true, who would believe that? For years, I felt he was bound for the White House." She leaned farther forward, her shrewd eyes glinting. "Now I know it's *me* who's bound for the White House."

In that moment, I had no doubt, absolutely none, that I was looking at a future President of the United States.

"Why are you doing this for us?" I asked. I wondered what kinds of things Jed had told her about me. I was certain all of it would have leaned towards making him look good and me look bad. But Willa didn't seem the type who would be willfully ignorant to her husband's defects.

She shrugged her slightly padded shoulders. "I'm Italian-American. We take family very seriously. I consider you and Arial to be family. She shares blood with my children and that's good enough for me. *Benvenuta*."

She smiled. She had the kind of smile that, though wide and glistening with superb dental care, sent a sliver of fear down the spine. If she was on your side, you were golden. If she wasn't, God help you.

"Did Beckett know you knew?"

Now that she was only a few feet away from me and I was getting the full blast of her intelligence and backbone, I couldn't believe I'd ever imagined that I or Jed or Beckett—or anyone for that matter—could have fooled her.

"Oh, no," she said, almost laughing. "They say it's the wife who's last to know. In this case, I was the *first* to know when Jed came to me blubbering for money. I wouldn't say we have the type of marriage that—let's just put it that Jed and I had the same ambitions."

I noticed she was already talking about Jed in the past tense even though life was still pumping through his veins at the hospital. This didn't come across as cold-blooded but more that Willa was imminently practical and didn't hold tightly to sentiment, even if that meant swiftly and definitively recategorizing her still-breathing husband from alive to dead.

"Americans put so much store in sexual fidelity," she sighed. "Why? That's the last thing we should put so much value in. There's nothing more tenuous on this planet than a man's sexual fidelity. I'd rather concern myself with keeping Social Security funded, the middle class not taxed to death, and terrorists off our shores than trying to keep a man's dick in his pants."

She gave a knowing grin, then relaxed into her chair, glancing approvingly around the porch.

"I'm glad I could buy you this house," she said, genuinely smiling again. "Did you good to get out of the city after that horrible tragedy."

I nodded, a lump of nerves in my throat. I was starting to like her and yet was deathly afraid of her at the same time. I didn't know her well enough yet to understand what might provoke her and thought it prudent to say as little as possible.

"So, Neely," she said in a clipped, no-nonsense way. "I'll let you know the date of the funeral, should you and Arial decide to come. It will be at Frank Campbell's, of course. I won't mention her in the obituary unless that's something you want. And, I hope, sincerely hope, in the near future, she can meet Gia and Toni. They're wonderful girls. I have no doubt they'd want to know their little sister. I haven't told them yet but plan to soon. I wanted us to have a talk first."

She glanced at her watch and abruptly stood. Then she stuck her arm out for a handshake. I, too, stood and offered her my hand, which was humiliatingly soft and uncertain inside of her strong, competent clasp.

"If you need anything," she said. "Let me know."

Chapter Forty-Nine

"*Mommy! Moooooommmyyy!*"

I jolted awake, heart hammering. It wasn't the first time I'd been thunderbolted out of sleep in the middle of the night by my daughter calling for me but with everything that had gone on lately, the sound exploded me into action.

I had left my bedroom door open and hers was only a few steps away. Flying from my room, I saw her door was wide open even though I'd locked it. Hadn't I? I quickly turned the dimmer up to its full light.

My daughter was not in bed.

"Arial!" I shouted, rushing down the hallway. "Honey!"

"Mooommmmmyyyyy!"

Her voice was tiny and far away, slightly muffled. Hitting the kitchen, I slapped the overhead light switch on and darted my gaze around.

The basement door was agape. Nearby was one of the kitchen chairs. The immediate impression was that she'd climbed atop the chair to lift the latch lock just as she'd climbed on a chair to reach the top shelf in the cabinet. She'd somehow figured out I'd put the candy in the basement.

I was so frantic that the fact she'd gotten out of her locked bedroom was muddled in my brain, not fully comprehensible. The tumbler of wine, the highly unexpected visit from Willa. Had I been distracted to the point where I hadn't locked her door and only *thought* I had?

I stood at the top of the musty basement steps. "Arial?" I called, turning on the light at the top. Halfway down the staircase hung another light, a bare bulb that had to be turned on by pulling a loop on a string.

"Mom, I fell! Help me!"

I didn't see her anywhere but knew I'd have to turn on the hanging bulb in order to illuminate the bottom of the steps. I started down one step, two, three, then jerked to a stop.

When your child calls for you, you react. You're a train hurtling down the instinctual track of motherhood. A distress call from your baby sends every fiber into action mode. And yet the idea of continuing down the stairs had seized hold of me with visceral, acute fear. My body was frigid and paralyzed. I couldn't move forward.

"Baby!" I called tremulously. "What's your favorite book?"

"Moommmeeeeee!" She started to sob, ragged, choking tears catching in her throat. The kind of cry that happened when she was truly distraught and not exaggerating for attention. The kind of cry that meant she was in pain, that I heard when she fell on pavement, scraping her hands or knees.

"Quickly, Arial, please! A book you love. Hurry!"

When she only continued to wail, my body started to shake uncontrollably. I grasped the rickety old railing. The steps were perilously steep. I felt unbalanced, as if I was hanging over a cliff-face that I might plummet down any moment.

My jaw started to tremble, my teeth chattering. I realized the shaking wasn't only fear—but that the basement had turned ice-cold. Glacial as a subzero winter. Visible white wisps of my breath rose in front of me.

"No," I said before being cracked on the back of the head.

The sudden bomb of pain was star-bursting, my vision blind-white as I collapsed down the steps, down, down, down, and crashed onto the cement floor, my body crumpled into a broken ball, my head screaming with pain.

I lay there for a long time trying to pull the pain into something manageable so I could look up. My eyes were bleary, unfocused, feeling as if they'd been poked directly in the corneas with something long and sharp.

"Arriiiaal," I moaned.

I could not accept what had happened. I was still worried that my daughter was down here somewhere and injured, even though I knew this had been a ruse to get me to the basement, and that my daughter was no longer my daughter. The maternal instinct is so fierce, so all-encompassing. Even though I was in dire danger, my first concern was for Arial and not myself.

"You dumb, dumb, dumb cunt," I heard from above. The voice was guttural, coarse, and sent gushes of cold terror through my smashed body.

I began slowly, slowly trying to move my limbs, clasping my fists, sliding my feet out, attempting to get a sense of what body parts still worked. The wooden steps creaked as footfalls came down them. I agonizingly pushed myself up enough that I could turn my pain-seared head.

The thing stood halfway down the stairs, staring at me. The rubbery face and bluish lips, the eyes phosphorescent with volcanic reds and oranges glowing in the darkness of the basement.

"What do you want?" I rasped.

When the thing didn't answer, only continued to stare at me with otherworldly hatred, with fiery, burning hellfire eyes, the anger that I'd let go of, that I'd managed to release, reassembled completely, reformed into roaring rage.

"What do you want?" I screamed despite the sharp stabbing in my head. "What do you want from me? What do you want from my child? WHAT DO YOU WANT?"

At first, the thing said nothing.

Its poker-red eyes pulsed and blazed malevolently. Then it opened its purple-blue mouth, showed me its little rat's teeth, and howled, "I want a childhood!"

The soul-searing lament, howled in a guttural growl, sent the frail old steps shaking, and I felt the volcanic vibrations through the cement floor.

The thing craned its veined neck towards the ceiling,

arms groping upwards, little hands like claws. No longer a trace of my daughter, but a small, beastly, distended thing, climbing towards the sky, towards its pain. This is when I realized it had a long knife in one hand.

"Maybelle," I groaned. "I can't give you that. I wish I could." With an agonizing effort, I continued trying to push myself up, dragging my broken body away from the bottom of the staircase.

Her childhood. She'd had her childhood stolen from her, so she was forever a child. Forever a child searching for something that she'd never get, demanding something unobtainable, nonexistent.

Her deep-soul calling for a childhood could have been me. Only, I'd wanted a return to the childhood I'd been given, a reclamation of a time of safety and love. And she only wanted to be *given* a childhood, to be regifted the one that had been violently yanked away from her when her mother was hanged.

I pushed my palms on the ice-cold cement floor until I was leaning against a tall shelving unit that had been down here when we'd moved in. I had nothing to store so it was empty but gave me something solid to lean on.

I looked full at her, something I hadn't done before. Trying to see her as a sentient human spirit, not as a *thing*. Something was torturing her so badly that she could not rest, not even after she'd discarded her flesh.

Whatever the source of her rage was, it seemed more than what I knew of already—more than her mother being executed in front of her. The look on her waxy, stippled face, the smoldering hatred in those red-coal eyes, the monstrous, infinite, open canyon of her pain. There was more inside of her than I'd been told.

The idea formed… slowly. As she turned her attention back to me, turned those eyes glowing with the depths of hell in my direction, it came to me. The complete, horrid, profane truth was passed down through the collective unconscious, from her womb to mine.

The first words I'd ever heard from her.

I killed him.

He deserved to die, the cheating son-of-a-bitch.

Are you happy?

"My God…" I breathed, intensifying the throbbing pain in my skull. "You killed someone. Your mother's companion. And… you killed *all* those people, didn't you?"

"Of course!" she shrieked. "Are you just figuring that out, stupid cow?"

This was too much to take in. It was absolutely impossible. She must have been younger than ten when the murders started. A child that young could not be a serial killer. And if by some horrific perversion a child did have the urge to kill people and knew the means to do so, a small child couldn't have buried all those heavy adult bodies. There had to be more here. Something so heinously inhumane as to be inconceivable.

Unspeakable things happened to her when she was too young to fight back or even understand them…

"She made you," I said lowly, still hardly able to fathom the reality. "Your mother. She forced you."

The beastly little vision that was my daughter but

not my daughter didn't respond, her lava-red eyes glittering with savage fury and intelligence.

"What—what did she do to you? To force you?"

"What didn't she?" she bellowed. "Beat me, starve me. Whip Carrie in front of me and tell her it was my fault. Carrie, who didn't understand anything, who'd scream like an animal. I'd do anything to stop that screaming. I'd bring them the tea. They thought it was sweet, a pretty little girl with curled hair and a bow bringing them tea. They'd drink it even if they didn't want it, to be polite and please me. That's why she had me do it, so they'd always take it. With a smile and a thank you. Then they'd collapse in front of me, black blood pouring from their mouths, gasping, begging to know why I'd done that to them. Do you know the sickest, most twisted part of all? I couldn't stop loving her. I tried. But she was my mother."

I shook my head even though that increased the sharp throbbing sensation in the back of my skull. "None of that was your fault," I said. "None of it. You were a child! You were protecting your sister!"

"I became like this because I had to. I turned off anything good. All feeling. Shut it off like a spigot." Her hellfire eyes gleamed, her blue lips twisted into a macabre grin. "Now I kill for myself. Now I like it. If I didn't like it, I'd be in hell."

"No, you don't like it. You don't. It's what you did to survive. What you did for Carrie. You're not a killer. You're the bravest person I've ever known."

She came down the remaining few steps, the knife gripped in her small, clawed hand. "Dumb pig," she growled. "You think your empty compliments will save your life?"

"Then kill me. With that knife." I made a plunging motion into my heart. "Kill me then."

"You think I won't?"

"I think nothing. Do it if you believe it will make you happy. But leave my daughter alone."

She tilted her grotesquely rubbery face as if these words were curious conundrums.

"I'm sorry you weren't mothered. You should have been loved and protected. I wish I could go back and be a good mother for you. You deserved none of what happened to you. But I can't. I can only mother my own child. If killing me puts an end to your agony and frees her, then do it. I can't give you a childhood. I can only give one to my daughter."

I reached towards her, towards the knife.

"Take my life and give my child hers!"

She took a step forward, raising the knife. I braced myself. She would stab that immense blade into my heart and I would let her. I would let her because then she'd leave, free my little girl. I had no idea what would happen to my daughter in a world where it would appear she'd murdered her own mother, but I presumed because of her young age, she wouldn't be imprisoned. Who would take care of my baby? Willa's visit gave me hope it would be her.

"Kill me and release my child!" I ordered. "If you truly are a killer, then kill me!"

Suddenly, she stiffened her back and convulsed as if she was having a seizure. Her burning red irises levitated upward into her sockets until all that could be seen was the hazy, milky white sclera.

She howled, a beastly, mournful sound, raised the knife, higher and higher over her head, then violently threw the blade down where it clanged onto the cement floor.

Chapter Fifty

THREE WEEKS LATER

"Then, Grandma and Grandpa, we'll see Niagara Falls," Arial said.

She was giving a rundown of our travel plans to my grandparents—or rather to their gravestones.

"I've always wanted to see it. Do you know what caused it? Glaciers, like big icebergs" —She stretched her arms as if to convey the glaciers' phenomenal size— "that smashed into each other." She clapped her hands together. *Smash.*

"Very good, hon. I'm sure they enjoyed that geology lesson." I grinned.

School started soon and we had just enough time for a road trip. After everything she'd been through, I wanted to make one of her dreams come true, so we were off to see Niagara Falls, which was about a six-hour drive away.

"Say goodbye to Grandma and Grandpa for now, we have someone else to visit," I said.

It was a crisp, clear day. The sky was boundlessly

blue, the air fresh and clean. I figured it would get hot pretty soon so we were leaving early, it wasn't quite nine a.m. But Arial had insisted we tell my grandparents about the trip before we got on the road.

We traipsed through the stubby, emerald grass until we reached a flat gravestone. It said simply, "Maybelle Lula Hubbard Pfau - Mother" and the dates of her birth and death. She'd died at the ripe old age of 89.

At the historical society, I'd found the records for the cemetery and, sure enough, saw the number of her plot. Not in the same plot as my grandparents.

I assumed it had been my grandfather who'd bought his mother's plot and arranged her burial as her other sons had predeceased her. It was also at the historical society where I'd learned that Maybelle's mother, Viola, had been buried in a potter's field outside of town.

"This is your great-great-grandmother," I told Arial as we looked down at the slab of pinkish marble. It was free from lichen and the etching of her name hadn't been worn down at all. Earl's choice of stone had held up well over the decades.

"She had a very hard life so we're going to include her in our visits from now on," I said.

"What do I call her?"

"Well, her middle name is Lula. That's kind of nice."

"Yes!" Arial said, bursting out with her little *I'm excited* jump. "Lula!"

"Good morning," I heard. I turned around and saw Pearl about thirty feet away, moving slowly towards

Henry's grave. "Oh! There's your aunt," I said to Arial, and we headed over to greet her.

"Well, now!" Pearl enthused, staring at Arial. "It's good to see you. You feeling well?"

"Yes!" she said, gyrating again. She had on her favorite pink leggings patterned with gold stars, a ladybug t-shirt, and her hair was in two braids pinned to her head. "I'm sooooo good."

Pearl looked at me questioningly and I nodded to let her know things were fine. I hadn't seen any signs of possession in the near-month since my confrontation with Maybelle in the basement.

I had a concussion that was almost healed but I still wore sunglasses everywhere. Otherwise, I'd miraculously survived the staircase fall without any broken bones, though my neck was still bothering me a great deal.

This was part of the reason we were driving rather than flying to the Canadian border, so I could get out and walk around whenever I needed to. It would also give us the opportunity to detour through the city where we had dinner plans with Willa, so Arial could meet her half-siblings.

Arial had been astonished and excited hearing the news of having older half-sisters. "I have two big sisters!" she'd randomly announce to herself. "Gia and Toni. They're older than me. They're grown up!"

About a week ago, the girls had spoken to Arial by phone. They were so incredibly nice to her that it repelled me that I'd spent so many years feeling jealous and resentful of them. But these days, I was making an effort to go easy on myself. I was human. Jealousy was natural. The important thing was working on creating a relationship with them for my daughter's sake.

Arial seemed rather unaffected about my news that her real father, Jed, whom she'd always only known as my friend, was in heaven with Grandma and Grandpa.

"I hope 9/11 Daddy won't be upset," she'd said, concerned that the stranger with the memorial bench would be sad that he'd lost his "daughter." I assured her he would completely understand and we could still visit him if she wished.

Salem was doing well, recovering at home. His sister Jordy had come from Nova Scotia to help him out, accompanied by her one-year-old son. There had been a playdate at the park: the three high school pals—Jordy, Debbie, and myself—and our children. My hawk-eyed oversight of Arial had eventually waned as she continued to show no hint of aberrant behavior.

Salem and I had every intention of continuing our thus-far highly dramatic courting. You had to love a man who not only didn't mind that I had a daughter, but was also tolerant of the fact that she'd tried to kill him.

I told Pearl about Arial and my travel plans and she smiled approvingly. We had a brief discussion about how to remove lichen from gravestones without damaging the surfaces. I promised to be in touch as soon as we returned so Pearl and I could get down to decluttering and organizing her house. She was my first official client.

"The church is having a potluck in a few weeks, hope to see you both there," she added.

"What's potluck?" Arial asked.

Pearl bent down a little. "It's when everyone in the community cooks their favorite dish and brings it to share with everyone else."

"Ooh!" Arial exclaimed. "I'll make fettuccine Alfredo. I don't eat animals!"

"That sounds wonderful," Pearl said, glancing up at me with a *she does seem alright!* look on her face.

"So," Pearl went on, straightening. "You found Maybelle's grave."

"Yes. Was that my grandfather's handiwork?"

"I believe so. It certainly wasn't mine. But Earl was a kind-hearted soul. He was going to help her out no matter what." She shook her head as if to say *he's a better person than I am.*

I explained that we had to get on the road. Then I gave her a quick hug and looked at Arial who spontaneously did the same. Pearl couldn't have seemed more pleased.

At the car, Arial got in and I checked to make sure her door was fully closed. But I didn't lock it or glide up her window. By now, I trusted that Arial was Arial.

"Boo," I said. "I forgot to ask Pearl if she'd come pick up our mail while we're away."

We'd only be gone a few days. But I was expecting an important notice from my health insurance company and was uneasy with such sensitive mail sitting right on the road for that long.

With Salem not fully operational, I wasn't sure who else to ask. It didn't feel right to request a favor of Ben, our neighbor. Not with what I suspected caused the demise of his cat. And Pearl lived a lot closer than Debbie did.

"Okay, Mom," Arial said, wriggling into her seat and picking a book up off the floor. "I'll wait here. Benny and Belinda just got to Paris. Can we go to Paris?"

"Maybe someday." I smiled. It was only yesterday that she'd taken Kevin's gift from her keepsake trunk.

I crossed the street and headed back into the cemetery, scanning the tombstones for Pearl. I noted that she was wandering away from Henry's grave. Her back was to me and she didn't see me approaching.

I wondered where she was going and it dawned on me that she was headed in the direction of Maybelle's marker. I was about to call out her name but instead only observed silently as she moved ever closer to what I now saw was definitely Maybelle's headstone. It was a surprise to see Pearl getting so near to it. I'd assumed she'd want nothing to do with her late mother-in-law. Not even a slab of stone with her name etched on it.

I wanted to keep a respectful distance but I also had to get on the road. Perhaps I'd just call her later. But something kept pushing me forward. I got near enough that I could see the side of Pearl's face and noted her lips moving. Then I heard her voice. At first, I couldn't tell what she was saying, a gentle breeze whisking the words away.

But as I got closer, and then was only several feet from her, the sound traveled to me, forming words clear as the bright summer day.

"You didn't do right by me, Maybelle," she was

saying. "And you know it. But you did right by that little girl, leaving her be. Because of that, I forgive you for all you did to me."

She bowed her head, her arthritic hands clasped in front of her, and stood like that for several moments. Then she lifted her head and began to walk in my direction.

I opened my mouth to call to her. But when she caught my gaze, the pale morning sun sparked off her cerulean eyes, giving them a momentary infernal red glow. Her skin was rubbery and stippled, her bluish lips twisted into a feral grin. She opened her cavern-mouth, showing little sharp rat's teeth.

I couldn't move as she closed in.

The shaft of sunlight passed and the shadow of an overhead tree branch dangled on Pearl's face. She was suddenly my great-aunt again, lined and warm and smiley, her expression slightly taken aback at my reappearance.

It's her, only her. Really her. I had a moment, that's all, just a bad moment...

"I thought you'd left, Neely," she said. "Everything alright? You look like you've seen a ghost."

* * *

THANK you for reading *The Trauma Child: A Thriller*. If you enjoyed this book, please leave a review at your favorite retailer. Reviews are so important and can make the difference between a book being shown to new readers or not.

Today, authors face more hurdles than ever. We've always competed with other authors but now we compete with software programs that churn out full-length novels. To ensure that writers keep writing, please support us with reviews.

Also by C.G. Twiles

About C.G. Twiles psychological thriller, *The Perfect Face*:

"An out of this world thriller." —Liz Alterman, author of *The Perfect Neighborhood*

Looks can be deceiving

Reporter Maddie is ecstatic to be on a picturesque Greek island for her summer holiday. But then she meets a beautiful 12-year-old girl, Ruby, traveling with a woman claiming to be her mother.

Soon, Maddie suspects the girl is being trafficked to a nearby private island, one owned by the brilliant and reclusive billionaire Dexter Hunt. To help the girl, she joins forces with a local man and a rival reporter.

Maddie may have checked into the billionaire's notorious island—but can she ever leave?

Other psychological thrillers by C.G. Twiles

The Little Girl in the Window: A Psychological Thriller

At 14, Romy accidentally killed the town's beloved prom queen, Misty. Years later, when a crisis forces her to return to the scene of the crime, a little girl with eerily blue eyes begins appearing in her window, taunting her. Who is she? And how does she seem to know Romy's darkest secret?

The Little Girl with a Secret: A Psychological Thriller

Romy heads to Amish country to get away from her cheating fiancé and duplicitous best friend. Soon she becomes embroiled with the locals' many secrets. One of them is so explosive it will change her life forever.

Brooklyn Gothic: A Modern Gothic Romantic Thriller

A young, idealistic reporter working in a Brooklyn Gothic mansion begins to suspect that her new boss—and lover—is keeping dark secrets. For fans of the Brontes, Daphne du Maurier, Darcy Coates, and Ruth Ware.

The Neighbors in Apartment 3D: A Domestic Suspense Novel

Cintra's compulsive lying has torn her family apart. But when she notices a chilling sign taped to her neighbors' door — "I'm being held" written in childish handwriting — she's determined to help the kidnapped boy, regardless of who believes her… —BookBub

The Last Star Standing: A Psychological Thriller

A forgotten talent show winner has a second chance at success. But first, she'll have to kill the runner-up.

How far will Piper go to save her family and reclaim her former glory?

The Ghost Wife: A short tale of suspense

Tabitha wants one thing for the holidays: For her family to face reality. And the reality is… she's dead.

So why are they acting like she's still alive?

Neighbors and Other Dangers: A Psychological Thriller Box Set

Three heart-pounding, up-all-night psychological thrillers in one economical box set: *The Neighbors in Apartment 3D, The Last Star Standing, and The Little Girl in the Window.*

About the Author

C.G. Twiles is the pseudonym for a longtime writer and reporter who has written for some of the world's largest magazines and newspapers.

She enjoys traveling, animals, old houses, ancient history, and cemeteries. She lives in Brooklyn.

Please find her on social media, she'd love to connect!

facebook.com/cgtwiles

instagram.com/cgtwiles

goodreads.com/cgtwiles

bookbub.com/profile/c-g-twiles

Acknowledgments

There are people I need to thank for their friendship and support. This was a special book, much of it inspired by my hometown and by my family. Eternal love to Earl, Mary Jane "Mae," and Olive. And to my wonderful childhood house that will live forever in my memory. It truly was the magical place where I felt loved and safe.

I must mention Lavinia Fisher, whose story as the "first female serial killer in the United States" was the muse for Viola Hubbard. While innumerable possession stories have been written, I salute the best one: *The Exorcist* by William Peter Blatty.

Gratitude to my usual support group: Megan Easley-Walsh, Polly Kahl, and Liz Alterman. Without you, I'd never get this done. As always, I'm honored to be part of Bookstagram.

And to my regular readers (including Mom!): You are the reason I write, it's as simple as that. I can't thank you enough for your support.